THE TRUST

Tom Dolby

THE
TRUST

A SECRET SOCIETY NOVEL

KATHERINE TEGEN BOOKS
An Imprint of HarperCollins Publishers

Katherine Tegen Books is an imprint of HarperCollins Publishers.

The Trust: A Secret Society Novel
Text copyright © 2011 by Tom Dolby
All rights reserved. Printed in the United States of America.
No part of this book may be used or reproduced in any manner
whatsoever without written permission except in the case of brief
quotations embodied in critical articles and reviews. For information
address HarperCollins Children's Books, a division of HarperCollins
Publishers, 10 East 53rd Street, New York, NY 10022.
www.harperteen.com

Library of Congress Cataloging-in-Publication Data
Dolby, Tom.
   The trust: a secret Society novel/by Tom Dolby.—1st ed.
   p. cm.
   Summary: Four wealthy Manhattan teenagers who have been initi-
ated into a secret society that promises to fulfill their every wish
must now try to extricate themselves from the dangerous and corrupt
Society.
   ISBN 978-0-06-172164-9
   [1. Secret societies—Fiction. 2. Wealth—Fiction. 3. Interpersonal
relations—Fiction. 4. New York (N.Y.)—Fiction.] I. Title.
Pz7.D7003Tr 2011   2010009495
[Fic]—dc22   CIP
                                                             AC

Typography by Amy Ryan
11 12 13 14 15   CG/RRDB   10 9 8 7 6 5 4 3 2 1
                          ❖
First Edition

"Delusions are as necessary to our happiness as realities."
—Christian Nestell Bovee

*"If I'm wrong, I'm insane . . . and if I'm right,
it's worse than if I'm wrong."*
—William Goldman, *The Stepford Wives*

For my family, old and new,
and especially for W.D.F.

PROLOGUE

NEW YORK CITY, 1992

Outside the Metropolitan Museum of Art one cold February evening, photographers swarmed around the entrance, pushing and jostling, angling for the perfect shot. The Met's grand staircase, swathed in black carpet and dotted with snowflakes, was the runway for a flock of Manhattan luminaries who ascended the steps to the museum and into the event of the winter season, the Dendur Ball. Most posed and preened for the cameras, savoring their moment in the spotlight before they were ushered into the museum.

An exquisitely beautiful woman in her late twenties, with long dark hair, fair skin, and a thin, regal neck, walked across the street with her husband, dodging the limousines and town cars that were stacked three deep on Fifth Avenue. She clutched her dress so it wouldn't catch on her heels, and held her petite handbag in one hand and a sheer wrap that fluttered in the wind in the other. She didn't come in a chauffeured car or a taxicab like the other guests at the ball. She didn't need to, for she lived right across the street.

The crowd parted ways for the two of them, as if they carried an electric charge, an irresistible field announcing to all that she was in their path. He was handsome and dressed in a classic black dinner jacket, but it was she who commanded attention as she ascended the staircase, photographers and reporters shouting her name. She appeared barely to hear them as she climbed slowly and carefully. At the top of the steps, she turned around and glanced not at the crowd, not at the white-hot flashbulbs, but at the swirling snow around her.

She delicately stuck her tongue out and caught a snowflake on it, closing her eyes, as if to make a wish.

Her name, photographers whispered to the uninitiated, was Esmé Madison Evans. She was wearing an ivory column dress that had been designed by Sebastian Giroux, the up-and-coming young couturier. Around her neck was an exact replica of the new jewel of the Met's Egyptian wing, an artifact temporarily on loan from the Museum of Egyptian

Antiquities in Cairo for a special exhibit. Around the neck of Esmé Madison Evans, wife of Patchfield Evans, Jr., was a replica of the Scarab of Isis, a necklace that, until tonight, had never been viewed in New York City.

I

NEW YEAR

CHAPTER ONE

They gave me two choices," Patch said.

It was New Year's Eve on Isis Island, a small, private body of land off the coast of Maine, and Patch was sitting on a rocky overlook, surrounded by his friends. The four of them were united once again after several trying months: Patch, Nick, Phoebe, and Lauren, as well as a new addition to their group, Thad.

Patch had known Nick for so long, it was as if they were two sides of the same coin, and yet tonight it felt like he hadn't seen his friend in years. The two had been at odds with each other during the fall semester, and it was only as of the previous evening that they had reconciled. Nick was now sitting with his girlfriend, Phoebe, while Lauren and Thad sat together as well, though the latter two were only friends.

Unlike the others, who wore the latest cold weather gear, Patch was bundled in a ratty, oversize parka. On his head, where his brown hair had been shaved close to his skull as part of his disguise to get onto the island, he wore a wool hat. His left eye, swollen and bruised from a scuffle with Nick a few days ago, was slowly healing.

He was, he imagined, a sorry sight.

Patch had not had the luxury of packing carefully. Everything he was wearing he had carried on his back when he had snuck onto the island several days ago, posing as a member of the catering crew.

Now he was with friends, was ostensibly safe. As safe, he thought, as any of them could possibly be, given everything that had happened.

What had really happened? How had they all ended up here?

Patch knew the facts, but they didn't settle the unease that he felt settling over the group. It was the evening after all the Initiates in the Society had been advanced to the level of Conscripts, the evening after so much had been revealed to them. Last night, Patch had been reborn into the secret group, and the fate of Alejandro Calleja, their classmate and Lauren's boyfriend, had been divulged by Nick's father, Parker Bell, the Chairman of the Society.

Alejandro had disappeared after a Society party two weeks earlier, but now they learned that his cold cadaver was sitting in a morgue downtown, where toxicology screens would reveal the drugs he had taken. The fourteen new Conscripts had all been told that his was a cautionary tale, a warning about the dangers of drugs and alcohol.

But Patch knew the truth, as did the other four. Alejandro had not done this to himself, nor had any of their classmates been complicit in it, even though the rest of them believed that they had been. The Society's Council of Regents, aided by their private security force, the Guardians, had been responsible.

The older members—the Elders and the Council—had gone home that morning to spend New Year's Eve with their families. Isis Island now seemed empty in comparison to the chaos of the past few days.

The five of them sat on a lookout point that had a view of the Great Cottage, the shingled building on the island where the majority of the Society's activities took place at its remote retreat. Below them, Patch could see the other Conscripts blithely popping open bottles of champagne on one of the rustic porches off the foyer, ready to ring in the new year. Unlike the five of them, the rest were oblivious to what the Society was really about. Even if Patch and his friends tried to convince them, they wouldn't believe them anyway.

"What were your two choices?" Lauren asked Patch, as she rubbed her hands together in an attempt to stay warm.

"I had to agree to turn over the material I had filmed from the initiation—there was no question about that. I could then either be set free or I could become a member. The second option was the only one that I knew would truly keep me safe. Whatever that means."

"You really think we're safe now?" Lauren asked.

"I don't know," Patch said. "After what they did to me, not to mention to the others—I can't believe that it couldn't happen to any of us."

They all looked out at the horizon, at the clear sky, full of stars. The previous four days had been so filled with uncertainty and tension that it was a relief to have some quiet. Patch's joints were still stiff from the time he had spent in captivity, but he tried to block it from his mind—the terrifying, wrenching feeling of being trapped in a coffin, fed nutrients from an IV in his arm. He shivered. The memory wouldn't go away.

"So what now?" Nick finally said.

Patch thought about everything he had been through, the horrible questioning by Nick's father, and how Patch had made the only choice that would guarantee his freedom. He had hoped being a member would answer the questions he had about his mother, Esmé, and her madness; he hoped someone might explain how, when he was six years old, she had developed a mysterious borderline personality disorder that had kept her institutionalized. He hoped it would answer the questions he had about the Bell family, and the ones he had about his grandmother, Genie. Patch thought about all the things he had needed to experience over the previous few months to get to this point: the Society initiation in the Meatpacking District, the visit to his mother in the facility in Ossining, his infiltration and kidnapping. The other members, even the four he was sitting with now, would never understand what he had been through.

Because of this, even if he was now officially a Conscript, now officially one of them, he would always remain an Outsider. It was a phrase he had heard the Society use in some of its communications: *Outsiders are those who do not belong.*

"Phoebe, you've been quiet," Nick said. He nudged her carefully.

"Yeah," she said slowly. "I've been thinking about something."

"What's that?" Thad asked.

"I think Patch is right that we should be careful. All of us. I don't believe the worst is over."

Fireworks went off in the sky above Isis Island, and they could hear the ten remaining Conscripts in their class and the fourteen in the class above them whooping and shouting, toasting the new year from the lodge's balcony. Before yesterday, the Society had succeeded in its goal to create two classes of fourteen each. They had started with fifteen in the fall; then there was the death of Jared Willson, from the class above them, and the death of Alejandro Calleja. In each class, someone had died, thereby binding together all the other members with the horrible truth about their classmate's death. It had forced them all to trust each other while as recently as four months ago, many had been strangers.

Classes of fourteen were supposed to be stable, immune to corruption. Classes of fifteen were unbalanced and open to insurrection. The Society had historically taken classes like theirs, classes in danger of anarchy, and had instituted this practice of reducing the group to fourteen members.

They called it the Power of Fourteen.

In short, Patch thought, it was an extremely genteel explanation for ritual murder, all under the justification of protecting a way of life.

"What do you mean? What do you mean by 'the worst isn't over'?" Nick asked Phoebe.

Before Phoebe even spoke, Patch guessed what she was about to say: The Power of Fourteen was no longer. With Patch having joined the class the previous night, they would be fifteen again.

CHAPTER TWO

It was no surprise to Lauren that St. Patrick's Cathedral was packed for Alejandro's memorial service. The Calleja family had even known to arrange extra seating for latecomers. Family members and friends had traveled from South America and Europe, all dressed in their best designer black—hats, veils, furs, enormous brooches—as if, grotesquely, they had been waiting for just the right moment to show off their finery. The church was decked out in white peonies, thousands of which had been imported from Brazil.

Lauren's mind flashed to her seventeenth birthday party, the black-and-white theme, the kiss she had shared with Alejandro on the dance floor. Now the sea of black dresses and white peonies seemed like a monstrous perversion of the beauty of that night, a night where anything had seemed possible.

She felt bile rise up in her throat, and she swallowed it down.

Lauren looked down at what she was wearing, and she didn't even recognize the dress. Something black, something she had pulled from her closet in a daze. Was it even formal? Appropriate?

It had only been a few days after their return from the island, a few days after she had learned the news. Not that a few days would be enough to process the shock of Alejandro's death, but Lauren had pictured herself as stronger than this. Had she even remembered to put on makeup this morning? Look in a mirror? Brush her hair? She couldn't remember. She touched the right side of her forehead to feel the awful, stinging sensation of a pimple forming, a result of too much stress, too many sleepless nights, and too much caffeine.

She wondered if she had covered up the blemish adequately. Then she realized she didn't care.

Nick and Phoebe were sitting next to her, and Thad was on the other side. Phoebe held her hand throughout the entire service, but Lauren could barely feel the sensation of her friend's touch, and the sentiment behind it. It wasn't Phoebe's fault. It was that parts of Lauren had gone numb.

After the service, Alejandro's body would be flown back to Argentina.

There would be no burial to attend.

In that church, amid throngs of people she had never met, was Lauren's last chance to say good-bye.

It was a Catholic mass, complete with a performance of Mozart's *Requiem*. Lauren thought the whole thing was overdone, not to mention completely impersonal, given that Alejandro had never shown the least bit of interest in religion or classical music.

But it was for the family. Lauren knew that.

The family that didn't want to accept that their son had been a drug addict.

Perhaps it wasn't fair of her to think like this. Yes, Alejandro had a drug problem, but he had been able to manage it—not that this made it okay. He had gotten himself into trouble over the years, but he had never overdosed. Not until the Society caused him to do so. Lauren didn't know the exact details about it, and she didn't want to. It was too horrible, the thought of what they might have done to him, feeding him the poisons that his body craved.

Alejandro might have screwed up his life, but he didn't deserve to die. Not at seventeen years old. Not with people in his life who cared about him.

Not with her in his life. Whatever their problems—his drinking, his inability to take responsibility for his life—she still cared for him. For his sweet smile, his playful sense of adventure. No matter his faults: she missed him.

Their relationship had ended so abruptly when he was dragged out of a nightclub two weeks ago on the Lower East Side by the Guardians, never to be seen again. How could she have let that happen? And now, how was she supposed to deal with all the mixed emotions: guilt and regret about not taking better care of Alejandro; fear and anger at the Society for what they had done to him.

What therapist would ever understand what she was going through?

Lauren raised a fist to her face, rubbing her eyes, and found that she was crying. It was for Alejandro, of course, but it was also for herself.

How could she have gotten herself into such a mess? Part of her wanted to find out the truth about Alejandro and what had really happened, and another part of her wanted to let it drift into the past, to be a coldhearted girl who didn't even care that her boyfriend had died.

She would never be like that. But if dwelling on it made the raw, biting pain stay with her, then she wanted to leave it behind.

Today, arriving at the service, sitting in the pew, she felt as if she were being followed by his ghost: she could see it in people's eyes, the pity.

Elders from the Society and members of the Council of Regents sat in the first several rows behind Rocío and Federico Calleja, Alejandro's mother and father; his older sisters, who had flown in from Argentina with their husbands; and other members of the Calleja family.

Most of the attendees were weeping through the service, and Lauren spied Gigi and Parker Bell, Nick's parents, both of whom were making a big show of dabbing at their eyes with linen handkerchiefs, along with Palmer Bell, Nick's grandfather. She wanted to scream, to bound over the pews and strangle them all: Parker and Palmer for arranging Alejandro's murder, and Gigi for her hypocrisy, for pretending that she was nothing more than an innocent bystander. It didn't matter that Nick was Lauren's friend. Even Nick knew how evil his parents and grandfather were—they were the leaders of the Society and its financial and charitable arm, the Bradford Trust. She wanted to shout at them, to wail, to scream: *You killed him, you evil bastards! None of this would be happening if it weren't for you!*

She wanted to tell everyone everything she knew. To go to the papers. To tell her mom and dad. To tell the police.

But how could she?

Parker Bell had made it quite clear how their futures would be jeopardized if they revealed anything about Alejandro's death. Was that enough of a reason to stay silent? Lauren didn't know. If she came forward, would anyone believe her? She had seen what had happened to Phoebe when she had gone to her mother with doubts about the Society last fall. The minute Phoebe had said anything, she was sent to a doctor who treated her as if she were crazy, giving her tranquilizers and hinting that she should be placed under observation.

As Lauren looked around the cathedral, she realized that it was decorated more lavishly than for most weddings, with candles everywhere, garlands of flowers even in the rafters, not to mention an abundance of not-inexpensive flower wreaths, an Argentinean tradition. All that money that could have been spent on rehab was now wasted on flowers and candles that would end up in the trash. She glanced over to the Callejas. Rocío Calleja was wearing more jewelry than Lauren had ever seen anyone wear at a memorial service: rubies, diamonds, gold. She had greeted Lauren when she had entered, embracing her as if she were a family member.

In death, it seemed that Lauren's position as Alejandro's girlfriend was more secure than ever.

Lauren knew one thing: she was done with bad boys. In fact, she might be done with dating altogether, at least for a while.

As the service ended, she got up with Thad and ducked away toward the exits in an attempt to avoid the crush of people. Thad had been amazing over the past few days, taking her out to lunch and for coffee dates, anything to keep her mind off things. He even took her shopping, an activity he admitted that he hated. He was such a sweet guy, and she was especially glad that Thad was gay—it removed any awkwardness from their friendship. She may have been sleepwalking through the past week, but at least she had someone who cared about her to do it with.

As everyone started to leave the cathedral, there was a commotion near the front. Palmer Bell, Nick's grandfather, was halfway up the aisle when his cane gave way and he tumbled to the floor. Panicked voices rang through the cathedral, echoing over the organ music as everyone, but particularly members of the Society, crowded around him, calling 911 and shouting words of advice to try to revive him.

I hope he dies, Lauren thought. I hope he dies right here in this church, fifty feet from Alejandro's casket. That would serve him right.

The paramedics rushed in, heralded by the sirens of their ambulance. Palmer Bell was coming to, but he clearly needed serious medical attention. In all the commotion, it was as if the reason people were here—to mourn Alejandro's death—had been completely forgotten.

Once again, Lauren thought bitterly, it was all about the Bells.

CHAPTER THREE

After his grandfather's collapse, Nick slipped awkwardly out of the cathedral, following his family into the black limousine that was waiting for them. An ambulance that would take Palmer Bell to New York-Presbyterian Hospital had just pulled away from the curb. Nick agreed that he would meet up with Phoebe after he learned more about what was going on. According to what the paramedics had told his father, Palmer had suffered a stroke, indicated by his collapse, complaints of numbness in his legs, and general disorientation. The car pulled away and drove south, turning east on a side street and then uptown. The driver followed the ambulance, taking advantage of the path that had been cleared for them.

Nick loosened his tie and scratched his neck behind his

collar, realizing that he had been sweating. The panic of a crisis was almost a welcome relief from the charade they had all been playing. It had been devastating to sit through Alejandro's memorial service when he and his friends knew the truth about what had happened to him. And now his family was sitting in this warm cocoon of luxury while the rest of the horrible world went on. It was the first time in a week that Nick had been in such close proximity to both his parents—he had been avoiding them ever since returning from Isis Island on New Year's Day. His mother, with her fiery red hair; his father, though graying, lean and fit on a regimen of running and stress.

Nick's two older brothers, Henry and Benjamin, home from Yale for the funeral, were both idly texting and shooting worried glances at their parents and each other. They had proven to be nothing more than drones when Nick had asked them about the Society back in December. Nick wouldn't have been surprised if someone told him that his brothers had been lobotomized. He had always thought Ben might have rebelled against the group, as he had been more of a free spirit, a member of the Yale Pundits, the type of guy who would bring home *The Anarchist Cookbook* and leave it in the living room over Christmas break. Henry, conversely, was notoriously uptight and headed directly to law school. Nick sensed that Henry, as a senior, was already being groomed to become more involved with the group. Perhaps Ben was as well.

Nick's mother, Gigi, was on the phone and fussing with arrangements, calling Palmer's doctor, making sure that the hospital would be ready to see him. Nick's father was bickering with her, arguing that any doctor would do—whoever was on duty in the emergency room was fine. Just because Palmer had made a large bequest to the hospital several years back, he shouldn't expect to be treated any differently.

Yeah, right, Nick thought. The rich are always treated differently.

The limousine pulled up behind the ambulance, and Nick could see his grandfather being loaded out and wheeled to the emergency room.

As Nick stood in the hospital lobby with his mother and father and his two brothers, assorted hangers-on started trickling in: Family lawyers. Advisers. Friends. Society members who were concerned. *How is he? What room will he be in? Does he have the best doctor? My father had a stroke and . . .*

To Nick, it was like vultures gathering around a half-dead carcass, waiting for their share of the spoils.

He walked out of the hospital's revolving doors and headed home without saying a word to anyone.

CHAPTER FOUR

When Phoebe joined Lauren outside the cathedral after the memorial service, Thad gave her a knowing look. He had been waiting patiently with Lauren, but now that Phoebe had arrived, he seemed to know instinctively that the girls needed some time together. He parted ways with Lauren and Phoebe, giving them both hugs.

Phoebe walked with Lauren back to Lauren's apartment on Park Avenue. There was to be a catered reception at the Calleja apartment at the St. Regis, but Lauren hadn't wanted to go, and Phoebe agreed with her that they should skip it. Both of them knew that it didn't make any difference to Alejandro, and that in the swarm of travel-weary mourners, his family wouldn't even notice their absence.

Phoebe also knew that her friend needed her more.

Lauren was horribly depressed, as anyone would be about her boyfriend's disappearance and death—it had only been two weeks since it had happened, and the pain was still fresh. Even worse, though, was the knowledge that Alejandro had never needed to die. Sure, he may have played fast and loose with the rules, but no one deserved his fate: to be kidnapped from a nightclub, taken to a flophouse on the Lower East Side, and forced to take all the drugs he could? Alejandro may have had a drug problem, but he hadn't been out to kill himself.

Phoebe, Lauren, Nick, Patch, and Thad were the only ones who knew about any of this. Parker Bell had told all the other Society members that Alejandro had overdosed of his own free will, that it was a terrible tragedy that could have been prevented.

Only the five of them knew the truth—that the Society killed Alejandro because he was in danger of revealing its motives to the world. Alejandro had had a series of bad nights in the fall, one during which he was quoted as saying that he knew important people, and everyone would be sorry.

A simple comment like that was enough to make the Society concerned—it put the Society's secret existence, not to mention the assets in the Trust, at risk. More than anything, though, Alejandro's death fulfilled the Society's goal of creating a class of fourteen. A class that would be stronger. A class that was bound by a secret.

For what? Amidst all the commotion and the threats,

it was hard to understand what the Society was so worried about. During the retreat, Parker Bell had made repeated references to a way of life that the Society had to uphold. Phoebe understood that its secrecy was its power. The Society, she had learned, was a network of wealthy, educated people who recruited their sons and daughters, as well as other talented, educated young people. Phoebe had fallen into the latter category, while Nick, with his family's involvement, was in the former.

The group used this network to gain and grant advantages to its members, sometimes legitimately, and other times in ways that were illegal. By the time members learned about the Society's criminal ways, they were in too deep; they were either culpable for some of the Society's deeds, or the Society had enough information on them to blackmail them effectively.

The Society also had a public face: the Bradford Trust Association. The members used the Trust as a cover, sometimes giving the group the appearance of a benevolent charitable foundation. Phoebe suspected that some of the members didn't even know about the Society's misdeeds, that they were only aware of it as a social group associated with the Bradford Trust.

Trust was a funny word: Phoebe couldn't think of a single person in New York City, apart from Nick and her three friends, whom she truly, honestly, could trust.

Like the others, Phoebe yearned desperately to get out of it, to tell the world about the Society, but she couldn't. If she and her friends were going to reveal anything, they didn't want to do so until they had a plan. It had seemed unwise to make a move until Alejandro's memorial service had taken place. The fact that Nick's family was so directly involved in the coverup—a revelation that had become apparent to Phoebe only in the last week—made things even more complicated.

Nick was, after all, the first and only boy she had ever loved. And she wasn't about to ruin that.

At the moment, though, Phoebe didn't want to come up with a plan or do anything remotely strategic—there would be plenty of time for that later. She wanted to comfort her friend. This was Lauren, after all: Lauren, who had approached her in a nightclub four months ago and taken her under her wing; Lauren, who had made Chadwick bearable.

Lauren, who had encouraged Phoebe to follow her to the Society initiation when both of them had been invited.

Phoebe looked at her as the two of them rode up in the elevator to Lauren's mother's Park Avenue apartment. Even when she was exhausted, Lauren was so beautiful. Phoebe had always felt like the ugly duckling next to the swan. Lauren had blond hair while Phoebe had reddish brown; Lauren was lithe and graceful, while Phoebe, though still slim, worried about her hips. Before they reached her floor, Phoebe reached forward and grabbed her friend, giving her a private hug.

She couldn't say it was going to be okay, because she didn't honestly know if it would be.

When the two of them arrived at the apartment, Lauren's mother, Diana, was already home. She had taken a car from the cathedral and arrived ten minutes before them. In the kitchen, it was as if Diana was hosting a wake for three. Lauren's little sister, Allison, was already away at boarding school, and Lauren's father lived across town.

Diana Mortimer was not exactly the most nurturing person Phoebe had ever met; she was so thin that Phoebe imagined hugging her might not be a pleasant experience. Today, though, she had come through with exactly what Lauren needed. On this Saturday afternoon, she stood with a mimosa in her hand and welcomed the girls into the kitchen. There was a beautiful spread of food that had been prepared: two kinds of quiche, a salad, Lauren's favorite variation on eggs Benedict, pastries, a Linzer torte, coffee, tea, and freshly squeezed orange juice. Phoebe found herself touched at the sight of it all. From what Lauren had told Phoebe about her mother, Diana had never been one to equate food with love— her wavelength was more handbags and jewelry—but right now luxury goods weren't going to cut it.

Lauren sat down in the breakfast nook and smiled weakly at Phoebe and her mother. "You know something? I'm actually hungry. For the first time in days, I'm hungry. I'd better eat, before the feeling goes away."

Phoebe knew what this was like, the feeling of fear-induced nausea that was so constant that as soon as it went away, you tried to get a little food down. Lately Phoebe's stomach had been in knots as well, and so instead of trying to control her hunger as she might before a big night out, she found she was actually grateful to be able to eat a few bites without feeling sick.

The two of them dug in, asking the cook to pile their plates with eggs Benedict, quiche, and pastries. Diana asked them if they'd like mimosas, but they both declined. There was something about the Society that made them not want to drink too much—it was the drinking, after all, that had gotten their friends into so much trouble. Jared at Cleopatra's Needle, freezing to death and dying of exposure after a night of bingeing. Alejandro, making a fool of himself at a club in the Hamptons, and then, of course, overdoing it that night at Prohibition, the club on the Lower East Side where the Guardians had kidnapped him.

No, Phoebe knew, and she sensed Lauren did, too, that staying sober and aware would be the best policy, at least for the next few weeks.

Lauren was silent as she took small bites of her food, and Phoebe resisted the urge to check her phone, which kept buzzing in her purse. It was probably Nick, but she felt it would be rude to answer. Her relationship with Nick had gone so well during all of this that she wondered what they would do if they weren't facing an external crisis, if they didn't have the constant outside stimulation to keep them going. They had started dating at Thanksgiving and had made it through the stress of exams, the aftermath of Jared's and Alejandro's deaths, the Society retreat, and Patch's disappearance and initiation. Though it had only been a few weeks, Phoebe did worry a bit about whether things, once they settled down, would seem slow.

After eating, Lauren assured Phoebe that she really didn't need her to stay, that she hadn't gotten much sleep the night before and was going to take a nap. Phoebe gave her friend a hug, said good-bye to Diana with a double air kiss, and let herself out.

She wasn't going home, though, to the town house where she and her mother were living on Bank Street.

Via text, Nick had asked her to meet him in Central Park, at a location she remembered all too well from the fall: the chess tables.

CHAPTER FIVE

omehow, this felt appropriate," Nick said. He was sitting on a bench near one of the chess tables outside the Chess and Checkers House in Central Park as Phoebe approached.

"You couldn't have picked a place that wasn't freezing?" Phoebe said, giving him an anguished grin. It was late in the afternoon, and the Chess and Checkers House was closed. He handed his scarf to Phoebe, who wrapped it around her neck. In an attempt to warm up, she stomped her shoes against the ground as they sat on the ice-cold bench.

Nick gave her a big bear hug, but it didn't seem to help. "Sorry," he said, slightly embarrassed at not having realized how cold it would be inside the park. "We can keep walking."

Phoebe gave him a kiss on his ear. "Hey, it was a valiant effort. I feel like I haven't been inside the park in weeks."

They looked around. The wisteria, so lush in the summer, had gone dormant. No one was playing chess. Nick remembered back to that night several months ago when they had been challenged to decode the address of the Society's town house, and how new and exciting it had all seemed: the perks, the thrill of membership, the doors that would open for them. And that second Society event had almost seemed like a second date between Phoebe and him. He thought back to how he had imagined she would never like him, and how they were both so happy when they had finally gotten together over Thanksgiving. Now they started walking together out of the park.

"How's your grandfather?" Phoebe asked.

Nick shrugged in frustration. "I didn't stay," he said. "The paramedics said he had a massive blockage. To be honest, I was sick of all the family drama."

Phoebe touched his shoulder as they walked. "But don't you—I mean, don't you care about what happens to him? I mean, he is still your grandfather."

Nick shook his head bitterly. "Yeah, I guess I care, in that way that I'm supposed to care. But do I really care? No. What they've done is inexcusable. He may not be in charge of the Society anymore, but I still hold him responsible, along with my dad and everyone else. And why he had to have a stroke during the funeral, I have no idea. He certainly succeeded in taking people's attention away from the real event."

Nick kicked the muddy leaves on the ground as they walked.

"You don't think he faked it for that reason, do you?" Phoebe asked.

Nick smiled grimly. "No. He's a bastard, but I don't think he's able to spontaneously give himself a stroke. Anyway, he's in the hospital now, recovering."

"I'm sorry," Phoebe said.

Nick shrugged again. "I really don't think about him the way I know you're supposed to feel about family."

Nick wondered, as they walked, if these feelings would ever change. His family had betrayed him. First they had covered up their involvement in the Society. Next they orchestrated the deaths of two people Nick knew. He had been blocking it out during most of the past two weeks. And then Patch had come into the fold, had been instantly declared a member of the Society after he had infiltrated the retreat. Nick was happy that their rift was starting to heal, but it had brought up a host of other issues. Would Patch ever forgive him for shutting him out during those months? And would Patch accept the truth Nick now knew, the secret his father had told him the morning after Patch's initiation?

Nick had decided, for now, that that conversation had happened to a different Nick Bell, that he and Patch were good, that there were no rifts to be mended, no awkward subjects to be broached.

"Are you doing okay?" Phoebe asked.

He realized he hadn't said anything in several minutes, had been staring at the ground as they walked. He appreciated how Phoebe would, most of the time, leave him alone to his thoughts when she knew he needed it.

"I'm so angry at all of them," Nick said. "I mean, how can we be part of this when we know everything that they've done? And now, with my family, I can already sense it. If we tell them we want out, they're going to deflect it: it's going to be all about my grandfather and his health. 'Don't bother us now, Nick, not when your grandfather's health is at risk. Stop worrying about petty things, Nick.' As if our friends dying is somehow petty."

"Maybe going to them isn't the answer," Phoebe said.

"So what can we do?"

Phoebe paused. "Boycott the mandatory meetings? Not just us, but the five of us—you and me and Lauren and Patch and Thad. That's a third of our class. It would drive the point home, don't you think?"

At that moment, Nick's phone started buzzing. Phoebe motioned to him to answer it, and he picked it up, even though it was not a number he recognized.

"Your grandfather would like to see you," a male voice said.

"Who is this?" Nick asked.

"It would be in your best interest to visit him at the

hospital. The other family members are gone." Whoever was calling didn't want to identify himself.

"Why should I visit him?"

"He knows about your wishes. He wants to help you."

The line clicked off.

"You're not going to believe this," Nick said. "We're being summoned—well, officially, I'm being summoned—to go see my grandfather at the hospital because he 'knows about our wishes.' Whatever that means."

Phoebe shook her head. "Do you really think you should go?"

"I don't know," Nick said. "Would you go with me?" He thought back to that moment in the fall when he and Phoebe had promised to look out for each other.

Phoebe paused, and for an instant he thought she might turn the other way, catch a cab downtown, never speak to him again.

She nodded slowly, taking his hand. "Let's go."

CHAPTER SIX

Like most people, Nick hated hospitals. They creeped him out, and New York-Presbyterian was no exception. Not only was it a hospital, but its lobby's architecture was like a Gothic cathedral, with vaulted ceilings and dark wooden plaques on the walls and even a little chapel near the entrance where people could pray for their loved ones' speedy recovery.

All in all, it was not a fun place to spend an evening.

Nick and Phoebe took the elevator to the intensive care unit. He was grateful that Phoebe had wanted to accompany him on this trip.

The word was that Palmer's condition had stabilized, though his doctors were keeping him under close observation. Visiting hours were officially over, but Palmer had left word at the desk that Nick was to be let up.

Outside Palmer Bell's room, one of the Guardians was standing watch in a dark suit. He nodded to Nick and Phoebe as they entered, though Nick ignored the brutish guard.

Nick's grandfather was conscious, but his movements and speech patterns were slow. It felt so strange to see the handsome older man lying in a bed, powerless.

"How are you doing, sir?" Nick asked. "You remember Phoebe, right?"

"Mmmmpph," Palmer grumbled.

"Is there anything we can do for you? Do you need anything?" Nick knew he was asking more out of reflex than anything else, as he knew all his grandfather's needs were taken care of.

Palmer cleared his throat and began speaking slowly. "I'm glad you came. I do need you to do something for me."

"Of course, anything." Nick realized that he was being polite to his grandfather out of tradition and habit, not out of any genuine sense of respect.

There was a pause, as if Palmer were collecting his thoughts. Nick heard Phoebe shifting awkwardly as she stood beside him.

"Your father won't understand this, your brothers won't understand this. I will not tell them about it, and I suggest you don't, either."

Nick nodded.

"I don't know how much longer I'm going to last. And I know you want to get out."

Nick looked at Palmer, then at Phoebe. "What do you mean, sir?"

"I know you want out of the Society. It has been obvious from the first week. Your actions last month on the island made it very clear."

"Well, I—I mean—" Nick stammered. He didn't know what to say. "Why—why would you say this?"

"Nicholas, I want you to live the life that you want to lead, not one that has been set up for you by your family. I have seen—I have seen how destructive that can be. How much can be ruined when families tell their children how to live."

Nick nodded. "What about my friends?"

"If you do this one task for me, you and your friends will never hear from the Society again."

Nick paused. This was a major breakthrough, the chance to gain freedom from this group that had terrorized them over the past several months.

"What is the task?"

Palmer chuckled, and then started coughing. When it subsided, he spoke again. "Now just telling you—that would be too easy, wouldn't it?"

"I suppose so." Nick looked glumly back at Phoebe, as she shrugged.

Another day, another riddle. It seemed as if that was what

their life was amounting to these days. Nick heard Phoebe sigh.

Palmer clutched Nick's hand. His grandfather's fingers felt dry and brittle in his own.

"Son, you must go to the beach. You'll find everything you need at the beach. At both beaches."

"I'm not sure I understand. What's at the beach?"

"All the treasures are buried in the sand. You remember the beach: the sand castles, all the shells, the jellyfish, the pieces of driftwood you would bring back to the house. You and your brothers used to spend all day on the beach."

Nick scowled. His grandfather was playing them like puppets. "And you want us to go there because . . ."

"You must go to the beach, you must go down below. Below the surface of things."

"Sir, I don't understand. Which beach? The house in Southampton?"

"You need the key first. You need to find the key."

"Where do we find the key?"

"Both beaches."

Nick looked at him, confused. What did he mean? Southampton had several beaches: Cooper's, Fowler, all the others. Not to mention the rest of the beaches in the Hamptons, all the way east to Montauk.

A nurse knocked on the door. "I'm sorry to cut this visit short, but Mr. Bell needs to take his medication."

"Wait!" Nick said to his grandfather. "You've got to tell us more than this."

"You have enough," Palmer said. "Nicholas, you may not realize this, but you have always had everything you need."

CHAPTER SEVEN

As they went down in the elevator, Phoebe didn't know what to make of Palmer's request. Would he really grant them an exit from the Society? As the group's Chairman Emeritus, did he have the power to do this? Phoebe was skeptical. She had been burned by the elder Bells before—namely, Nick's father, who had some of her paintings taken out of her gallery show last year—and so she was hesitant to trust the old man. More importantly, she knew that Parker Bell and Palmer Bell were responsible for Jared's and Alejandro's deaths. Why would Palmer go against his son's organization, a group he had spent so many years leading?

"Are you really sure this makes sense?" Phoebe asked Nick. "I mean, it could be a trap, right?"

Nick shook his head. "I don't really know."

"He seemed remarkably lucid," Phoebe said. "I thought he had suffered all sorts of brain damage."

"He did, supposedly," Nick said. "That's what's so confusing about this. I can't tell if he's faking it, or if he really is out of it and he's just spouting nonsense."

"It's another riddle. It almost sounds like a treasure hunt. But once again, we don't know what the treasure actually is. What was that about things being buried in the sand?"

The elevator doors opened. Phoebe nudged Nick in the ribs, motioning down the hall with a nod. They needed to stay quiet. At the lobby entrance was Gigi, Nick's mother, with a packed monogrammed tote bag. Phoebe had acknowledged Gigi earlier that day at the service, but hadn't said hello to her.

"Phoebe, darling!" Gigi said, as if the two of them were meeting at a cocktail party instead of a hospital lobby that smelled vaguely of disinfectant. "It is so sweet of you two to visit Palmer. I'm sure it meant so much to him. I'm just bringing him some fresh clothing—those nurses are such Nazis, but I think they'll let me in. How did he seem?"

Nick paused, as if he wasn't sure quite how much to say. "Better than I thought. But a little bit strange. I think maybe it's that thing where people have a stroke and they start reminiscing about the past."

Nick clearly didn't want to tell his mother about the conversation. Gigi was an Elder of the Society and took very seriously her role as the wife of the Chairman.

His mother sighed. "Sweetie, you can't pay any attention to him. They've got him on so much medication. You know how it is." She looked down at the bag. "I'd better bring this up to him." She gave Phoebe an air kiss. "Nice to see you, darling."

Nick pushed his way out of the hospital into the cold night air. The two of them started walking west.

"What should we do?" Nick asked.

"We have to call a meeting, just among the five of us," Phoebe said. "It's going to take more than you and me to figure all this out."

CHAPTER EIGHT

Whenever Patch found that his world was closing in on him, he liked to go to the Metropolitan Museum to help clear his head. There were little nooks and crannies that he knew about, away from the tourists, among the more obscure collections. European Decorative Arts was one of his favorites—it was basically a fancy word for antiques. There was something cool about thinking that people had sat on these chairs, eaten on these tables, conducted their affairs and intrigues. And that we, today, would never know what had transpired.

It was such a universe apart from his own problems, it made him forget them momentarily. On Sunday afternoon, he could almost forget everything he was thinking about the Society, all of his questions. A Society meeting had already been called for the following evening at the town house. Would he go? Would Nick and the others? He didn't know.

Patch's phone buzzed as he was examining an antique harpsichord. It was a text from Phoebe, confirming the details of a meeting at Lauren's that night with just the five of them. It made sense that they would do it there; Lauren was the only member whose parents didn't have any connection to the Society. Phoebe had told Patch about Daniel Fullerton, the guy her mom was dating, who was in the Society; Nick's parents were involved, of course; and Patch's grandmother, Genie, would likely overhear whatever they were planning and have an opinion on it. This new guy, Thad—they didn't know much about his family, but Patch imagined that Phoebe figured he was too recent a friend to take a risk on. Patch had learned that trusting people hadn't been so easy these past few months.

A few hours later, Patch arrived at Lauren's apartment. Despite the nap she said she had taken, Lauren looked exhausted, her hair messy and matted. The five of them stood around her kitchen, and at her urging, helped themselves to the refrigerator full of food. It was stocked, which surprised Patch; it seemed welcoming, like a normal house, not that of a fashionable socialite, which was Lauren's mother's reputation. He and Nick and Thad dug in.

Lauren, who wore jeans and a baggy sweater, carried her cup of tea into the living room. Nick accepted a beer, and Patch decided he would have one, too—just one, to help him

44

relax. Phoebe sat protectively next to Lauren on the sofa in front of the windows with the gauzy curtains that faced Park Avenue. What had happened in the past few months had been hard on all of them, but Lauren was particularly feeling the blow right now. Though Patch had heard her admit that she didn't even know if things with Alejandro were going to last, he imagined that it still burned, to have someone in your life disappear like that, as if they had never existed at all.

For a moment, he realized that this was how he felt about his parents. He had been too young when his father died to have any clear memories of him, and his mother had been hospitalized since Patch was six.

"How are you holding up?" Nick asked Lauren.

Lauren shrugged. "As well as can be expected, I suppose. I haven't done any of the winter reading, I feel like I'm going to be floating through my classes tomorrow. Sebastian wants me to come up with new jewelry designs—I guess he thought it might distract me or something? All I want to do is sleep and watch stupid movies."

"Do you think . . ." Patch paused, not wanting to say anything inappropriate. "Do you think it might help for you to talk to someone about it all? Like a professional?"

"Not that Meckling freak," Phoebe said, jumping in. "He's like the Nurse Ratched of shrinks. I still can't believe my mom took Daniel's recommendation. I guess she didn't know that he was part of it all."

"I know someone good," Thad said. "He helped my older brother when he was going through a lot of stuff."

Lauren nodded. "I guess so. I don't know. I just want it all to go away."

"I'm not sure we can make it go away," Nick said. "But I think we can get out of it." He looked at Phoebe. "My grandfather gave me a challenge yesterday to search for something."

"To search for what?" Thad asked.

"We don't know exactly," Phoebe said. "I'm worried it might be a trap."

"We might as well try," Thad said. "And you think this would get all of us out of the Society?"

"He said that if we solve this, 'you and your friends will never hear from the Society again,'" Nick said. "The search starts at the beach."

"Which beach?" Patch asked.

"That's what we don't know," Phoebe said.

"Phoebe and I will start this coming Friday," Nick said. "For now, we need to figure out what to do about these meetings, right?" Nick said. "In particular, the one tomorrow night."

"Honestly, I don't know what we have to meet about," Phoebe said. "Like they couldn't just let us digest everything that's happened so far?"

"I'm not going," Lauren said. "I can't go on any longer with it."

"Me, neither," Thad said.

"Pheeb, what about you?" Lauren asked.

She looked at Lauren and Thad. "I'm with you guys. I'll skip."

"Maybe Patch and I should go," Nick said. "You know, so they don't think something's going on?"

"I guess so," Phoebe said.

"I'm just so angry about it all," Lauren said. "I think we should go to the police. What could the Society do to us? We could tell the cops everything we know. I don't even care if I don't get into college, if they bust us for being drunk that night. We weren't responsible for Alejandro's death. We were partying with him. It wasn't that part that killed him."

Everyone looked uneasy.

"Do you really think the police would believe us?" Nick said.

"They would have to believe something," Phoebe said. "Don't you think? I mean, we've made this mistake before. We should have gone to the police the night that Alejandro disappeared."

"We didn't know what was happening. We didn't know how bad it was going to get," Nick said.

"Honestly, inside the club, most people didn't even see him," Thad said. He turned to Patch. "What do you think?"

Patch shrugged. "I, um, I don't really know. It's hard for me to say, since I wasn't there."

Patch realized, at that moment, that this was part of his

uneasiness. Even though he should have felt like a real member, he didn't. He would never feel like as much of an insider as they did. Even though they all greeted him warmly and treated him as a friend, he still felt like an interloper. They were the chosen ones, and that was the way it was always going to be.

And why, he wondered, did he want to feel like an insider to this group that he and his friends were now trying so desperately to escape?

CHAPTER NINE

One of the perks of being a member of the Society was that its town house on East 66th Street had a private, glassed-in rooftop swimming pool. The text message that Nick, Patch, and the others had received said that on Monday night there would be a pool party, a rare treat in chilly January.

As Nick approached the doors of the classic brownstone with Patch, he thought about how, for the first time, the two of them would be going to a Society meeting together. For a moment, it felt as if this was the way things were supposed to be, as if the world had righted itself and all had been put back in order.

Of course, that was far from the truth of the situation. Nick sighed inaudibly as the door was opened for them by

Anastasia Lin, who was Phoebe's mentor in the class above her. She was dressed casually, in jeans and a cashmere sweater, though she wore her usual dramatic red lipstick.

"Nick! Patch! It's so good to see you," she said as her eyes darted from one to the other. "Is Phoebe with you?"

Nick noticed Patch giving him an awkward sideways glance. "No, um, she's coming separately," Nick said. "She might be a little late. She said she wasn't feeling well." He hoped the lie would allay any suspicion when it later became clear that Phoebe was skipping the meeting.

Anastasia led Nick and Patch up several flights of stairs in the direction of the rooftop pool. Nick wanted to give Patch the full tour of the town house, but he also didn't want to attract suspicion from any of the other members who were roaming about. Like a classic gentlemen's club, the place had the odor of cigars and worn leather, and its walls were adorned with aging oil paintings of mediocre quality, along with framed medals, photographs, and letters from politicians, all yellowing at the corners and wrinkled in their frames.

With everything Nick now knew about the Society, being at the town house felt cheap. He wouldn't exactly describe the first night there in the fall as *magical*, but it had possessed a certain aura of exclusivity, of the idea that they were part of something special. There had been a richness that the building held; now, in its place, all he felt was a troubling emptiness, the feeling of promises broken, of betrayal.

"So this is it," Patch said as he looked around. They were on the top floor. The entryway to the swimming pool had a white marble floor and a tiled dome ceiling. Through the entryway, blue light from the pool flickered against the potted palms that lined the sides of the room. The roof of the swimming pool was glass, so you could see the stars as you floated in the water.

A bar had been set up against one wall, and Emily van Piper, one of the members of the class above them, was mixing drinks. She was wearing a blue swimsuit with a wrap tied around her waist. With her blond hair, she fit in perfectly with the pool party atmosphere. Nick knew Emily was Lauren's mentor and would surely notice she was missing as well. Nick and Patch got ginger ales, but luckily, Emily didn't ask about Lauren.

Nick stood with Patch on the side of the pool. "Are you going to put your suit on?" Patch asked, motioning to Nick's messenger bag. Both of them had dutifully packed swimsuits, as per the instructions they had been given, but swimming was the last thing Nick wanted to do.

Nick shook his head. "No."

As he looked at all the members splashing around the pool and relaxing so easily, Nick thought back again to the first time he had been here, in the fall. It had all been fun and entrancing and mysterious. Most exciting of all had been meeting Phoebe, seeing her in a swimsuit a mere twenty-four hours after they had met. He couldn't pretend that it hadn't interested him, that he hadn't been paying attention.

Charles Lawrence walked over to Nick. He wore a bright red square-cut bathing suit and had a towel draped around his neck as if it were the middle of summer and he was a lifeguard at the country club doing his hourly patrol.

"Having fun?" Charles asked.

Nick gave Charles a blank look. It was difficult to know how to act around Charles—he was, after all, the de facto leader of the older class of Conscripts. He had started out as a friendly guy, someone everyone liked, but as last semester progressed, Nick suspected Charles of having a hand in Jared's and Alejandro's deaths. He was the one who had handed Alejandro a drink before his collapse, and he was the first one who had discovered Jared at Cleopatra's Needle. Nick didn't know whether to be afraid of Charles or to scorn him.

"I need to talk to you about something," Charles said. "Actually, to both of you. I've been asked by the Council of Regents to be a mentor to both of you, since neither of you has one currently."

It was true. Jared had been Nick's mentor, and Patch hadn't been assigned one yet.

"What about Jeremy?" Nick asked. "And aren't you already Bradley Winston's mentor?" Jeremy Hopkins had been Alejandro's mentor, so it would have been logical to pair up Jeremy with Patch.

Charles laughed. "Bradley is doing just fine. And I'm not really sure Jeremy's up to the challenge. He's a little busy right now with some kind of art project that he's doing with Anastasia." He looked at Nick. "Your dad asked me personally that I be a mentor to the two of you."

"Whatever," Nick said, shrugging. "I guess it's fine."

"Why don't you and Patch go get changed?" Charles asked. "The water feels great."

Nick scowled. "Not tonight." He laughed a little, mostly out of nervousness. "I don't see how you can just relax after everything that's happened," he muttered.

"What do you mean?" Charles asked.

"Um, I don't know," Nick said. "Maybe that two people died last semester? Why does no one seem to care about that?"

"Nick, accidents happen. Everyone knows that. You can't dwell on the past. Come on, have a drink, come and hang out with the other members. People are starting to think you're a bit of a snob, the way you only talk to your friends."

"There's a reason for that," Nick said. "We're fine where we are. We'll watch from the side."

Nick knew he was supposed to pretend that nothing was wrong, but when someone like Charles came along and provoked him, he couldn't stay silent. He wasn't going to let on about his grandfather's challenge and his offer to get him and his friends out of the Society—that would just be stupid. But he also figured that Charles and the others might be suspicious if he and Patch suddenly seemed like they were going along with everything, no questions asked.

"Suit yourself." Charles shrugged and walked away.

As Nick looked at the other members, they disgusted him as they horsed around in the pool. Two of the guys, both slim and tan, tried to throw one of the girls in, the three of them fell in together, and then she retaliated by dunking their heads underwater. He heard snippets of conversation echoing around the room: *I got my early acceptance a few days ago . . . Yale . . . Harvard . . . vacation in St. Barts . . . ski house in Aspen . . . I know! . . . Grab me another drink? . . . SAT scores? Well, I'm not going to worry about something that doesn't even affect me!*

Nick nudged Patch. "What do you think?"

His friend seemed chagrined. "I don't know. Would I be wrong to say that it actually looks like fun? I know I'm not supposed to think that. But I can see how everyone's gotten sucked into it. The perks aren't bad. And the view—I think this might be the most beautiful view I've ever seen in Manhattan."

"It's true," Nick said. "But we can't let ourselves be so enchanted by it. I need to be more careful, though. I thought I was going to lose it in front of Charles."

"He's a snake," Patch said. "He's become, like, your father's little errand boy."

"Yeah, right—since I never exactly fulfilled that role, and

my brothers are away at school."

"Hey, don't beat yourself up," Patch said. "You're doing what's right. Charles will get what's coming to him someday. What I want to know, though, is, do you think it was always like this? I mean, if our parents were—or, in your case, are—in it, I can't believe that all the terrible stuff we saw on the island is what it's always been about. Why would they ever join a group like that?"

Nick shook his head. "I'm not sure. Maybe there was some kind of golden age for the Society that we missed. My father said that the Power of Fourteen"—his voice lowered—"started in the 1960s. In this pool, actually. Which is totally wacked, I know. Someone drowned during a ritual and they all had to keep it quiet, since everyone felt like it was their fault."

"Maybe it's like with a lot of things," Patch said. "It starts out good and then it turns evil. It gets corrupted when it doesn't know what to do with its own power."

Nick nodded. "But I think everyone here—or at least a lot of the people here—have no idea how bad it is. They think it's a social organization, with all the charitable stuff and the parties and the donations made by the Bradford Trust Association. But that's all a smoke screen."

The Administrator approached Nick and Patch from across the room, and Nick knew they had to cease their conversation.

"Hello, Nicholas," she said. Katherine Winthrop

Stapleton, known to many members as the Administrator, was a longtime member of the Society and was in charge of keeping records. She was an older woman and didn't tolerate any nonsense from the younger members. She also protected their parents, many of whom were Elders themselves, from having to discipline their own children about Society matters.

Nick nodded a wary hello.

"I've noted that everyone is present tonight except for Phoebe Dowling, Lauren Mortimer, and Thaddeus Johnson. Do you know their whereabouts?"

Nick shook his head. "I think some of them were sick."

"It was made very clear early on that if someone is ill, they are to check in with me beforehand in order to get permission to miss the meeting."

"I don't know what happened, Miss Stapleton," Nick said. "Maybe they were too sick to remember."

She made a few notes on her pad and then retreated to the paneled anteroom. She pushed one of the panels, it opened, and she stepped inside, closing the panel behind her.

Charles appeared at Nick's side. "Did she give you the inquisition about your missing friends?" he asked. "I told her I didn't know anything."

Nick nodded. It seemed so obvious that Charles was pretending he was on their side.

"You guys had better be careful," Charles said. "You may

think that because of your family and everything, you're above all this. But you're just the same as the rest of us."

Claire Chilton, a member of their class, joined the boys after getting up from a chaise longue. That evening, Claire was one of the few who hadn't gotten her hair wet at all. She was dressed in a white robe and sandals, like a Park Avenue matron at a spa retreat. "Hello, boys. Are we discussing the absence of your three friends?"

Nick ignored her, though he was unsure of whether he should respond to Charles's earlier comment.

Thankfully, Patch saved him. "You know, we'd really better get going. School night, you know."

A few of the Society members were looking at Nick and Patch strangely. Hunter Jones and Emily van Piper had stopped their conversation by the bar, and Jeremy Hopkins was looking at them from across the pool. Nick wondered if he was being paranoid.

"Same old, same old," Patch muttered to Nick. "You get into a club, and you still feel like you don't belong. Let's get out of here."

CHAPTER TEN

On Tuesday afternoon, Lauren ran into Claire Chilton in the ladies' lounge at the Ralph Lauren store on Madison Avenue. The flagship store was housed in a Gilded Age mansion, and even its restrooms were gorgeous, with brass fixtures from England and lovely prints on the walls. Lauren had been shopping the post-holiday sales, which so far, had worked as a distraction.

Running into Claire had just ruined that for her.

"Funny seeing you here, Lauren," Claire said. Lauren had forgotten how underneath her veneer of snobbery, Claire was, at heart, extremely awkward. What was funny about seeing her here? Not much.

Lauren gave Claire an icy stare before looking ahead at the mirrors. They weren't at a Society event, and Lauren didn't have to be nice to her. After all, Claire had never returned the favor.

"You were missed at the meeting last night," Claire said as she washed her hands. "It was a lot of fun, hanging out at the pool. Strange how three people were all sick on the same night. None of you seemed sick at the memorial service for your boyfriend."

Lauren shot her a look that said *How dare you bring up Alejandro?* but Claire continued.

"I overheard my mom talking and she said that in her day, they never had issues with things like attendance. People were so much more devoted to the cause."

"The cause? What cause?" Lauren didn't know what Claire was talking about.

"You know about the museum benefit, don't you?" Claire started carefully drying her hands with a cloth towel she took from a basket.

Lauren shook her head. "I'm afraid I don't."

"You'll find out soon enough. I think you'll realize that the group is about much more than parties. It's about helping make the world a better place."

Lauren nodded noncommittally and examined her lip gloss in the mirror, as Claire leaned forward to meet her eye.

"I know that you all skipped the meeting together—you, Phoebe, and Thad," Claire said. "Everyone knows. It's completely obvious. You'd better be careful."

"What are you going to do, Claire?" Lauren said. "Tell on me to your mom? Ruin my chances to get into the Junior League? Maybe it's a big surprise to you, but I really don't care about any of it. For some of us, our world is bigger than all that."

Claire looked shocked, then confused, before gaining her composure again. "I don't know what you mean," she said as she patted down her straight hair.

Lauren leaned against one of the sinks and looked at the large oak door to make sure no one had entered. "Claire, hasn't it ever occurred to you that this group is about a lot more than philanthropy and social opportunities? Haven't you considered that it's a truly evil group that we've all been indoctrinated into, and that we won't truly be free until we leave it?" Lauren took a breath. She knew she was getting into risky territory here.

"I think you're crazy," Claire said. "There's nothing evil about the group. My parents have been members since they were teenagers themselves. They've never said anything bad about it. What happened last semester were tragedies, but we can't let that bring the group down. Chin up, Lauren. It'll get better."

Claire clasped her purse closed and started to move toward the door before turning around.

"Look, Lauren, I like you."

"Oh, I'm so glad," Lauren said as she tried to control her sneer.

Claire ignored her tone. "I think you should know that you guys are all on secret probation. There was a word my mother used: *Infidels*. They're calling the five of you 'the Infidels.' Anyway, I hope to see you at the next meeting."

"I'd rather eat broken glass," Lauren said. She had never gotten this angry at someone like Claire before, but somehow it was all bubbling to the surface now.

Claire smiled, as if she hadn't even heard what Lauren had said. "There's really no reason, Lauren, that you have to ruin everything for yourself."

CHAPTER ELEVEN

The following morning, Phoebe woke up to a strange sound coming from above her. A rustling, then a squeaking.

She crawled out of bed and cautiously tiptoed in her bare feet up to the third floor of the town house. It was a floor she and her mother didn't use much, except when Phoebe had been working on her art. Tatiana Lutyens-Hay, the sculptor friend they were house-sitting for, had a studio, and Phoebe had been storing some of her paintings and art supplies on the third floor.

When she reached the studio, Phoebe gasped, covering her mouth and stifling a scream.

The floor was covered in rats: huge, gray rats scurrying around the worktables and behind the file cabinets, crapping on the carpet and gnawing away at several of the canvases. Two of them ran between her legs, over her feet, and down the stairs.

"Mom!" Phoebe yelled, before remembering that her mother was staying with her boyfriend, Daniel, in Park Slope. Phoebe hadn't minded her mother being away, until now.

She shut the door of the studio and ran downstairs to grab her phone. Who should she call first? Her mother? Nick?

Nick would be a better choice. Her mom probably wouldn't believe her anyway.

She got him on the first try, grateful that he had set up a special ring for her on his phone.

"You what?" he said, still groggy. "Rats? Like real rats?"

Upstairs, the squeaking and scratching seemed to be getting louder.

"Yes!" she shouted. "Can you come over and help me? This is really freaking me out. I'll call an exterminator."

She grabbed her laptop, and after four tries, was able to get someone on the phone who could be there in half an hour. She put on shoes and waited in the kitchen.

Nick arrived twenty minutes later. He insisted on seeing the situation, though Phoebe didn't want to go up there. Reluctantly, she followed him and peered through the cracked door. She could see why the rats were swarming. What looked like dog kibble had been dumped onto the floor, and the rats were gobbling it up. Someone must have snuck into the house the day before to dump the food and then released the rats early that morning. How could they have gotten in? Security at the town house wasn't the best; there was a fire escape in the back, and Phoebe and Maia regularly left the windows unlocked. This had to be a major operation, though—there must have been at least fifty rats scurrying around the room.

Amidst the chaos, she could only imagine that the Society had done this to her. She felt like she was about to throw up as she thought of the implications of her suspicion.

"Did you get bitten?" Nick asked.

Phoebe grimaced. "I think I might have. I'm not really sure. Two of them ran over my feet." She looked down. Inside the sneakers she had thrown on, her feet itched, though maybe it was only her anxiety causing this.

"We should get you to a doctor for some shots. After we get these little beasts out of here."

The rats upstairs were too big to go under the door frame, but their squeaking seemed to carry through the entire house, a revolting, haunting echo.

"I don't ever want to be barefoot again in this house," Phoebe said. "This is so disgusting!"

The doorbell rang, and it was the exterminating team. They would be spreading traps and bait stations all over the town house, which would kill the rats, and then they would remove the bodies. The thought of it was vile.

It would also cost fifteen hundred dollars.

Nick handed over his credit card to one of the exterminators.

"You don't have to do that," Phoebe said. "My mom can cover it."

"I feel like it's my fault that it happened," Nick said. "I shouldn't have let you guys boycott the meeting."

"You're sure it was them?"

"Who else would it be?" Nick asked. "I've seen rats in New York City, but you usually get one or two in the basement, not a swarm on your third floor."

"We all went along with it, Nick. It's my fault as much as anyone's."

The guys started working on the problem, advising Nick and Phoebe that they might want to leave the house for a few hours. "I've got to warn you, you might want to call a cleaning service afterward," one of the guys said. "We can get all the vermin out, but there's still—well, there's still everything they leave behind."

"Like what?" Phoebe asked.

The guy made a face. "Rat droppings. They're messy creatures."

Phoebe sat down at the kitchen table and put her head into her arms, unable to process this last bit of information. "It's like the worst part isn't the actual rats—it's that it gets inside your head."

She started hyperventilating, as Nick tried to comfort

her. "Let me get some clothes for you, and you can shower and change at my place. You can always stay there for a few days if you need to."

"No, I don't want to do that. We need to get this place cleaned up," Phoebe said. "I feel like the longer we wait, the more nasty it's going to get."

"Should we just skip school?" Nick said. "I mean, you're a mess."

"I think we deserve it," Phoebe said. "I know that I'm still completely exhausted." It may have only been the third day of classes, but Phoebe felt a tiredness that ran so deep, she didn't know if it would ever leave her.

Nick found a cleaning service that specialized in unusual situations, and within a few hours after the exterminators left, the studio was almost back to normal, though Phoebe's paintings were still chewed up. Nick took her to her doctor, who gave her a series of shots, as she had a small bite on her foot.

By four P.M., they were sitting at a neighborhood café, having a late lunch that was little comfort. Phoebe picked at her croque monsieur, but found she wasn't hungry.

"This whole thing is so messed up," she said. "You really think this is their way of telling us that we can't miss a meeting? Wouldn't it have been easier to send a note?"

Nick looked at her seriously. "Come on, Phoebe. Would a note really have had the same effect?"

CHAPTER TWELVE

Now that the semester had started, Lauren had resumed her internship at Giroux New York, though she had been promoted in her responsibilities after the success of her jewelry line in the fall. Not only was she designing the line, but she had been given the chance to work under the merchandising director in setting up the jewelry displays at the store. Giroux was always known for its elegant and creative displays: last year they had displayed jewelry inside giant fish tanks with real fish, and the year before, they had rented a grove of potted Japanese maples on which the pieces had hung.

On Wednesday afternoon, she met with Antonio, the merchandising director, about the display, and then went downstairs to the design library, where they kept a collection of reference books and magazines. The concept was the zodiac, with a different set of jewelry representing each astrological sign. She felt like she was hit in the gut when she got to the images for Leo, which was Alejandro's sign.

His birthday would have been in August. Since they had met in September, she had never even gotten to celebrate his birthday with him. She gulped back her tears and tried to focus on her work.

About an hour into her research, the intercom buzzed. It was a salesgirl from the first floor. "Lauren, there's someone here to see you."

Lauren walked upstairs, wondering who it could be.

When she saw that it was Claire Chilton and her mother, she rolled her eyes, only realizing as she did it that she was fully in their view.

"Lauren," Claire's mother, Letty, said. "What a treat."

Letty Chilton was a stout woman who was known for her personal frugality, even though she sat on the boards of several multimillion-dollar institutions and was known to give generously. She would wear Oscar de la Renta suits from the eighties until the elbows were nearly worn through, and she hadn't redecorated their apartment since Claire had been born. Recently, however, her husband had come into a great deal of family money, and the word was that she was spending more freely. Still, the main thing Lauren always associated with her was that she stank of stale Chanel

No. 5. Today was no exception.

Lauren greeted her and Claire civilly.

"I'm hoping you can help us out," Mrs. Chilton said. "In fact, I *know* you can help us out. Claire needs some new clothes for the season, and I've heard you have the best eye."

"Well, I can recommend you to a stylist," she said. "I'm really focusing on the jewelry now."

"That's right, your little jewelry line," Mrs. Chilton said. "So sweet."

"We want your employee discount," Claire said.

Mrs. Chilton glared at her daughter, and then smiled at Lauren. "We wouldn't want to impose, of course."

"You know, I'm really not supposed to do that," Lauren said. "They don't even let us use it all the time. And I'm not really a full-fledged employee."

"Of course you're not. So what does it matter? Anyway, we so appreciate it. I know you'll do a marvelous job picking out some outfits for Claire."

"Actually, I don't really have time—"

"Thank you, Lauren." Mrs. Chilton turned and walked away, as if the matter was settled and there was nothing more to discuss.

"I'll give you the name of a stylist," Lauren said to Claire. Lauren wrote a name down on a card and handed it to Claire. "If you want a discount, you'll have to talk to Sebastian. Here's his extension. He'd be happy to talk to you, I'm sure."

After Lauren had said good-bye to Claire, she was fuming. How dare Claire march in there and demand that she serve her like a shopgirl? Even Lauren didn't like using her employee discount too often for herself, as it made her look like a spendthrift in front of the other employees, who could barely afford clothes at a designer sample sale, let alone at Giroux. The thing that really annoyed Lauren was that Claire would probably get the discount from Sebastian, if she spent enough.

At the end of the day, after Lauren had finished her work downstairs and created a look board for the concept, there was a flurry of activity near the door.

Sabrina Harriman, the store's creative director, stood near the front door. The store had closed for the evening, and the staff was getting ready to leave.

"People, listen up, we have a problem! The pair of limited-edition sapphire earrings is gone from the jewelry case. They were here this afternoon, so I don't know what could have happened. We didn't even show them to any customers."

Everyone gasped. The sapphire earrings were one of the most expensive items in the entire store and were kept in a locked glass case. They retailed for four thousand dollars.

"I'm so sorry to have to do this," Sabrina said, "but we're going to need to search everyone's bags before you leave."

Lauren stood in line, annoyed that this would make her late in getting home. What kind of person would work at the store and steal a pair of earrings? Not only that, but a pair that would certainly be missed?

Lauren reached the front of the line. "Hey, Danny," she said to the security guard. He was a sweet bear of a guy, and she had always made an effort to greet him by name. He took her bag.

"Sorry about this," he said, muttering under his breath. His eyes suddenly opened wide. "Lauren, what the—"

"What?"

"Lauren!" He pulled out the earrings, still in their box, and held them up for Sabrina and everyone else to see.

"What!?" Lauren felt her neck growing hot. "That's absurd!" She turned to Sabrina. "Sabrina, you know I would never do anything like this."

She grabbed the earrings from Danny and handed the jewelry box back to Sabrina.

"Lauren, I don't know what to say," Sabrina said as she took the box.

Sebastian Giroux had come up from his office. "What is going on?"

"We have a problem here. Lauren, I'm afraid we might need to press charges."

Lauren glared at her, though inside she was completely mortified. Someone must have planted the earrings in her bag while she was working. Her bag had been in her locker most of the afternoon. The lockers were in an employee staff area, and anyone could have gained access to it—that is, anyone with the master combination.

Who would have done it? One of the Society's lackeys? A Giroux staff member? Sebastian himself? Sebastian was a member of the Society, but Lauren couldn't imagine him doing this to her.

It didn't matter who had done this; it only mattered that it had happened. She was being sent a message, just like the handbag she had received back in September. Only this time, it was a message of a different type: a spiteful reminder that she shouldn't miss any more meetings.

"No charges will be pressed," Sebastian said to his staff. "We'll handle it internally. You can all go home for the night. Lauren, please stay behind so we can discuss this."

Everyone filed out, a few of them giving Lauren sympathetic looks and others averting their eyes.

Lauren sat down on a chaise where customers usually tried on shoes. "Look, I am completely horrified, but you've got to believe me, I have no idea how those earrings got into my bag. It was in my employee locker for most of the afternoon— could someone have slipped them in there? I mean, come on, Sebastian, you know me. If I really wanted those earrings, I would have asked my mom to buy them for me. Why would I do something to jeopardize my relationship with the store?"

Sabrina shrugged.

"She's right," Sebastian said. "Sabrina, you and I can discuss this between the two of us. Good night, Lauren."

Lauren zipped up her bag and slinked away. No one at the store would have done this to her. Even though Sebastian was in the Society, she knew that he liked her. The horrible thing, of course, about being accused of something like this was that even if you didn't do it, you still felt guilty.

And that, she imagined, was exactly what the Society had wanted her to feel.

CHAPTER THIRTEEN

That afternoon, Patch went downtown to shop for some new music. The kind of stuff he really loved he couldn't find on iTunes: remixes, obscure tracks, bootlegs. He had even bought a used pair of direct drive turntables and was starting to expand his record collection so that he could start DJing using real vinyl. The store he had wanted to check out, East Village Sounds, was on Sixth Street, and was two steps down from street level. It was a dank, musty shop, with walls covered in posters, stickers, and graffiti, each year's tastes obscured by the next. At the front, they sold T-shirts, and the countertop was covered in flyers for shows at local venues: $2 COVER! FIRST HOUR, FREE WELL DRINKS! OPENING ACT: BEEL-ZEBUB'S KITTEN!

It was a far cry from the posh, slick nightclub world that

Nick and his friends inhabited, but Patch liked it.

He browsed around the store, carefully tracing the perimeter of the room and avoiding contact with the girl with dark eyes and jet black hair who was staffing the counter. She had on her earbuds anyway and seemed disinterested in the fact that Patch was in the store.

There was a listening booth near the cash register, like in the old days, where you could bring a record to the front and they would unwrap it for you. There was one Patch wanted to hear, but it was forty-five dollars. It was a limited-edition press of an album by some obscure French DJs; he had read on a blog that it was huge all over Europe.

He brought it up to the front and smiled at the girl. She was pretty, lithe, half Asian, perhaps. She wore a baggy sweater, one shoulder off, over a long black Goth skirt, over leggings. Though it might have made some girls look sloppy, on her it looked cool.

Patch had grown more confident lately, which made him less shy about interactions like this: his arms were muscular from his trips to the gym, his hair was shorn in a way that, even though he had done it himself with a pair of clippers, didn't look half bad, and he had noticed that his new attitude had somehow made his skin look clearer, brighter. What had changed in his life on the outside that could have caused this? The Society, for one thing. But maybe he had changed on the inside as well.

She sighed as he handed her the album, giving him a weary look. "You want to listen to that one?"

Patch nodded. "Is that okay?"

"Oh, you'd only be about the eighth person this week who's requested it. No one ever wants to buy it because it's too expensive."

"What if I do want to buy it?"

She scoffed. "Why would you buy it when you can rip it off the net so easily?"

"Maybe I like vinyl."

She paused. "Oh. Seriously?"

"I just bought a pair of turntables last week."

"Last week? Wow, you must be really experienced." She gave him a shy smile.

Was she making fun of him? Or was it possible that she was flirting with him?

"Come on back here," she said, placing the record aside. "I'll show you some stuff that's far better than those Parisian twits."

Patch's eyes widened. "Don't you have to watch the store?"

"It's cool, there's a sensor on the door so I can hear when someone comes in." In the storeroom in the back, she grabbed a box cutter and for a moment, Patch was cautious. She started opening several UPS boxes. "We just got these in," she said. "I've been waiting for the right moment to open them."

"Why is now the right moment?"

She smiled. "I don't know. You're the first semi-normal person to walk in today."

"Maybe someday I'll make it to normal," Patch said. It was a weak attempt at humor, but she didn't seem to mind. He felt happy here, a warm feeling that seemed miles away from Chadwick and his life on the Upper East Side. "So what's so special about these albums?"

She held them up in their slick plastic wrappers, the wild colors of their artwork flickering in the light. "You know when music can completely transport you?" she said. "That's what I'm after. I don't do drugs, I don't drink, I don't smoke. These are my drugs." She motioned to all the record albums and grinned. "They will get you more messed up than any drug can."

Patch knew what she meant. He wanted to stay off drinking himself, but around Nick and the others, it was hard. Now, standing there with this girl, it was cool to meet someone who didn't need chemicals to keep herself entertained.

She turned on the music, and it washed over them both, track after track. It was their own private listening booth, much more exclusive than the little phone booth–sized compartment in the front. She smiled at him. She had a gap between her two front teeth, which was cute.

"I'm Lia, by the way," she said.

Patch nodded. He realized, half a song later, that he

probably should have told her his name, but the moment had passed.

In between one of the tracks, she cracked a smile for no reason.

"What?" Patch said.

"It's nothing."

"No, tell me!"

"You really want me to? I barely know you."

What was it? Did he have bad breath? Did his socks not match?

She leaned forward and touched a spot on his jawline. "You have a patch where you missed shaving," she said. "That's all."

Patch felt his face turning red.

"Oh, now you're blushing!" she teased him. "It's not a big deal. My ex-boyfriend used to do it all the time. He was always in such a hurry, he would miss a spot."

"Sorry," Patch said, chagrined. "Though I'm not sure why I'm apologizing to you." He felt like such a dork.

"What's your name, anyway?" she asked.

Now it was Patch's turn to laugh. "You're not going to believe it."

"What's so funny?"

"It's Patch."

She paused, and then smiled. "No, seriously."

"Really. It's Patch Evans."

"Okay, Patch, patch. I get it. Is that like your trademark or something?" She reached out again and quickly stroked his cheek. It wasn't romantic or anything—more like playful.

"No, it's—"

He was cut off as the buzzer in the front sounded, and Lia jumped up. "Party's over," she said. "Back to work."

"Can I buy the other album?" Patch asked. It was a big purchase—he could get four albums for its price on iTunes—but he still wanted it. He would put it on his credit card, though he knew it was a little irresponsible, given his financial situation.

"Why don't you just take it?" she said. "I'll tell my boss that someone scratched it and it was ruined. It happens sometimes."

"Hey, you don't have to do that."

"Okay, I won't." She went back to sorting receipts at the counter while keeping an eye on the customers who had just walked in, two tattooed guys with a Rottweiler.

Patch laughed. "No—that's not what I meant. I mean, it's really cool of you. I don't have much cash right now, and I've wanted something by these guys for, like, forever. You're sure it's not a problem?"

She shrugged. "We comp small stuff to our good customers all the time. I'll just pretend you're a really good customer."

"What can I do for you?" Patch asked.

She scribbled her number on the back of a show flyer, as he felt the blood rush to his neck again. "Here's what you can do: call me sometime."

CHAPTER FOURTEEN

After parting ways with Nick, Phoebe wanted to tell her mother about what had happened but decided against it. Despite the undeniable evidence in the studio that the rats actually had been there—the room reeked of cleaning supplies after the crew had given the floor a thorough scrubbing—she didn't want to get into it with Maia. Her mom would probably never notice the rips in Phoebe's canvases anyway; she might just think it was part of the work.

When Phoebe had mentioned the Society to her mother back in the fall, Maia had sent her to Dr. Meckling. The psychiatrist, who was part of the Society himself, had implied that Phoebe was suffering from delusions and should possibly be hospitalized. After returning from the retreat at Isis Island, Phoebe had been afraid to say anything to her mom about what had happened there, for fear that her mother would, once again, think she was crazy.

Now she didn't even want to mention the rats to Daniel; though he was in the Society himself, he might not believe her.

Her mother and Daniel arrived home, and Maia busied herself in the kitchen. Phoebe sat in the living room with Daniel and tried to concentrate on the reading for her literature class, a book of Kafka stories. As the fire he had lit started to crackle, Phoebe found that the text was starting to blend together on the page. She looked up from her book and tried to relax her eyes.

"Is everything okay with school?" Daniel said. "You look exhausted."

"Thanks," Phoebe said drily. "That's always nice to hear."

"Anything going on? It's only the first few days into the new semester, right?"

"I'm not sure you would understand," Phoebe said.

"Is it about the retreat?" he asked quietly.

"Well, yeah, for starters." After he had told her mother to send her to Meckling, Phoebe didn't know whether she could trust him or not. But he was being nice to her tonight, and she thought that if he opened up, it might help her piece together answers to some of the many questions she had.

"I think—" Daniel paused, as if carefully measuring what he was about to say. "I think you may be taking all this stuff with the Society too seriously. The work the Society has done over the years has been exemplary, and I think you're ignoring that in favor of a few minor incidents. There's the work they've done philanthropically, and the connections they help people to make. All that stuff, the initiations, the stuff on the island, that's all just to get people excited about it. Sort of like a pep rally."

Phoebe scoffed. "Um, a pep rally where they burn coffin effigies of two people? Come on, Daniel, two people my age *died*! That certainly wasn't smoke and mirrors."

Daniel looked back nervously at the closed door leading to the kitchen. "You know we need to be discreet about this, Phoebe. It's a privilege to be picked for the Society, and you're treating it like it's some kind of high school prank."

"What will happen if I tell my mom again? Will you get in trouble?" Phoebe sneered at him. She was surprising herself; it wasn't like her to act this way.

"I think you know. The Council won't tolerate insubordination. You're ignoring all the good that the Society has done, and focusing on the bad. Have you heard about the renovations at the Met? Ninety percent of that has been funded by Society contributions."

Phoebe sighed. "My friends and I are just so sick of all these rules. You really believe in all this?" She was starting to wonder herself. Maybe she had overreacted to everything. Maybe Jared's death had been an accident. But Alejandro's death: Parker Bell had admitted to them that he had orchestrated it. She didn't know why she kept doubting herself. The Society was corrupt, and within her first two weeks in New York, she had gotten involved in it.

She should have known better.

Daniel leaned toward her. "I believe that if we live according to the best ideals that have been set forth for us, we can achieve our maximum potential."

Phoebe nodded blankly and turned back to her reading. Talking to Daniel wasn't going to do any good.

When Phoebe had arrived in Manhattan four months ago from California, she had wanted her New York to be like the one she had seen in the movies.

Now it was, in a sense.

The only problem was that it was the wrong kind of movie.

CHAPTER FIFTEEN

After parting ways with Phoebe, Nick took the subway back home. He decided to get off several stops early, on Lexington Avenue in the Sixties. It was a chilly night, but with everything that had happened, he wanted to take a walk and clear his head. As he was about to cross the street and go west toward Fifth, Nick got a call from Thad.

"Did you hear what happened to me today?" his new friend said. "I've just spent the last four hours in the headmistress's office." Thad attended the Whitford School on West End Avenue, but gossip about people Nick knew usually reached him, even if they didn't go to Chadwick.

"What did you do? I wasn't at school today, so I didn't hear."

"I didn't do anything! I opened my locker between first

and second period, and a bottle of gin fell out. It shattered all over the floor, and you know how gin smells like—"

"Like my parents in the summer?" Nick interrupted.

Thad laughed grimly. "I was going to say like gin, but yeah, whatever. Anyway, you couldn't miss it. I was pulled in by the headmistress, and she was not pleased. You know how crazy they are about drinking. I guess it's the same at Chadwick."

"Don't remind me." Nick had been admonished for hosting a party that was featured in *New York* magazine, and he was still trying to regain credibility at school as someone who wasn't a complete screwup.

"I've been suspended for a week," Thad said. "I would have been expelled, but I told them there was no way the bottle was mine. My father threatened to bring in a lawyer and do a forensic test on the broken bottle and everything. That got them to back down. But I'm still suspended, and the incident may go on my permanent record."

"We've got to figure out a way to end this," Nick said. "Let me think about it tonight, okay?"

Just as Nick was hanging up, another call came through from Phoebe, who said that Lauren had just been accused of theft at Giroux New York.

Nick shook his head. "I'm not surprised." He told Phoebe about what had happened to Thad.

"We need to get together again with the others," Phoebe said. "Let me figure out a good meeting place."

Nick slowed down his walk as he hit Park Avenue. Traffic was light, and there weren't many pedestrians. "I'm worried about you," he said quietly. "Are you going to be okay? Staying at home, with, you know . . . I mean, what if something else happens?" Phoebe had mentioned that Daniel, Phoebe's mother's boyfriend, would be staying over that night.

"He's not going to do anything. This is all coming from far higher up—I feel like it's coming from the Council of Regents. Seriously, talking to Daniel, I think he believes the Society is this amazing organization that's only out for the greater good. Besides, there's no reason why my being close to Daniel is any more dangerous than you being around your parents."

There was an awkward pause on the line as Nick let this sink in. "I guess you're right," he finally said.

He knew his dad had done all these terrible things, but he had mentally separated those actions from his father's role as his parent.

Maybe it was time to accept that it was all coming from the same man. He didn't want to, and it had been so difficult for him over the past several months to see his parents change from people he trusted and believed to people who trafficked in deception. Nick knew that his father wanted to draw him into his world, but he had resisted. On New Year's Eve, before everyone left Isis Island to go back to the city, Nick's father had confided in him, telling him a secret about Patch that was far too momentous for Nick to reveal. Nick hadn't wanted to tell it to Patch a mere day after they had reconciled, and then as each day passed, it became more difficult to reveal what he had learned. Now that it had been more than a week, Nick had pushed the information to the far recesses of his mind.

Phoebe said she had to go, as Daniel and her mother were still downstairs.

As he walked up Park Avenue, Nick thought about what had happened to his three friends. The Society was punishing them for not attending the meeting on Monday night. Nick had always heard that meetings were serious and not to be missed; it was one of the Society's rules. But all these horrible acts? It wasn't right.

Alejandro's and Jared's lives had already been sacrificed. Should the five of them remain steadfast in not allowing the Society to control them? Should they skip more meetings?

Nick didn't know the right answer.

Soon he arrived home at his family's apartment building, across the street from the Metropolitan Museum. He considered stopping at Patch's floor to talk it over with him and Genie, but he decided against it.

Nick's fingers and toes felt frostbitten, so he took a long, hot shower, which eased the pain.

The soapy water swirled down the drain, and he gradually regained sensation in his extremities. He thought of the comforts that the Society provided for all of them. Like a long, hot shower on a chilly winter night, the Society wanted to placate them all into submission with perks and luxuries, to make life so comfortable that it would be easy to ignore the darker side of any situation.

Nick dressed carefully in jeans and a nice shirt. Running into his parents these days was an awkward affair, and he almost pretended that he didn't know them, as if he were in a hotel and was passing another guest in the hallway.

But tonight he couldn't avoid them. Not when his girlfriend had been sabotaged.

Downstairs he heard his father in the library. Nick walked in.

"Nick, it's nice to see you," his father said. "You look a bit flushed. Did you go running today?"

Nick tried to keep his bitterness in check. He sat down on one of the leather couches and took a deep breath before answering.

"No, I didn't. I had to help Phoebe. Her art studio was filled with rats."

His father raised an eyebrow. "Rats? How odd." He took a sip of his scotch.

"Thad was suspended when a bottle of gin fell out of his locker, and Lauren was accused of theft. Dad, we know that the Society is responsible for all of this."

His father looked at him. "Maybe you'll think about these occurrences the next time that you decide to miss a Society meeting. After everything that happened in the fall, I'd think you would take your responsibilities more seriously."

"Dad, what happened in the fall was that you *killed* two people. Maybe not you personally, but the Society. And as far as I'm concerned, and from what everyone has told me, you pretty much are the Society. Or at least you're the only part of it that I have any access to."

"Calm down, Nick. At this time, your family needs you. You haven't even asked about how your grandfather is doing. What kind of a selfish person are you?"

Nick's mother appeared at the entryway to the library. He glared at his father. "Oh, forgive me if I put self-preservation and caring for my friends above my grandfather. It's not like he's exactly helped with this situation."

"Your grandfather has made more possible in your life for you and your friends than you will ever understand," Parker said as he stood up and moved toward the door. "So I strongly suggest that you get yourself in line."

CHAPTER SIXTEEN

On Thursday nights, Genie went out, a rare weekly event when she attended a ballroom dancing class and then went to a diner afterward for coffee and pie with her friends. Because of this, Patch decided to offer up their apartment for the emergency meeting. For a few hours, they would have the place to themselves. He had wanted to make it nice for everyone, and though there was no way it would ever compare to the opulence of Lauren's apartment, he had straightened up the living room and even bought sodas and baked a roll of chocolate chip cookies.

Thad, Phoebe, and Lauren recounted all the sabotage that had happened in the last forty-eight hours. Thad was still lobbying his school's administration to keep the incident with the gin bottle off his permanent record. Phoebe was recovering from the vermin infestation and would need a follow-up meeting with her doctor to make sure she hadn't been infected by the bite. Lauren was waiting for the verdict from Sebastian Giroux about the jewelry found in her bag.

"There's something else," Lauren said. She pulled out her phone from her handbag and showed everyone a text message she had received that day.

It read:

AQ EKEPRLE FMPYD QZP OQL RMYD QPDRL?

"Looks like gibberish," Phoebe said.

"It's not gibberish," Thad said. "It's a cryptogram."

"A crypto-what?" Nick asked.

"It's a code where each letter stands for a different one. Lauren, give me your phone."

She handed her phone to Thad, and he punched the series of letters into his own iPhone, copying over the cryptogram.

His face grew dark. "I think I know what it means. I used a cryptogram solver. It's a little bit . . . well, it's a little bit scary."

"Come on, what is it?" Phoebe asked.

He looked at Lauren. "Go ahead," she said.

"It reads—and I think this is correct: 'Do sisters watch out for each other?'"

"That's weird," Phoebe said. "Does that make any sense to you?"

"It makes sense to me," Lauren said.

"Why's that?" Nick asked.

"The text wasn't originally sent to me. It was sent to my little sister, Allison."

The group was silent for a moment.

"She's not even in the Society," Phoebe said after a moment.

"Maybe that's the point," Patch said. "They want us to know that they're not afraid to get to our families."

"Why Lauren, though?" Phoebe asked. "Why not any of the rest of us?"

"They think Lauren's vulnerable right now," Thad said. "And she's the only one who has a younger sibling who's not in the Society."

"That's true," Patch said. "I'm just trying to figure out a pattern here. The rats were destroying Phoebe's canvases. Phoebe's an artist; that hits her where it hurts. Lauren, they put your job designing jewelry at risk. And the message to your sister is a further warning. But what about the bottle of gin? They could have done that to mess with any of us. Why Thad?"

"You're right; it doesn't match up," Nick said.

Thad spoke slowly. "They must know more about my

family than I usually tell people. My mom has been sober for ten years, but she used to have a drinking problem. They must have known that this would really bother me."

Lauren gave his arm a supportive squeeze. "Hey—it would have bothered anyone."

"What kind of sick stuff is this?" Phoebe said. "I can't believe this—they're not only messing with us physically, it's like they're trying to get to us psychologically. How do we know what's next? If they could manage to screw up our lives this much in the last forty-eight hours, who knows what they could do?"

"We need to lay off," Lauren said. "I mean, this is my sister we're talking about. She's a freshman at boarding school. It would be so easy for them to get to her. We need to go to the meetings. We need to do what they say."

"I have a plan," Nick said. "And it won't put us in danger. I just need to work it out a little more before we get going on it."

"What kind of plan?" Patch asked warily.

"I need you guys to hang tight for a couple of days. Can I fill you in on the weekend?"

Everyone nodded.

"In the meantime, maybe we all need to pretend to be model citizens, at least for a little while," Thad said. "We need to get to know the other members."

"I just don't know if I can bear it," Phoebe said. "They're all like zombies. Claire Chilton going on about how the Upper

East Side isn't like it used to be. Who the hell cares?"

Lauren jumped in. "Speaking of Claire—I had an odd confrontation with her on Tuesday. Phoebe, I told you about this, right?"

Phoebe nodded.

"I ran into her at the Ralph Lauren store. She said that everyone had noticed that three of us were missing from the meeting, and then she started going on about how the Society was all about cultural advancement and how there was going to be a benefit for the museum. About how the Society was all about making the world a better place."

"Oh, if only that were true," Nick said sarcastically. "She's totally bought into the whole thing. Her parents are both members. You know how seriously they take it."

"There's something else: they've given us a name. The five us are 'the Infidels.' That's what the older members are calling us. I looked it up; it's like when you don't believe in a religion that everyone else believes in."

"Well, that would be us," Phoebe said.

Nick gave a half smile. "Maybe we should print T-shirts."

"Yeah, right," Patch said. "Talk about wearing a bull's-eye on your back."

"So let them call us that," Thad said. "Let them think the group is about cultural advancement. We still need to fly under the radar. Don't let them think we have anything planned."

"Because the truth is, we don't," Patch said.

"That's not entirely true," Nick said. "I think I can figure something out. I just need some more time."

"What should I tell my sister?" Lauren asked.

"Tell her that she'll be fine. Tell her it doesn't mean anything," Nick said.

"How can you be so sure?" Phoebe asked. "I mean, we all thought that skipping a meeting wasn't a big deal, and look what happened."

"They've made their point," Nick said. "From now on, we don't miss any more meetings. Give me a few days—in fact, clear your Saturday, if you can. I'll keep you posted."

"You're sure you can come up with something?" Patch asked.

Nick nodded. Nothing more had to be said. Patch trusted his friend, and the rest of them did as well.

After everyone left, though, Patch kept wondering about the Society, about its methods, and how they had gotten to Lauren by threatening her sister.

All he had in his family were Genie and his mother. And he wondered which one of them could be next.

CHAPTER SEVENTEEN

On Friday morning at school, the junior class had a meeting with Chadwick's director of college advising, Mr. Gregory. He went on and on about the importance of their grades and extracurricular activities, particularly in the second semester of their junior year. This would be the second-to-last official set of grades that admissions committees could use to evaluate the candidates from Chadwick, and for those who were applying for early admission to places like Yale, it would be the last full set of grades available before an admissions committee would make its decision. Phoebe noticed some of the students sitting in the back, their feet perched rudely on the desks in front of them, as if none of this applied to them. Phoebe wasn't going to make any assumptions; she knew she still had to keep her grades up. She had met with a few alumni who were on different admissions committees last semester at a meet and greet sponsored by the Society. It had all been done under the auspices of a "private gathering sponsored by a group of helpful alumni." But she didn't feel like she could just coast on through.

Phoebe tried to focus on Mr. Gregory's talk, but something had happened last night that she couldn't get out of her mind. When she asked to use the bathroom at Patch's apartment, he had directed her to Genie's, as he said that his own was a mess. Phoebe had developed a terrible habit of snooping when she was in other people's houses, and she couldn't help taking a peek into Genie's medicine cabinet. Besides, she was curious about the woman. There was something Genie wasn't telling all of them about her past, and Phoebe was anxious to know what it was.

Just a few weeks ago, Genie had told Phoebe and Nick about her broken engagement with Palmer Bell in the 1940s. But Phoebe sensed that there was more to the story. Why had Genie ended up in the same apartment building as Palmer's son and his family? Was it simply coincidence that Nick and Patch had become such good friends?

Phoebe imagined that Genie's secrets might help them unravel the mysteries about the Society that they had been trying to uncover. She hadn't wanted to pry Patch when he was so new to the group, but there were things she had noticed: the wistful, far-off look in Genie's eyes when she had talked about Palmer that afternoon a few weeks ago, the way she fiddled with the locket around her neck, how Patch seemed to have such a strange relationship with the Bell family, as if he were both an outsider and a close family friend.

"Phoebe!" Nick tapped her on the shoulder. "We have to go. The presentation's over."

She nodded distractedly, only able to think of one thing: as she had stood in Genie's bathroom the night before, amidst cold cream, perfume, and prescriptions, she noticed a blue glass bottle of tuberose perfume. It was vintage, not something Genie would have bought recently. From the gold script on the bottle, it might have been forty or fifty years old. Phoebe gently opened the bottle and held it to her nose, and the smell brought her right back to the same scent in that velvet-lined sarcophagus in the warehouse on Gansevoort Street at the Night of Rebirth.

CHAPTER EIGHTEEN

Adding to all the confusion over the past week, Patch had been unable to reach Simone Matthews, his producer on *Chadwick Prep*, the television show that they had been hoping to pitch to a number of network and cable TV outlets. In the fall there had been some real traction on the project, and they were getting interest from foreign as well as domestic networks. It had been everything Patch ever wanted, from the first time he had picked up a video camera: to have his own show. And now it had been so close, so within his grasp, it was almost as if he had already reached his goal.

Almost.

Ever since Simone had started putting together the footage that Patch already had, she had said she needed something more. Something more exciting, something with what she called "a throughline." She wanted real drama, and the only way Patch could deliver that was by giving her access to the inner workings of the Society. She had been the initial impetus that had sent him to Isis Island, in the hopes of getting some footage of the Society's retreat. Unfortunately, he had never had the chance to capture a single frame. While he had gotten an insider's view, all he had were his own memories. And now, after having been kidnapped and becoming a member, the Society had the original memory cards of his footage. In addition to messengering them to the Society's town house the day after the retreat, he had signed an affidavit that he no longer had any duplicate copies in his possession.

What he didn't tell them was that a week ago, he had contacted Eliot Walker, the older of the two Walker cousins who were on the lobster boat he had taken out to Isis Island. As a favor to Patch, Eliot had set up a safe-deposit box for him at the Coastal Bank of Maine. The key had arrived in the mail today. In the safe-deposit box were several memory sticks containing all the raw footage, plus the rough cuts that Patch had put together.

Patch knew he wouldn't be able to use any of it now, but at least he had it as leverage if he ever needed it. He figured he hadn't technically broken the affidavit, as the material wasn't in his possession.

Now, this afternoon, as he headed to the loft that housed Simone's production company, he hoped he might be able to revive the project, even without the Society footage—to make the show more about Chadwick and less about the Society. He had tried to get back in touch with Simone, but she wasn't returning his calls.

When he showed up at the building in the West Thirties, though, his key card no longer worked. He waited for a few minutes and then was able to gain entry as some members of a production crew left for the day.

Patch went up to the third floor and looked for Eyes Wide Open Productions. There was no sign on the door anymore, and the office was unlocked. Patch walked in to discover that it was as if the company had disappeared. All the editing decks had been removed; the same went for the file cabinets, the bulletin boards, the posters on the walls. All that was left was what the space had come with: empty cubicles, phones with dead lines, and the detritus of moving.

Patch called Simone on her cell. Perhaps they had recently moved, and she had been preoccupied.

He felt the lightbulb on one of the office lamps. Confirming his suspicions, it was still warm.

Simone picked up after a few rings. "Patch," she said. "You're probably wondering what's going on."

"Um, yeah, that would be one of my questions."

She sighed. "I had to move my editing suite uptown. I was given an opportunity—it was something I couldn't turn down."

"What kind of opportunity?"

"I'm not really supposed to talk about it. I guess it's okay to mention it to you. I got a grant from this group that gives out awards to filmmakers, sort of like the Guggenheim or the MacArthur grants. The Bradford Trust Association?"

Patch groaned. Even though the Bradford Trust Association was the parent corporation for the Society, everyone thought it was a philanthropic group that was improving the world by writing checks.

"Anyway, they gave me a hundred thousand dollars to work on my documentary, a pet project I've been doing."

"What are their terms?"

"I had to sign a confidentiality agreement about where I was getting the money. And, well . . ."

"And what?"

"I had to commit to working in film for the next two years. It's really exciting—they think this new project of mine could make it to Sundance next year. They don't want me distracted by my television projects."

"Where does that leave us with *Chadwick Prep*?"

"I'm sorry, Patch. We're going to have to drop the project. Our option runs out on it in June. After that, you'll be free to pursue other venues. But to be honest, I just don't know if I see it going anywhere. I mean, until you get some more footage of that secret group—"

"Simone! Don't you see? That secret group *is* the Bradford

Trust Association! They shut down the project by giving you that money."

She laughed. "Um, right, Patch. And let me guess: they killed the Kennedys, too?"

"Simone, you've got to believe me. You really don't want to get involved with these people. Is there any way you can get out of it?"

"The papers are already signed. I thought you would be happy for me. I'm sorry about your show, Patch. I really am. But it just wasn't the right time for me. These things happen. It took me years before I got my first TV project on the air."

"Simone, I have a limited amount of time in which I can do this! I'm graduating from high school next year. It's not like I'm going to be able to go back to Chadwick and film stuff after I'm gone. If the option expires in six months, then I'll have wasted my whole junior year."

"I know, I'm sorry. Maybe we can work something out, let you out of your contract early. You might have to give back some of the option money."

"How much of it?"

"I don't know. I'd have to talk to my agents about it. Maybe half?"

Five thousand dollars. He had already spent most of the money on equipment and personal expenses. He had put twenty-five hundred into a CD at the bank, at Genie's insistence, and he had about a thousand dollars left. The rest he had invested in a new AVID machine at home and a new computer monitor. And some new shoes and his new DJ equipment. Now he realized that it had been stupid of him to spend so freely. But he had thought *Chadwick Prep* was a done deal. He definitely didn't have five grand to buy back the rights early. And he wasn't about to ask Nick for the money. He was too proud for that.

"I'll think about it," he said, bluffing.

"So tell me one thing," she said. "Whatever happened on that island? I'm dying to know."

Patch paused. Should he tell her? What good would it do? She couldn't produce his TV show. And he certainly didn't want her knowing that now he was a member of the Society himself.

"Nothing," he said. "The ferry schedule was off, and I never even made it."

CHAPTER NINETEEN

Lauren was encouraged that her friends had immediately decided to back down upon hearing that her sister had received the creepy text message. They didn't have any proof that the Society was responsible, but the mere possibility that there could be more violence in the future was enough to keep them all in line.

Of course, this was exactly what the Society wanted them to think. But maybe it wasn't a bad idea to work more covertly. Lauren trusted that Nick and the others would come up with some kind of plan. The best she could do was to play along once she found out what it was.

The next Society meeting was held on Friday night at a special location: the Metropolitan Museum of Art. The twenty-nine Conscripts—the older class of fourteen and the younger class of fifteen—were asked to meet in the lobby of the museum at seven P.M. Claire Chilton's mother, Letty, appeared when the group had assembled and motioned for everyone to follow her into the Egyptian wing. Security guards stood by the cases of artifacts, just as they would during museum hours. When the group entered the main area, the Temple of Dendur was lit up beautifully in a wash of red and lavender, as if for a special event. Four rows of chairs sat facing the temple, and everyone took their seats.

Letty Chilton stood in front of the group and began speaking.

"You're probably all wondering why you're here," Mrs. Chilton said. "We wanted to bring you here tonight so that you could all see the beauty of the temple up close. I know many of you have grown up with Dendur practically in your backyard, but you may not have had the chance really to look at it. We'll have the opportunity to do that later. For now, we're going to discuss a very important event that is coming up."

Nick yawned, and Claire glared at him as her mother continued speaking.

"I have some exciting news that I think will send you all over the moon! On February 13, Valentine's Day eve, the museum is throwing a benefit party, a revival of the Dendur Ball, an event that last occurred in the early 1990s. The Met will be celebrating the renovations on the new Egyptian wing—work that, as you know, was funded by the Bradford Trust Association. Anonymously, of course. The museum has asked us to take a leadership role in the planning of this event. And I know it will be a lot of fun!" Letty Chilton punched the air with her wrinkled fist as if at a pep rally, and a few members of the group twittered at the intense awkwardness of the presentation.

Lauren shifted in her seat. How could the Society be so cavalier about hosting another event after so much had gone awry? She focused on Phoebe, Nick, Patch, and Thad, which gave her the courage to stay.

Mrs. Chilton continued. "We're excited to announce that all of you will be serving on the Junior Committee. My daughter, Claire, will be chairing the committee and handling its meetings. Your job will primarily be to get the younger generation involved in the museum. You can sell tickets to your classmates, to your friends. We have a special price for the under-twenty-ones. Remember, patronage of the arts starts at a young age. This is our cultural heritage, this museum and others in the city. It's our job to make sure that it is preserved."

Not another committee. It all seemed like a ruse to steer people's attention away from the awful things that had happened in November and December. Lauren cast a sideways glance at Phoebe, Nick, Patch, and Thad. They all looked bored.

Later, over refreshments—sugary punch and stale butter cookies—she talked to Phoebe. "What do you think about all this?" she asked.

"I guess going along with this is part of our keeping in line?" Phoebe said.

"Something like that."

Claire came up to Lauren. "How are you, Lauren? It's nice to see you here."

Lauren nodded.

"I was so sorry to hear about the little incident at Giroux this week. It must have been a mistake, right? I mean, when I was talking about it to Sebastian, I told him I know you, and there is no way you would ever steal a pair of earrings!"

She gave Claire a frigid look, but it didn't stop Lauren from reddening. "Sure, whatever, Claire. Thanks for having my back."

Phoebe pulled Lauren away, rescuing her. "Let's go talk to Nick."

Lauren gritted her teeth. "Claire just makes me so angry, sometimes I feel like I could kill her."

"I know, we all do," Phoebe said. "She's a loser; you can't let it get to you."

They walked up to Nick, who was drinking a glass of punch.

"You really sure you want to be drinking that?" Phoebe said.

"If I die of cyanide poisoning, I guess we'll know what happened," Nick said.

Lauren and Phoebe gave him blank looks.

"Sorry, bad joke," he said.

At that moment, Patch joined the group. "Nick, there's something I need to show you."

"Now?" Nick put down his glass on a side table.

Patch nodded. "Right now."

CHAPTER TWENTY

Before grabbing Nick, Patch had been roaming around the portion of the Egyptian wing that had been kept open while the last part of the renovations were being completed. In the main room, there were large placards along the wall that explained the history of the temple and how it came into existence. The story centered on the area of northern Nubia, along the Nile, where the Temple of Dendur was built. The temple, removed from its original site in Egypt in 1963 and opened at the Met in 1978, was considered a smaller temple, though it was still thought to be one of the prime examples of Egyptian architecture in the world. The temple had been erected in the year 15 B.C.E. to honor Isis, Osiris, and two brothers, Pedesi and Pihor, who had drowned in the Nile during Roman times.

But this wasn't what Patch wanted to show Nick.

"You've got to see this," Patch muttered to his friend. "Just don't be too obvious about it."

Nick followed as Patch led him to a skirted table that was displayed with a scrapbook, invitations, photographs, and clippings from Dendur Balls in years past, specifically the last one, which took place in 1992. Claire's mother had said the display was there to provide some background and get everyone excited about the party.

"It's just a bunch of New York socialite stuff," Nick said.

"Right, well, look at this," Patch said, pointing to a picture of a woman.

There was a spread from the *New York Times*'s social pages, a grouping of pictures by Bill Cunningham, the well-known photographer. At the center was a picture of a woman, identified as Esmé Madison Evans. She was wearing a simple column dress and was staring straight at the camera, her eyes wide, a strange combination of an otherworldly spirit and a deer caught in the headlights. Her photo was next to those of prominent socialites of the time, names Patch recognized as important social leaders, the types of women who chaired committees and would find their names, along with those of their husbands, carved above the doorways of the Met's galleries.

"It's my mom," Patch said. "From before I was born."

"Wow," Nick said. "She looks beautiful. I mean, I always knew your mom was beautiful, but I—well, to be honest, I don't remember that much of her, since she, you know—"

"I know," Patch said. "Neither do I." What he did recall was mostly from after her breakdown: when they had to shave her head to keep her from pulling her hair out, and the baggy hospital-issue clothing that she was forced to wear. His mother had probably spent the last ten years wearing nothing more glamorous than a stained nightgown.

"Look," Nick said, pointing to another spread from a magazine. "Here's a picture of my parents."

It was a picture of Georgiana and Parker Bell. Patch marveled at how young and innocent Nick's parents appeared in the photograph.

As he looked at the picture, Patch felt a tap on his shoulder. He turned around to find Mrs. Chilton standing behind him.

"Patchfield," she said warmly, as he nodded. "I'm wondering if you can help us out with something. I've heard that you're quite wonderful on the—I don't know what the kids are calling it these days. Disc jockey? On playing music?"

"Sure, I can spin," Patch said.

"Would you be willing to provide the music for the Dendur Ball? It is so important that every dollar we make goes to the museum, and you wouldn't believe what some of these so-called professionals charge! It would be such a treat if you would donate your services. You just tell our deputy chair exactly what you need in terms of equipment, and we'll provide it for you."

Patch nodded. "Um, sure, that would be great. I can do that."

"And we need a name for the invitation. I mean, we can't just write 'DJ Patchfield Evans,' can we? What would your parents think?"

"My parents are, um, they're not around."

Mrs. Chilton ignored this. "What would your name be? Something fun, right?"

Patch thought about it for a second. His vlog was called PatchWork, and though he hadn't been posting to it regularly since the television option, people knew the name—he did, after all, have tens of thousands of followers on his MySpace and Facebook pages. "How about 'DJ PatchWork'?" he asked. "Is that ridiculous?"

Claire had come by to stand next to her mother.

"I think it's adorable," Mrs. Chilton said.

"So cute!" Claire agreed.

"Yeah," Nick ribbed him. "*Totally* cute."

"I guess so," Patch said. Strangely, the only thing on his mind was, what would Lia think about this? He wasn't really sure.

Still, it was a good gig, and if it got his name out there, it might lead to other jobs that actually paid. He could be on his way to making the five thousand dollars he would need to buy back the rights to *Chadwick Prep*.

Mrs. Chilton turned to Nick. "And dear, I hope you'll be able to promote this evening to all your nightclub contacts— we really want to attract a young crowd. Claire's told me all about the parties you've been having."

Nick stood there awkwardly. "I've actually sort of gotten out of that. Ever since Jared died. It's been hard."

"Well," Mrs. Chilton said with a plastic smile, "I'm sure you can muster up the energy to do it for charity."

"Of course," Nick said, clearly straining to keep his sarcasm in check. "Patch and I will do absolutely *anything* for charity."

After waving good-bye to Nick and Phoebe on the steps of the Met, Patch walked across the street to his apartment building. Nick and Phoebe had to go to Southampton to execute the first part of Nick's plan, though Nick had been vague about the details. Patch didn't mind—he was tired of being the one who was always investigating everything. Besides, he still wanted to sort mentally through everything he had experienced today. For starters, the picture of his mother and her connection with the Dendur Ball. He knew his mom had been social and that his parents had been friends with the Bells, but seeing a picture of her in a newspaper clipping made it concrete. Before this, his primary image of Esmé had been as a crazy person. In the black-and-white newspaper photograph, though, she looked so composed, so beautiful. Like someone he had never known.

Patch was also incredibly frustrated by his chat with Simone and the prospect of buying back the rights to his show. The possibility of DJ gigs in the future might help, but it would take a lot of bookings to make five grand.

While he felt distracted by everything going on, he was also amped up about Lia. After his visit to Simone's former offices, he had met Lia for a coffee date at the Pink Pony on Ludlow Street. She was the only girl he had ever met who knew more about music than he did. He liked, though, that she didn't lord it over him the way she could have—for the most part.

As Patch ducked under his building's awning, he saw Parker Bell get out of a town car that had been idling at the curb. He looked at Patch, as if surprised to see him.

"Patchfield, it's nice to see you. Are you just back from the meeting?"

Patch was momentarily surprised, as Parker was not usually so nice to him. The last interaction he'd had with him was at the initiation on a remote island in Maine.

Patch nodded as Parker handed his briefcase to the doorman and asked that it be left in his foyer.

"Will you walk with me for a moment?" Parker asked. "I'd like to confer on a few matters with you."

Patch nodded, figuring that out on Fifth Avenue he wasn't in any immediate danger. He still didn't trust Nick's dad after everything he had been through in December.

"What's up?" he asked.

"I just wanted to see how you were adjusting to Society life. You've entered our group in a rather unusual way, and I want to make sure that you feel fully acclimated. Of course, I know you are already friends with some of the members, my son included."

"I've been fine. I know some of the other kids. It all seems pretty straightforward." Patch knew this was a lie, but he wasn't sure what else to say. "They told us about the Dendur Ball tonight. Sounds pretty cool."

"The Dendur Ball." Parker seemed almost wistful. "It's amazing that they're reviving it after all these years. You'll have fun that night. The event is black-tie. Do you have a dinner jacket?"

"I think I have one that used to belong to my dad," Patch said, thinking of the threadbare, moth-eaten tuxedo his father had. He would probably need to have it altered, but it still wouldn't look right.

"I want Nick to take you to our tailor. He will make one for you. There's nothing to make a young man look more handsome than a bespoke dinner jacket."

"I don't think I can afford—"

"You're to put it on our account. You understand?"

Patch nodded. He wasn't sure he was comfortable accepting something like this, but it would be nice to look sharp for the ball instead of having to wear hand-me-downs.

"Sir, can I ask you something?"

"Of course."

"Why are you being so nice to me?"

Parker Bell smiled. He was a handsome man, tall and trim, with silvery gray hair. Patch had always seen him as foreboding, but there was something about him tonight that seemed friendly. Patch understood how Nick could have such mixed feelings about his father. The man was like a chameleon.

"Patch, I care deeply about my children. About their future and about their happiness. I care about who they spend their time with. You have always been close to Nick, and I know that he values your friendship. What happened between the two of you last fall was regrettable. We should have realized that you were Society material from the start. I am sorry for that choice, and I hope that we can make amends."

Patch nodded, and there was a silence between the two. As if by unspoken agreement, the two of them turned around and started walking back toward the apartment building. Patch didn't know what else to say. As Patch put one foot in front of the other, the thoughts swirled around in his head: *This is a man who is evil. This is a man who killed people. This is a man I cannot trust.*

II

INFIDELS

CHAPTER TWENTY-ONE

Twenty minutes after the meeting at the museum ended, Phoebe and Nick were headed east on the Long Island Expressway toward the beach. The weekend had finally arrived, and they could focus on Palmer's challenge from the previous Sunday. Nick was driving his old beat-up Jeep Cherokee that he parked at a garage on 106th Street with the rest of his family's cars. The garage's location amused Phoebe; it was right on the edge of where the Upper East Side turned into Harlem, and yet the Bells parked their cars there for one simple reason: the prices were cheaper. Garage rates in Manhattan were notoriously exorbitant, and parking their cars twenty blocks away had never struck them as an inconvenience.

As they left the city behind them, Phoebe was pretty sure

they were breaking some kind of New York State law about driving without an adult present, but Nick didn't seem to care. It was more important that they figure out Palmer's riddle. Besides, Nick looked older than his age, he was a savvy driver, and he even had an illegal radar detector so he knew to slow down when cops were nearby.

"I feel like we should have done this five days ago," Phoebe said as Nick passed several cars. "We should have driven out the day your grandfather told us about it."

Nick shook his head. "It wouldn't have made sense. We had the first day of school coming up. And then everything happened with you and Lauren and Thad."

Phoebe gave a half smile. "Well, at least the way you drive, we'll be there before midnight." She sat back in her seat. For the first time in weeks, it felt like they were on the right track. Phoebe had also noticed a lightness in Nick's step as they were walking to the garage. It was the happiest she'd seen him since the day that they had officially started dating.

Nick picked up a soda and Phoebe opened it for him so he could keep his eyes on the road. After taking a gulp of root beer, he reached over to stroke her knee. "It's sort of an adventure, right? I mean, no one knows we took the car, no one knows we're going to the house."

"I like it," Phoebe said. "We should do it more often."

"Under better circumstances," Nick said.

They were silent for a few minutes, and Phoebe watched

the sea of red taillights ahead of them. She thought she might doze off, she was so exhausted, but she fought to keep her eyes open.

"This is going to sound weird," Nick said, "but do you think we would have ever met if it wasn't for the Society?"

"You tell me."

"I think we would have. I noticed you, that first day, when I handed you the flyer."

Phoebe laughed. "Yeah, right! Amidst the ten thousand other people you were inviting to your party."

"Do you think we would have met if we didn't go to the same school?"

"I think so," Phoebe said.

"Why's that?"

Phoebe took a deep breath. "Because I believe things happen for a reason. That certain things are, I don't know, not necessarily predetermined, but if they're meant to be, they're meant to be."

"So would you say the same for the Society?"

Phoebe looked out the window. Was it meant to be? If she could do it over again, would she have wished for none of it to happen? Or was it somehow part of a bigger picture?

"I don't know," she said. "We might feel completely trapped right now, but I think there's going to be a reason for all of this."

"You've certainly become very Zen about it," Nick said.

"Maybe it's just getting off the island," Phoebe said. "Getting away, especially with no one knowing where we are. Did you ever think about that? What if we turned around and started driving west, out of New York, across the country? Just got the hell out of here? Couldn't we leave all this behind?"

Nick frowned. "What about the others? And can you imagine leaving our lives here? Besides, what would we do? How would we live? I can't just—I can't just leave everything I've ever known behind me." He gripped the steering wheel tightly.

"I'm sorry, I didn't mean to upset you," Phoebe said.

He softened a bit. "No, it's not that at all—you're so damn smart. You're the only person in my life who would ever even suggest that option. And it's, like, by bringing it up, even if we never do it, just knowing that it's there, that you thought it—it makes me feel like . . . I don't know. It's just cool."

Phoebe smiled. Nick had a habit, when he was bordering on something profound, of backing away from it. Tonight she didn't want to push him.

His face grew serious. "Anyway, we should think about what my grandfather said. Are you worried at all?"

"What I want to understand," Phoebe said, "is why would he decide to help us? Why would he go behind your father's back?"

Nick kept his eyes focused on the highway as he answered. "My grandfather and my father haven't always gotten along.

They hide it well, especially in front of strangers, but they've disagreed bitterly about a lot of things over the years. When he was a member in his early years, my father tried to rebel against the Society himself. And I think there's something in my grandfather—it's almost like regret. Why, I don't exactly know."

Phoebe nodded.

"All I know," Nick said, "is that I don't want my life to be like that."

"If your grandfather doesn't believe in rebelling against the Society, why is he trying to help you do it?"

"I don't know exactly, but I'm not going to turn down the chance to make this right, to get us and the others out. I don't know if we have any other option. We can't work against them. We can't skip the meetings. The police wouldn't believe us, because we have no evidence. The only way to get out of it is to be officially released."

"Has anyone ever done that?" Phoebe asked. "They don't exactly seem keen on letting anyone out."

"It's not a question I want to pose to my father, not after what we saw on the island. I think we need to figure out this Palmer thing first."

When they arrived at the Bell family estate two hours later, it looked as if it had been shut down for the winter. All the lights on the property were off and the ground was frozen. After parking on the gravel driveway, Nick opened the front door with his key.

"Home again," Nick said as they stepped inside. The house was kept at a chilly fifty-five degrees in winter, and Phoebe shivered.

"Ugh, I wish I could just flop into bed," Phoebe said. "Do you want to start our search tomorrow? For whatever we're looking for. I guess we really should start now."

"Oh my God," Nick said. He stood in the central foyer facing the living room.

"What?" Phoebe asked.

Nick pointed to the space above the fireplace, and Phoebe looked up.

The Jackson Pollock painting, the one Nick had mentioned his mother had purchased at Sotheby's for ten million dollars, was gone.

CHAPTER TWENTY-TWO

Nick sat with Phoebe in the living room, and they both looked up at the blank space above the fireplace where the Pollock had hung. There was nothing on the mantel, just a few family photos.

"Is this what he wanted us to find?" Nick asked. "This isn't what I would call finding something."

"More like the absence of something," Phoebe said. "Maybe that's part of the clue. Maybe we're supposed to look for what isn't there."

"So we're looking for something that used to be there in the first place? That doesn't make any sense." He rubbed his temples. A headache was starting to come on.

"Hey—more importantly: Should we tell your parents about the painting being gone?"

"We don't have to. The caretaker will see it on Monday morning. Remember, we aren't even supposed to be here."

"Nick, they're going to have police here eventually. They'll see our fingerprints."

Nick felt nervous for a moment before he relaxed. "We'll just say we thought it had been sent out for restoration. My mom is always saying that the frame needs to be cleaned."

"So what do we do now?"

"Search the place?"

They went through each room of the house, which was no easy feat, considering that it was a six-thousand-square-foot house with eight bedrooms and multiple public rooms. Luckily, because the house was built in the 1920s, it was not enormous in the way of newer houses in the area. Nick had always appreciated that; its size was manageable, and you didn't need to run through every wing to find someone.

The house was immaculately clean but had that musty smell from windows not having been opened in more than a week. New Year's Eve would have been the last time his parents were here.

After several hours of searching, however, they hadn't turned up anything. It didn't help that they had no idea what they were looking for.

It didn't help, either, that it was four o'clock in the morning.

They went back to the living room and flopped down on the couches across from each other. "Your grandfather told you, 'You'll find everything you need at the beach,'" Phoebe said.

"We have no idea, though, if he was in his right mind."

"Let's think about this," Phoebe said. "The one thing we've noticed is that the Pollock is missing. We don't know if your grandfather moved it, but it's all we've got to go on. So can we assume that this search has something to do with art?"

Nick furrowed his brow. "Maybe." He stood up and looked at the space above the fireplace where the Pollock had been. He examined the panel, slightly darker, where the painting had been hung. Nothing appeared unusual or out of place. He pushed the panel, to see if anything would happen. Nothing.

Then Nick noticed something strange as his eyes ran over the photographs sitting on the mantel: while there had always been family photographs below the painting, they had now been switched out for specific ones. Every single picture of the Bell family was taken down in Palm Beach, where his grandfather lived during most of the year.

"I feel so stupid," Nick said, looking at the photographs.

"Why?"

"Remember, he said 'both beaches.'"

"Yeah, so what does that mean?"

"We're at the wrong beach."

It was a snap decision, but he and Phoebe knew that it was the right one. They had to find out what Palmer's babblings were about. Nick wanted to include the entire group of five, as he felt everyone should be involved. Besides, Palm Beach would be a welcome break from the chilly New York January, as well as from all the Society madness. Making good on his request for them to keep their Saturday clear, Nick called everyone early that morning and told them to meet Phoebe and him at La Guardia Airport for a shuttle flight down to Florida. As far as getting permission, half the group had parents who didn't care, and the other half would say they were staying over at each other's houses. Half an hour after Nick invited him, Patch called back: he wanted to bring Lia, as they had made tentative plans and Patch didn't want to cancel. Nick hadn't met Lia, but at school the previous day Patch had been going on and on about her to Lauren and Phoebe and him. Nick knew that she worked part-time in a record store in the East Village and went to Stuyvesant High School, but most importantly, Patch was really excited about her. Nick supposed he should have been worried about the secrecy of their mission, but part of him was exhausted from all the hiding. If Lia lived downtown and she wasn't in the Society, it wouldn't matter if she knew what was going on. After all, who would she tell?

Before booking six tickets on an inexpensive flight, Nick

placed a call to Horatio, his grandfather's caretaker and butler, who watched over the Palm Beach property and made sure everything was in top condition.

"I'll need to check with your grandfather, of course," Horatio had said. "I believe I can reach him at the hospital."

Horatio called Nick back in ten minutes and announced that his grandfather had said that whatever Nick wanted to do was fine. "I was quite surprised, actually, if you don't mind my being frank. Mr. Bell said, 'Whatever my grandson wants, you give him.' We haven't had this many houseguests since, well, since . . ."

"I know," Nick said. "Since my grandmother died."

"You will all stay in the east wing. I'll make sure that the bedrooms are ready. Three rooms, you said?"

"That should be fine." Nick figured that he and Phoebe could sleep together, Patch and Lia could share a room, and Lauren and Thad could share another. "Horatio, can you do me a favor?" Nick asked.

"Certainly."

"If my father happens to call, please don't mention this visit to him."

CHAPTER TWENTY-THREE

"Florida!" Lia said. "Are you crazy?"

She and Patch were already in a cab going across town, in the direction of the Midtown Tunnel. Patch had simply told her that he had a surprise, and that she should pack a change of clothing. It was only their second official date, so it was more than a bit unexpected, but Patch appreciated that Lia understood the value of spontaneity. The trip was like a present that had been dropped in their laps, the chance to escape from Manhattan.

"I thought maybe we were going to, I don't know, the Hamptons or something," she said. "But Palm Beach? What are we, like, eighty years old? Will it be warm there? I thought it would be freezing where we were going!"

"It's really nice there," Patch said as they entered the

Midtown Tunnel. "Nick's grandfather has a pool and everything. It has these stone dolphins that shoot water. It's kind of fun, in that old rich person sort of way, you know?"

"Well, I didn't bring a swimsuit," Lia said. "What are you going to do about that?" She frowned, pushing her black bangs away from her forehead.

"Don't worry, I'm sure Lauren packed five. Besides, it's casual. The girls will lend you some clothes."

She shrugged hesitantly. "Okay, so, what, is this like some kind of preppy ritual or something? Heading south in the winter?"

"Oh, come on," Patch said. "I'm not that preppy." He gave her a playful poke in the stomach.

"Whatever, preppy boy. You're right out of a Brooks Brothers catalog."

"Hey, no fair!" It actually did surprise Patch—he had thought that with his new haircut and new body, he was shedding the preppy image he had grown up with. Apparently not. "I don't actually feel like I'm that preppy," he continued. "I've always felt sort of—well, sort of different."

"How so?"

Patch wasn't sure he should get into his family history. He glanced at the cabbie in the rearview mirror. It seemed like a strange place to be sharing such intimacies.

"I don't really have the most traditional family structure," he said. He explained about growing up with his grandmother, his father's death, and his mother's hospitalization.

Lia's face softened as he told the story of his mother being put away. "And you still don't know exactly why she was sent there?" she asked.

"She has borderline personality disorder, but it can be quite severe at times. She just doesn't see the world the way that you or I do. Everything is a danger to her. I've never fully understood why she is the way she is." He didn't want to explain about seeing the Society's ankh branded on the back of his mother's neck last November, or about the picture of her that he had seen the previous night at the display of clippings about the last Dendur Ball. He didn't want to talk about how he now was questioning her entire history, everything that had happened to her. It was part of what was making the Society thing so confusing, and what made it different for him from the others. The rest of them wanted to get out of the group, whereas Patch had an additional goal: to understand what his mother's involvement with the group had been. He had tried talking to Genie about it over the past few weeks, but she wouldn't tell him anything. He knew that the obvious thing would be to go visit his mother at the hospital in Ossining. He had mentioned this to Genie, but she had discouraged the idea. It was so painful for Patch to see his mother in that condition. He hated visiting her, and it was not likely that Esmé would tell him anything. Her memories were so fragmented, like shards of glass.

He had a multitude of reasons for putting it off.

However he went about it, though, he knew that it would be his journey alone.

The cab pulled up at La Guardia, and Patch leaned forward to pay the driver.

Lia took a deep breath. "This should be interesting."

"Relax," Patch said. "You'll like my friends."

When they got to La Guardia, Phoebe, Lauren, and Thad were waiting by the ticket desk. "Nick is checking on a few things," Phoebe said.

Patch introduced Lia to everyone. Phoebe and Lauren were incredibly friendly to her, as if they were Patch's older sisters and Patch was presenting his first girlfriend to them.

"We've heard so much about you!" Lauren said as she gave Lia a hug. Patch was momentarily embarrassed that he had told Lauren and the others all about Lia the day before. Patch noticed Lia giving him a slightly uncomfortable glance, but he also sensed that she was grateful the girls were being so friendly. They invited her to come to a coffee place with them to grab some bagels before the flight.

As excited as he was to be with Lia, his mind was now jumping to the clues that Nick had told him about briefly on the phone. He didn't know what they meant, but he relished the chance to figure it out—and even better if it could help get them out of the Society.

Patch sat down in a waiting area outside of the security

screening checkpoint. Lauren joined him with her cup of coffee, a few steps ahead of the others.

He gave her a look that could only mean one thing: *What do you think?*

Lauren laughed. "Patch, relax, will you? You did well. She's adorable."

CHAPTER TWENTY-FOUR

As Nick's green and white cab pulled up at his grandfather's estate, he found himself smiling from behind his sunglasses. Palmer Bell's Palm Beach home was a coral pink beachfront palace, complete with elaborate plasterwork, multiple fountains, marble elephants guarding the gates, and columns held up by carved monkeys. It had been built by a film star in the 1930s and was known as a local landmark. Nick's parents had always derided the house as gaudy, but Nick liked it. It was so different from any of the other houses in the Bell family, which were more austere. The Palm Beach house was fun, like a momentary glimpse into fantasyland.

The front door was opened by Horatio, his grandfather's majordomo, a large, thick man with olive skin, dark hair, and eyes that were a little too close together. Horatio managed the household, rather like a butler, and, in Palmer's old age, attended to many of his medical needs as well. He made sure that the kitchen was stocked, that the pool was clean, that every inch of the house was dusted and polished by the housekeeping staff. He was of indeterminate age himself, somewhere between forty and sixty, and attributed his age-lessness to the dried goji berries that he ate with every meal. The Bells were grateful to Horatio, as he had taken care of Palmer after Elizabeth, Nick's grandmother, had died. Palmer had refused to move back to New York City, and so it was lucky that the family had someone to look after the eldest member of the Bell clan.

The other cab pulled up behind Nick's, and the six of them were led to the east wing of the house, where the guest bedrooms were located. The girls immediately changed into swimsuits—Lauren did indeed have a teal one that met Lia's approval for her to borrow—and they went out to the pool, where Horatio served them iced tea and lemonade. After changing into trunks, Nick reconvened in the living room with Thad and Patch, where the three of them stood in bare feet on the sisal rug. Nick's grandmother had decorated the room in classic Palm Beach yellow, and the room was punctu-ated by large linen couches and banana leaf trees in wicker baskets. Patch and Thad wore board shorts and T-shirts, which looked strange, as their arms were pale from the New York winter.

Nick and Phoebe had told the others about Palmer's challenge after everyone was checked in for the flight. They all had the same questions that Nick and Phoebe had mulled over, but ultimately, everyone agreed that pursuing Parker's enigmatic riddle was the best course of action. Nick mentioned the missing Pollock painting and the clue of the family photos that had led them down to Palm Beach.

"I don't know how much Horatio knows about all this," Nick said to the two other boys. "He might just think we're here to spend a weekend, so we can't be too obvious about snooping around. It's good that the girls are outside keeping him busy."

"And you still don't know what we're looking for?" Thad asked.

"Basically."

"I think that at least one of us should be at the pool at all times so it's not obvious that we're in the house," Patch said.

There was a voice from behind them, and Nick jumped. "Master Bell."

It was Horatio, holding a gold box engraved with images of Egyptian hieroglyphics.

"Your grandfather asked that I give this to you. A little 'welcome to the house' gift for you and your friends. You may play it while you are here."

"Play it?" Nick asked.

Thad took the box from Horatio and handed it to Nick,

who placed it on the white travertine coffee table. Nick opened the lid as Horatio excused himself from the room.

"Wow," Thad said.

"What?" Nick asked.

"I've only seen this kind of thing in museums. That is so cool."

"It would help if you told us what it was," Patch said, giving Thad a playful punch on the arm.

"It's senet," Thad said.

"Senate? Like in government?" Nick asked.

"No, S-E-N-E-T. It's the oldest board game in recorded history. Dates back to something like 3500 B.C.E. A senet board would be placed in a tomb with the ancient Egyptians—it supposedly gave you protection from the major gods. It was seen as a game of chance and fate."

"Um, okay, Encyclopedia Brown, how do you know all this?" Patch ribbed him.

Thad blushed. "I was really into Egyptian history in, like, the sixth grade."

Thad opened the board game and pulled out the pieces from a little drawer on the side. There were nine pieces and four sticks that each had a flat side and round side. "There's a piece missing," Thad said.

"Another thing that's missing," Patch said.

"What do you mean?" Nick said.

"So far, two things are missing: what you found at the

142

beach was a missing painting. Now you've got a missing piece on a board game."

Nick sat down. "So he's leaving these little clues for us. What does it mean?"

"You've got four things so far," Thad said. "A missing painting, family photos, the beach, though you don't know which beach. And an Egyptian board game with a missing piece."

"And where does that leave us?" Nick asked.

"This is just off the top of my head, but I think you're looking for something Egyptian," Thad said. "Maybe a family heirloom or something? Did your grandfather collect Egyptian art at all?"

"I think he might have. I never paid much attention."

"Okay, and if he had something that was special to him, where would he keep it?"

"In his study," Nick said. "Always in his study. It was the only place he wouldn't let my grandmother touch. That place is like a time capsule."

"So you should go to his study. I think I should go outside and teach the girls to play senet. You know, just so that Horatio doesn't get any ideas. Besides, we might come up with another clue."

Nick looked up to see that Phoebe was standing at the entryway to the room. He didn't know how long she had been there.

"What about this?" she said. "A missing piece is keeping

you from playing the game. I think that like so many things in the Society, the game itself is incidental. We can learn to play senet, but I think what Palmer's trying to tell you is that first you need to find what's missing, and then you can play the game."

"The game being?" Thad asked.

"The game isn't senet," Phoebe said. "The game is getting out of the Society."

CHAPTER TWENTY-FIVE

Patch, Nick, and Phoebe stood in the center of Palmer's study in front of a large Brazilian rosewood desk. It was a dark, mustard-colored room with a deep yellow shag carpet on the floor and electronically operated curtains that closed over a large picture window. The window looked out onto the property—the pool deck, the bathing cabins—and the beach beyond it.

"This is like a page out of *Architectural Digest*, circa 1974," Phoebe said.

Outside they could see that Lauren, Thad, and Lia were sunning by the pool and being served sandwiches by Horatio. Thad was trying to explain to them how to play senet, though Lauren seemed more interested in her copy of Italian

Vogue. They were using a golf tee to represent the missing piece.

Patch scanned the bookshelves that lined the walls, save for a small alcove behind Palmer's desk that was curtained in a fabric that was the same dark mustard color. In this room was Palmer's entire life, the life of a man who had always been mysterious to him. Books, awards, diplomas. Medals of commendation from various organizations. Photographs of Palmer with dignitaries. He was a man who couldn't have been more distant from Patch—he suspected that Palmer disliked him, for he had never paid him any mind. And yet there was something strangely comforting about the room, the way that a smell is familiar. It reminded Patch of his childhood.

"Hey, Earth to Patch. Come check this out." Nick had flipped up a raised wooden panel on the side of the desk. In it were two buttons. Patch and Phoebe went to take a closer look.

"Should we push them?" Phoebe asked.

"It could be an alarm," Nick said. "Horatio will know something's going on."

"Just make something up," Patch said. "Say you were looking for a notepad and you pushed it by accident."

"Prepare to be kicked out," Nick said. He pushed the top button and the three of them cringed.

At first, nothing happened.

Then, slowly, the set of curtains parted in the alcove behind Palmer's desk. It had seemed when they first looked at them that the curtains were merely a decorative element, but now, behind them was a piece of stone with some Egyptian hieroglyphics on it. It was encased in a Plexiglas box and a spotlight shone on it, as if it were in a museum.

"Have you ever seen this before?" Patch asked.

Nick shook his head. "He used to have a painting hanging on that wall. The usual Floridian crap."

The three of them turned to see that Thad had slipped into the room and was gazing with admiration at the piece of stone.

"If that's the real thing, your grandfather's been holding out on everyone," Thad said. "It's got to be worth a million dollars or something."

"What do you mean?" Patch asked.

"That's a serious piece of antiquity there."

"In plain English, please," Nick said.

"It's probably Egyptian," Thad said. "Possibly from a temple. I'm not an expert, but something like that belongs in a museum, not in some old man's study."

"What do you think the second button does?" Nick asked.

Patch shrugged. "Push it and see. We've gotten this far."

Nick pushed the button and the piece started swiveling around on a turntable, revealing the hieroglyphics on the back. Like the front, it was beautiful, with images of deities and animals on the glyphs.

Patch went closer to take a look. "There's something in the stone, a key of some sort."

There was a playing card–sized hinged door in the back of the Plexiglas box that corresponded exactly with a little niche in the stone. In it was wedged a key.

"Okay," Thad said. "That key is *not* part of the original stonework. They didn't have keys like that back then."

"You need to find the key," Nick said.

"Um, moron, the key is right there," Patch said.

"No," Phoebe said, "what he means is that Palmer told us, 'You need to find the key.'"

"And this key opens what?" Thad asked.

"I have no idea. But we need to get it." The little door was locked. "Can you guys open this?" Nick asked.

"I can pick the lock," Patch said. "But there's no way that it's not on an alarm."

Thad examined it. "It's a basic magnetic latch system," he said.

"Can you disable it?" Nick said.

"Give me half an hour," Thad said. "And tell me where your grandfather's maintenance room is. With the right tools,

Patch and I can get it open."

"So what do we do?" Nick asked, motioning to Phoebe.

"You go hang out with the girls," Thad said. "And keep Horatio busy enough that he's not going to come looking for us."

CHAPTER TWENTY-SIX

That evening, Lauren made a reservation for the six of them at an Italian restaurant on Worth Avenue that she knew her mother liked. It was a colorful scene, with a pastiche of Palm Beach socialites, their plastically altered faces frozen in time, overly tanned gay decorators, Manhattan celebrities in exile, and elderly dowagers dripping in costume jewelry who looked like they never left the island. Lauren and her friends were the youngest ones there, but thanks to Thad's flirting with the maitre d', they had scored an amazing table and had been comped several bottles of wine.

Nick had decided that after dinner they would make a small fire on the beach and roast s'mores. The boys were reveling over some kind of key that they had managed to find in the house, though no one knew exactly what the key would open. On the beach, as Lauren sipped the beer that Nick had offered her from a cooler, she only wanted to focus on things that were fun, diversions that would take her away from everything.

She sat with Phoebe and Thad on a towel near the crackling fire while Nick, Patch, and Lia tossed around a glow-in-the-dark Frisbee. Their marshmallows had burned to a crisp and were gooey and disgusting, and everyone shrieked each time they went up in flames. Thad helped them whittle down some sticks so that they could roast them without letting them fall into the fire.

For Lauren the trip had been a welcome relief from the city. Perhaps it was silly, but a tropical location like this, not to mention her friends' happiness, had made her think again of Alejandro. Palm Beach reminded her of that Saturday afternoon they had spent swimming at the house his parents had rented in Southampton, a chic, modern house that looked like it belonged in Miami. It reminded her of the dancing they had done under a background of palm trees to a Brazilian pop sensation singing "The Girl from Ipanema."

But Alejandro had been foolish. She had told herself this over and over again. Foolish with his life. He had squandered his opportunities. Even worse, he had broken her heart.

Perhaps it wasn't fair to blame him. After all, if it weren't for the Society, Alejandro would still be here today.

Lauren looked over at Thad, as he carefully held his

melting marshmallow over the flames. She had been so grateful for his friendship ever since he had pulled her out of her self-absorbed bubble several weeks ago. He had been so supportive and sweet, and she was indebted to him. She wished he would meet someone, though part of her also wished that she could keep him all to herself.

Lauren felt guilty for playing such a passive role in getting out of the Society, while her friends did all the work. But she was exhausted and depressed by it all. It was difficult to get excited about Nick's grandfather's challenge when her main personal struggle was getting out of bed each morning. She knew she would get through it, but for now, it hurt. Nothing, not even getting out of the Society, was going to change that.

CHAPTER TWENTY-SEVEN

Later that evening Patch lay next to Lia on the king-size bed in their guest suite. Aside from their coffee at the Pink Pony, they had barely even had a real date, and now he was in this incredibly romantic situation. They kissed for a few minutes before she broke the mood by asking the question he had been dreading.

"Patch, you've got to tell me, what's going on here?"

"What do you mean?"

"Well, let's see: The five of you all seem to speak in your own language, or at least you have your own vocabulary. You all have ankh tattoos on the back of your necks—at least, I'm pretty sure you all do, though I couldn't see Nick's too clearly in the pool. You're obsessed with keys and strange board games. Nick is leading you on some kind of quest, but he doesn't seem to know what the final goal is. What's it all about?"

"It's nothing. It's . . ."

"Patch, don't mess with me." Her eyes shone fiercely, and he realized he would have to tell her if he wanted the relationship to have any chance of working.

"We're not supposed to tell anyone. That's what they told us."

"Who's they? The boogeymen under the bed?"

Patch sighed and started speaking slowly. "The leadership of the group that we're in . . . it's sort of like a club. We're really not allowed to talk about it. I don't know. I guess we're sort of far away. Maybe the rules don't apply once we leave the city."

He knew that wasn't true. He knew that by telling Lia, he would be breaking the second rule on the scroll that had been handed to him on Isis Island: "*You will not speak to Outsiders about the Society, not to family nor to friends.*"

Screw that. Until recently, Patch was an Outsider himself. And he still felt like he wasn't truly a member, not a full-fledged one like the others in his class.

He started explaining to Lia how he had gotten involved in it all, about the Night of Rebirth, about the footage he had taken, about how he had been threatened and kidnapped after infiltrating the island. About how he had joined the very group that his grandmother had warned him about, which had left her none too pleased.

"I'm sorry," he said. "This is all so heavy. You don't need to hear this—the weekend was supposed to be fun, right?"

"I just don't believe—I mean, this stuff is really incredible. Secret initiations? Threats? Sneaking your way onto an island?"

Patch grinned shyly. "I know, crazy, right?"

"I'm actually sort of . . . well, I'm sort of impressed. I didn't think you had this kind of thing in you."

"Hey, it's not all fancy private school stuff," Patch said. "So does all this seem incredibly strange to you? You seem worried about something."

"No." She shook her head.

"Let me guess: You want nothing to do with any of it, including me." He knew he was being melodramatic, but he figured he should put his worst fears out there in the open.

"No, not at all," she said. "If you're in this, I want to be right there with you."

CHAPTER TWENTY-EIGHT

Sweetie, is that you?"

Phoebe had arrived back from Palm Beach after being dropped off at her house by Nick. She heard her mom's voice in the living room, so she popped her head in from the hallway. There was a fire going, and Maia and Daniel were drinking wine.

"I'm so glad you're back. How was the weekend? It was so nice of Nick to take you all to his grandfather's house." Phoebe had been able to tell her mother the truth about where she was going for the weekend, explaining that yes, Mr. Bell's caretaker would be on the premises at all times in case they got into trouble.

Phoebe could have sworn that she saw Daniel perk up at the mention of Palmer Bell's house. Maybe it was some kind of Society privilege to spend time at the house of the Chairman Emeritus.

"Um, it was really pretty there. Warm." She found herself fidgeting in the hallway, wishing her mom would let her go upstairs.

"We should get away more," Maia said, looking in Daniel's direction. "I guess work has sort of been preventing that." Maia had been printing photographs all the time for a new show she had coming up.

"We certainly can, if you want." Daniel smiled.

"Honey, we have a little something to share with you."

"What's that?"

"You'll be seeing a lot more of Daniel from now on."

Phoebe looked at her mom, confused. "Why?"

"Honey, he's moving in with us! Isn't that great?"

Phoebe stopped. After only a few months of dating? It seemed so fast. She didn't know what to think—she would now be living with a member of the Society under her own roof. It felt so odd, particularly since Daniel had only once made reference to actually being part of it. Aside from the conversation they had had a few weeks ago, he had never really been candid with Phoebe about the Society and his role in it.

"Don't you have anything to say?" Maia asked. "It's wonderful news. Tatiana has renewed her teaching contract in Paris, and the town house will be ours for another year." Officially, the reason they were living in such a posh house while paying only a pittance was that they were house-sitting for Tatiana, a wealthy sculptor friend of Phoebe's mom.

"Um, sure." Phoebe forced a smile. "That's great. I'm so happy for you both. I'd better get upstairs, and you know . . . schoolwork."

Maia and Daniel both nodded as Phoebe ducked into the hallway and went upstairs to her room. She heard them behind her, talking in hushed tones about teenage moodiness. Phoebe so desperately wanted to tell her mother everything she knew, but now with Daniel in the house and his direct ties to the Society, that would be impossible.

The following day, after school, Phoebe decided to take a route home that involved her walking past Nick and Patch's building. She didn't know if either of them were home, but she wanted to visit someone else.

"Will you ring Genie, um, I mean, Mrs. Madison, please?" she asked the doorman. Thankfully, he recognized her by now.

"Would you like me to tell Master Bell that you were here?" the doorman asked.

"No, just Mrs. Madison, that's all."

The doorman introduced Phoebe over the intercom and told her to go on up. Phoebe had to remind herself to stop at Patch's floor and not go all the way up to Nick's apartment. When Phoebe reached Patch's apartment, she was comforted by its sense of warmth, by the cracked and worn marble tiles in the entryway, scuffed with years of use.

Genie had already opened the door for her. "Phoebe, dear, what a nice surprise! I had no idea you were coming over. Is Patch expecting you?"

"No, it's actually you that I wanted to talk with," Phoebe said. "I hope you don't mind my dropping by like this."

"Not at all. Let me go make some tea."

Genie busied herself with the teakettle while Phoebe stood awkwardly at the entrance to the little galley kitchen.

"I wanted to talk to you about the Society," Phoebe said. "That's probably no surprise. I feel like I'm stuck in the middle of all of it. Not only in the Society itself, but stuck with Nick. I love Nick—please don't tell him that—but I just . . . well, it's just hard, everything with his family. And then getting to know Patch has been great, too, but there are so many things that we don't know. I'm sorry, I'm babbling. I just thought you might be able to give me some advice."

"Come into the living room," Genie said. "We should just let this tea steep for a few minutes."

"Thank you." Phoebe followed her.

Genie sat down on one of the two living room couches. "My advice to you and also to Patch is to stay away from it all. Nothing good can come from being involved with the Society."

Phoebe sighed. "It's too late for that, I'm afraid. It was

supposed to make our lives better, and instead it's made them worse. I was so ambitious last semester, while this semester I've done nothing."

"Now, Phoebe, come on. That's not the Society. That's all you. Patch is the same way, going on about his television show. You can do whatever you want to do. You don't need the Society to get you there."

Phoebe nodded. "I know. But we're trapped in it now. All I want is to get out, to get away from all the craziness."

"I don't know how you can get out. I know that others have tried, and failed."

"Others? Like who?"

"Why don't you go get that teapot and I'll tell you."

Phoebe walked to the kitchen. She wanted to find out as much as she could, but she wondered how much she could ask before Genie got too suspicious.

"My daughter was in your same position," Genie said as Phoebe poured two cups of tea in the living room. "She thought that being in the Society would make her life wonderful. And it was, for a time. She met her husband, she had a child. And then there was a disagreement."

"A disagreement with whom?"

"Let's just say that she upset some people with her words. She upset the people in charge. And then she had her psychotic break."

Phoebe thought back to her experience with Dr. Meckling,

160

how quickly he had labeled her as delusional.

"And that was when she was hospitalized?" Phoebe asked. She knew about the story from Nick.

"That's right. Patch doesn't know all the details, and I'd rather not get into them now. All I am saying is that you have to be cautious. Patch is looking for information about his mother, but I'm not certain he's ready to know everything."

"What about the Bells?" Phoebe asked. "I'm trying to understand—forgive me if I'm being nosy, but there's a connection somehow between you and Patch and them. I mean, beyond your engagement to Palmer Bell." She knew she was taking a risk, and she wasn't even sure if what she was saying was true, but there were too many connections for it to be a coincidence: Genie being in the same building as the Bells, years after her broken engagement with Palmer; Patch and Nick's friendship; Genie's knowledge of the Society; the bottle of tuberose perfume in Genie's medicine cabinet that smelled exactly like the scent used in the initiation ceremony.

"Our families have always been close," Genie said a bit stiffly. "Not so much in recent years, aside from Patch and Nick's friendship." She took a sip of tea. "I'm not really sure what else you want to know."

Phoebe sensed a defensiveness in her voice and realized that to push the issue would seem rude. She and the others needed to keep Genie on their side, and she didn't want to alienate her.

"I'm sorry," Phoebe said. "I've been so intrusive—it really isn't polite."

"Not to worry, dear. It was kind of you to visit. And yes, if you're wondering, I would have asked exactly the same questions myself when I was your age."

CHAPTER TWENTY-NINE

A week later, Claire Chilton announced the first meeting of the Dendur Ball Junior Committee at the Colonial Club. Lauren and Phoebe attended begrudgingly, knowing that they didn't have a choice.

Phoebe and Lauren arrived just as the meeting was starting. Nick, Patch, and Thad were already there, listening dutifully to Claire Chilton. What a charade this all had become, Lauren thought. Who ever thought that one's greatest role in life would be playing oneself?

After the meeting, which had mostly been a pep rally urging everyone to get their friends to buy the $250 tickets to the ball, Mrs. Chilton approached Lauren, with Claire behind her. Letty Chilton had been supervising the meeting from the back of the room, as if she didn't trust her daughter to do something properly on her own. Lauren and Phoebe were standing next to each other; the boys had disappeared somewhere else, into the vast maze of rooms that was the club.

"Lauren, dear, I've just had the most marvelous idea suggested to me," Mrs. Chilton said.

"Yeah?" Lauren cocked her head. She realized she was being a bit rude, but Mrs. Chilton didn't seem to notice.

"I'm very interested in your little jewelry company."

"Thanks," Lauren said.

"And you specialize in reproductions?"

Lauren bristled. She did not do reproductions. To suggest it was an insult.

Lauren smiled as sweetly as she possibly could, given that she wanted to walk away. "They're not reproductions. They're my own designs, and reinterpretations of classic jewelry." She paused. "Really old stuff. The kind of thing you might have worn while growing up."

Now it was Mrs. Chilton's turn to pay Lauren no mind. "We have had the most brilliant idea. You are familiar with the Scarab of Isis necklace?"

Lauren nodded. "I think I've seen pictures of it." The piece was a scarab, a winged beetle that was a popular amulet in ancient Egypt. The original was gold, inlaid with stones that were burgundy, navy blue, and turquoise. The gorgeous beetle was about the size of a silver dollar and hung on a gold chain.

"It's coming to the Met again from Cairo, on loan for the

new exhibit. We were thinking that the museum could give you the dimensions of it and the names of the original materials. We'd like you to make copies of it for all the members of the Junior Committee, using less expensive materials, of course. Won't it be darling when all the girls are photographed wearing such a stunning piece?"

"Absolutely," Claire said, nodding.

"Mrs. Chilton, I really don't make copies," Lauren said. "I wouldn't even know where to begin." That wasn't true at all, of course. It would be easy to make a copy. All Lauren would have to do is hand the specifications to her manufacturer in Red Hook, the one Sebastian Giroux had connected her with.

"Lauren, dear, I know you can make it happen. I'll have the marketing department at the museum contact you tomorrow with all the details. Oh, and say hello to your mother for me, will you? I'm going to call her next week, as a few of our rooms need a face-lift, and I think she'd be perfect for the job."

Claire gave Lauren a sneer as she walked away.

"I guess you've got yourself a jewelry job," Phoebe said.

Lauren scowled. "Isn't it ironic? You get the thing that you want all your life—or at least, for most of your life—and then you don't want it anymore."

"Tell me about it," Phoebe said. Lauren understood that Phoebe knew exactly how it was, having gone through a similar experience with her gallery show last November. A number of the paintings had disappeared, and Phoebe was never paid for them.

"Reproductions of jewelry," Lauren said. "What does she think I am, a supplier to the museum gift shop or something? So tacky!"

"Think of it as charity work," Phoebe said.

"I guess so." Lauren lowered her voice. "What I really want to know is, when are you and Nick going to figure out what the next step is in his grandfather's little treasure hunt? If that's what it is."

Phoebe shook her head. "We've been so busy with school, we haven't really had a chance to come up with a plan."

Lauren had a pleading look in her eyes. "Whatever you do, please come up with it quickly, okay?"

"We will," Phoebe said. "We'll do our best."

CHAPTER THIRTY

In the days following the Palm Beach trip, Patch thought about his situation and how similar it suddenly was to his grandmother's. After he had returned from Isis Island, Genie revealed to him that she had dated Palmer Bell in the 1950s, and they had been engaged to be married. Palmer's family intervened, however, and the night before their wedding, he had disappeared on an ocean liner to Italy. It had taken Genie nearly a year to recover from the shock, and she was grateful to have met Patch's grandfather, George, whom she married within three months. Now Patch was in the same situation, dating someone not in the Society. Would it always be a boundary that divided people?

Genie was sitting in the living room and working on a needlepoint pillow while watching television. She looked up, just enough to catch Patch's eye.

"I'm worried about you, Patchfield," she said.

"What about?"

"You don't look well. You're too thin. You're always sulking around in that ratty wool cap. What's going on?"

He sat down. "It's the usual. I mean, after everything that happened . . ." His voice trailed off. He had filled Genie in on the Society's retreat, and how he had little choice but to become a member. She had been upset with him, but she also understood the precarious position he was in. "I thought what happened in December would be the worst of it," he continued. "I thought joining would solve everything."

"Solve what?" Genie asked as she raised an eyebrow in suspicion.

"All my problems. I thought it would get me a TV deal, or at the very least, give me some new opportunities even if *Chadwick Prep* didn't work out. Big surprise: it didn't. It's the same with my friends. Phoebe's not painting, Lauren hates doing her jewelry, Nick hasn't organized any parties. Hey, at least I get to spin records at the Dendur Ball."

"The Dendur Ball?" Genie looked curious. "Imagine that. They're doing that again."

"Have you been before?"

"No, I haven't. By the time they started it, I was no longer running around with that crowd. But, your—well, Esmé, she cut quite a figure at the last ball."

"I know. I saw the photograph of her. I could barely recognize her."

"Those were the best days," Genie said sadly. "She was so happy then. Before everything happened."

"Did she and Dad go to things like that often?"

"Oh, yes," Genie said. "She and your father and the Bells, actually. Parker and Georgiana had only been married for a few years. The four of them were such a group: your father and Parker, Esmé and Gigi. They were the talk of the town."

"And then I came along."

"Oh, dear, that had nothing to do with it. Your mother had a decline. You know that. It's all . . . what's the word, hereditary. I read an article about it. You can't help what you're born with."

Patch sat down in an armchair and sighed. "Do you think she'll ever get better?"

"I don't know," Genie said. "I certainly hope so. For your sake. I know how devastating it is. I can't even remember what it was like to have her in our lives. It feels like she's already dead."

"Genie!"

"Patch, we have to be realistic about it. It's not your mother that we visit in Ossining. She's a shell, a reminder of the person she used to be."

"So what do you think I should do about all this Society stuff? My TV show project has tanked for now, which totally blows. And my friends are all being threatened."

"You take care of yourself first," Genie said firmly. "I know Nick watches out for you, but I don't know those other friends of yours. I'm sure they're good people, and I know you're a fair judge of character, Patch." She gripped his arm. "But still, you have to be careful."

CHAPTER THIRTY-ONE

After a few weeks everyone at Giroux New York had thankfully put the awkward incident of the stolen earrings behind them. Sebastian Giroux had first called it "a misunderstanding," as if Lauren had been some drug-addled starlet who had simply *thought* she had paid for something when she hadn't. No, Lauren insisted, someone had planted the earrings in her bag. While no one particularly cared how or why this could have happened, they accepted it as a reasonable enough explanation, and the matter was dropped.

Several weeks before the incident, Sabrina, the store's creative director, had set up a small office for Lauren in the basement, on the same corridor as Sebastian and the other designers. On the door was a placard that read: L. MORTIMER DESIGNS. Lawyers had drawn up papers specifying the exact relationship of her company to Giroux New York. Lauren would be licensing her designs to Giroux, and they would be in charge of the manufacturing. Sabrina handled the dealings with the factory in Red Hook, and Lauren visited the plant to view and critique prototypes.

Lauren dropped by Sebastian's office for a meeting with him and Sabrina to discuss the Egyptian jewelry plan. She didn't really want to do it, but Mrs. Chilton had upped the ante on her a few days after her initial request: she had, as promised, hired Lauren's mother to do some decorating in their apartment. Diana had let Lauren know how important the job was to her, and Lauren could see it for herself. Her mother was getting up early in the morning to source materials and prepare sketches. For the first time in a while, Diana Mortimer was actually excited about her job. Lauren wanted it to stay that way.

Lauren knew, then, that she had little choice but to do the job for the Dendur Ball, even if it would lower her to the level of making a reproduction.

"I tried to get out of it," Lauren explained to Sebastian and Sabrina. "I mean, I don't want to create some tacky thing that looks like you could buy it at a museum gift shop." The whole thing depressed her, but she felt as if she didn't have a choice in the matter.

"Let me guess," Sebastian said, laughing. "Letty Chilton strong-armed you. The woman can be very persistent. God, what her daughter has put our salespeople through recently!"

"Really?" Lauren was curious, but she wanted to stay on point. "I guess I've warmed up to the idea. It could be fun."

"The jewelry of that era is very beautiful," Sebastian said. "Can you imagine that they could create that kind of thing thousands of years ago? It's really quite incredible."

"What are the materials?" Sabrina asked.

"We would use enamel and semiprecious stones," Lauren said. "Nothing too expensive. Carnelian, lapis lazuli, turquoise. This would be a simulation, basically. But the important thing is that it has to look real. It will be really stunning to have all the young women wearing these, while the real thing is in a case just yards away."

Lauren handed Sabrina a manila envelope with the specifications from the curator at the Egyptian wing.

"Now, we need to talk about something more important," Sebastian said. "The jewelry is a hit. We're actually selling even more abroad than we are in New York. I told you that Colette picked it up?" Colette was a boutique-style department store, similar to Giroux, in Paris. It sold everything from limited-edition books to one-of-a-kind fashion to the latest DJ mixes to designer waters. Lauren knew that to have one's designs represented there was an enormous honor.

Lauren nodded. "That's fabulous."

"It's better than fabulous. They want to do a window display for spring this year featuring your pieces."

"Oh my God. Wow."

"There's a catch, though," Sabrina said.

Lauren groaned quietly. There was always a catch.

Sebastian continued: "They want the designs to be Colette exclusives. They would only be sold in the store on rue Saint-Honoré and online."

"Can we do enough volume there?" Lauren asked. "Does it make sense to do a line just for one store?"

Sebastian and Sabrina laughed.

"My dear, you take care of the designing," Sebastian said. "We'll worry about the business side of things."

Lauren smiled weakly as she flushed a little bit. She resented when Sebastian—or any adult, for that matter—assumed that just because she was in high school, she wasn't interested in the details. She wanted to learn all about fashion, not just about how to make jewelry or how to cut an A-line dress, but about merchandising, marketing, shipping, sales. Maybe she would have to wait until college to get that type of knowledge.

"So can you do it?" Sabrina asked.

"Of course," Lauren said, with the air of an old pro. "Just give me my deadline, and I'll make it happen."

CHAPTER THIRTY-TWO

The weeks leading up to the Dendur Ball passed quickly for Nick, though his grandfather's challenge was never far from his mind. When he wasn't thinking about it, Nick focused on his schoolwork, as he continued trying to repair the damage caused to his reputation during the previous semester. College applications were less than eight months away, and he had already started thinking about where he wanted to go. His entire family had gone to Yale, but he wondered if that option wouldn't be open to him anymore if he was released from the Society.

That was a risk Nick would have to take.

On a string around his neck was the key Thad and Patch had procured from the opening on the Egyptian slab in Palmer Bell's study. Nick couldn't stop thinking about it, though he was unsure what the next move should be. Ever since coming back from Florida, Nick had kept the key with him everywhere he went, whether at school, going running, or in the shower. It never left him.

It was an old-fashioned key, not the flat kind used to open most doors, but the type with a long, cylindrical base and a set of teeth. It was weightier than the average key; it could have opened a door, a chest, or even a set of drawers.

In short, it could have opened anything.

Or it could be a dead end.

Before leaving Florida, Nick had tried it on every door, locked box, secretary, and trunk he could find in the Palm Beach house, with no success. Because the clue that Palmer had given them involved "both beaches," Nick didn't feel like the solution—if there was one—would be found in Palm Beach. The Florida house was only part of the puzzle.

On the first Saturday morning in February, a few weeks after their last trip, Nick and Phoebe drove out to Southampton, to his family's house at the beach.

When Nick and Phoebe arrived at the Southampton house, they tried the key on every possible lock. When the caretaker, who happened to be on the grounds that weekend, asked what they were doing, Nick said they were picking up some ski equipment he had been storing up in the attic.

Nick and Phoebe searched every room meticulously, trying every chest of drawers, every closet, even an old campaign chest in the attic.

In the last guest bedroom, Phoebe wiped her forehead with her sleeve. "This feels hopeless," she said, stifling a sneeze. "We're kicking up dust you didn't even know this house had."

Nick nodded wearily. "I know. I'm just not seeing it here."

It was an unseasonably warm day for February, so the two decided to go for a walk on the beach. In contrast to the summer, the beach was completely empty, the surf frothing up and then retreating, the ocean behind it vast and gray and unknowable. There had been a storm the week before, and some of the dunes had been nearly demolished.

They walked for a few minutes, the light breeze nipping at their cheeks. It felt like they had accomplished nothing.

"I don't know where else to turn," Nick said after a few minutes, with the frustration of knowing he had complained to Phoebe about this more times than he could count.

"You've tried every lock in your parents' apartment," she said. "You've tried Palm Beach. We've tried Southampton." She reached out to him as they walked through the sand, to touch the key that was now hanging around his neck, grazing the V-neck of his cable-knit sweater. "What if it opens nothing? What if it's all just an elaborate ruse, something to keep us occupied while the Society continues to cover its tracks?"

Nick felt the wind rustling his hair. "Remember what he said about my brothers and me playing on the beach? About the treasures being buried in the sand?"

"So what are we supposed to do? Start digging?" Phoebe asked. "Do you really think he buried something under the sand?"

"I don't think so. I think he was just reminiscing. With all the winter storms, there's no way anyone could keep something buried for long." Nick stopped and glanced up at the dunes, just before the house, near the edge of the Bell family's property line. There was a stone block that he had never noticed before, a piece of rough-hewn granite lodged into the ground. Nick loped up the embankment to it and walked through a few yards of dune grass.

He gasped when he saw what was carved onto its face. Phoebe joined him. The block read:

P.M.E.

1962–1997

"Is that . . . a grave marker?" Phoebe asked.

Nick shook his head. "I don't think so. I remember my father telling me about this once, but I've never seen it. The storm must have uncovered it. It's a memorial marker."

"Who is it for?"

Nick paused. It was too much to think about—everything he knew, and everything he didn't want to believe. "It's for Patch's father," he said quietly. "He drowned near here. It was when our parents were close, and the Evanses were staying here one weekend. Patch and I were at summer camp. Patch's dad was caught up in the surf while swimming one evening at dusk. No one thought to look for him until dinnertime. That's what my father told me, when I asked him about it once."

Phoebe blinked. "Does Patch know this is here?"

Nick shook his head. "It's not really something we talk about. God, that memorial marker—I haven't thought about that in years. If you mention to Patch about us being here, I'd rather you didn't say anything—not that you would, but it just . . . well, it might upset him."

Phoebe nodded. "I understand. Though you do know he's trying to figure out what happened to his mother, right?"

"I know."

"Do you remember her?" Phoebe asked.

"No, not really," Nick said. "We were so young when she was taken away."

They were still standing in front of the memorial marker. "Patchfield Morgan Evans," he said. "I guess they left off the 'Jr.' Sort of hard to do that in initials."

"Why initials? Why not his full name?"

Nick shrugged and smiled sadly. "You've been around my family enough by now, haven't you? Everything's a secret, everything's encoded. Like they're afraid for anyone to know the real story about them."

Phoebe touched his shoulder. "Do you feel like you're the

first one to start asking all these questions?"

"Sort of. I know my brothers have, over the years. But they always get shut down. And they're so ambitious—they care more about success than about knowing the truth about the Society or the Trust. They're not screwups, like me."

"I don't think you're a screwup," Phoebe said. "And I guess, if you are, then maybe I'm in love with a screwup." She smiled shyly, as if embarrassed at her revelation.

Nick tried not to look surprised, but he felt his heart beating more quickly. He had felt this way for so long and had been afraid to say anything. Ever since the night last semester on the rooftop after Phoebe's gallery show, when they had almost kissed. Before they had gotten together, before they had started dating. She had always been the girl he thought he could never have.

Phoebe looked so beautiful, her reddish-brown hair whipping in the wind. He pulled her toward him and kissed her. "Then I'm in love with someone who's going to be a superstar someday. We're going to leave all this behind, right? Soon?"

She nodded. Her eyes were damp.

Nick felt tears coming as well. "I'm so sorry, Phoebe. I feel like all this is my fault. My family. The Society. Everything they've caused. You should have never met me. Your life would be so much better."

"Hey—I was asked to be part of this before I even knew you. You had no way of telling," she said.

"I know—but still, it's hard. It's hard not to feel like I'm partially responsible."

She shook her head. "I don't want you to feel that way."

He wiped his eyes on the sleeve of his sweater. "I don't think we should mention the memorial to Patch. I'll show it to him sometime in the summer. After things are more settled, you know?"

"You really think things will be settled?" Phoebe smiled. "You're certainly the optimist now."

"Yes," Nick said. "I do."

III
THE SCARAB OF ISIS

CHAPTER THIRTY-THREE

Over the past few weeks, Lauren had rushed through the prototype and manufacturing of the Scarab of Isis necklace. Now that she was finally walking up the plush black carpeted stairs of the Metropolitan Museum on February 13, the night of the Dendur Ball, she was happy about it. The fourteen girls on the Junior Committee—seven from her class and seven from the class above her—all looked stunning wearing the piece. Crowds gathered around the museum, hoping for a glimpse of the guests, and klieg lights had been set up on Fifth Avenue, swooping through the sky, movie premiere–style. A team of police officers manned the barricades as limousines, taxicabs, and town cars pulled up, one by one, and photographers swarmed anyone notable who hit the much-discussed black carpet, an innovation that the event designer felt was much more chic than red, and more in keeping with the Dendur Balls of years past.

Inside, the girls were photographed next to the actual Scarab of Isis, which was displayed in a glass case to one side of the Temple of Dendur. Everyone marveled at how similar the two versions looked. Lauren felt she couldn't take any credit for it—it was a copy, nothing more—but still, she was pleased that it had worked out.

She had been so busy lately, she hadn't even had time to think about finding a date for the ball. Thankfully, Thad had volunteered to take her. She was grateful to him, once again, for coming to her rescue.

A photographer stopped Lauren and Thad and took their picture. He looked handsome in his Ralph Lauren tux, and she wore a dress that Sebastian Giroux had designed for her, a simple sea-foam green strapless gown that was a perfect backdrop to the vivid colors of the scarab pendant.

The museum was breathtaking, with its classical columns lit up and the entire staircase of the Great Hall decorated with candles that made up the shape of an ankh. It frightened Lauren a bit, this symbol that had dominated their lives, but she admitted that its representation in light was beautiful. The central information desk in the Great Hall had been transformed into a bar, with a twelve-foot-tall floral arrangement of birds-of-paradise and other lush foliage. Champagne was poured by waiters in black tie, and hors d'oeuvres were served, all vaguely Egyptian-inspired: pickled cucumbers and smoked salmon on toast points, hummus and black olive tapenade wrapped in phyllo, and *batarekh*, or Egyptian caviar. Dancers worked their way through the crowd, dressed in skintight outfits, their faces painted with hieroglyphics and silver and gold markings, with jewels affixed to their features. Their glittering eyes, eyebrows, and cheekbones made them sparkle like otherworldly creatures.

Lauren and Thad followed the crowds to the right, into the Sackler Wing, where round tables of ten had been set up to seat people for dinner. Some chose to find their tables and sit down, while most milled around the entryway, awed by the stunning transformation of the room. The sandstone temple was lit up with a wash of oranges, blues, and lavenders, and the body of water in front of the temple was surrounded by hundreds of votives, reflecting everything going on around it. Tables were arranged with jewel-toned linens of turquoise, chartreuse, and magenta, classic gold Chiavari ballroom chairs, orchids combined with succulents, and tabletop lanterns lit with votive candles. A platformed DJ booth and a dance floor were set up in front of the temple.

Lauren made her way through the crowd, as she overheard all the praise the renovations to the galleries were garnering. In the galleries surrounding the temple, the lighting had been improved, the carpets had been replaced, and the placards had been updated and enlarged to improve readability.

Lauren noticed Parker Bell holding court with his wife, Gigi, at a prime table near the front of the temple.

She and Thad spotted Phoebe and Nick. Phoebe was wearing a 1920s flapper dress that she had found in a vintage shop; it was burgundy with gold beadwork and fit perfectly for the evening, as the Egyptian Revival–style was popular after the 1922 discovery of King Tutankhamen's tomb. The red of Phoebe's dress and the sea-foam of Lauren's were beautiful together, and photographers took several more pictures of them. Even though they had been drinking champagne, they were careful to put their glasses to the side for any photographs.

Patch arrived with Lia. She looked adorable in a Marlene Dietrich–style vintage suit made of blue shantung silk, and she had done her hair in a Bettie Page cut, with straight black bangs framing her face. She looked stunning and had the most amazing shimmering burgundy lipstick: it looked like red glitter itself.

"How did you do that?" Phoebe asked.

"It's a special thing I created," she said. "It's eyelash glue, and then you put glitter on it."

"Can you eat with it? Or kiss anyone?" Phoebe asked.

"It's a bit impractical," Lia admitted. "You end up getting a lot of glitter in your food. But it seems to be a hit!" She posed sweetly for another photographer.

"It's brilliant," Lauren said. "I love it." She looked at Patch.

"You're not looking too shabby yourself. New suit?"

"Thanks. Yeah, um, just got it the other day."

Lauren leaned forward to take a closer look at it, and then she laughed. Sprinkled on his neck and shoulders, like stardust, was a smattering of red glitter.

"Don't you have to start spinning?" Nick asked, looking toward the front of the temple. There was another DJ, a guy with a goatee, who was spinning.

Patch looked at his watch. "I go on in ten minutes. Can you believe it? I have an opening act! They didn't want me to start until eight o'clock. I'd better get going."

"Knock 'em dead," Nick said.

At that moment Claire Chilton came up to Patch. Lauren immediately recognized Claire's outfit: it was identical to a fabulous sketch that Sebastian Giroux had kept pinned to the concept board in his office for months, a sketch Lauren had thought would be reserved for next year's collection. It was a black and gold dress with intricate multicolored beadwork on the bodice, the kind of dress that would have taken three seamstresses several weeks to create. Being familiar with price points, Lauren also knew that it was the kind of dress that cost about ten thousand dollars.

It suddenly made Lauren's own relatively simple dress seem a bit drab.

Claire's dress was more Lauren's style, and she was feeling a bit hurt that Sebastian hadn't made the gown for her. She knew it was silly, but she had to ask.

"Claire, how did you get that dress?"

"Oh, Sebastian designed it for me," she said quickly, as if she couldn't be bothered with such a quotidian matter. "Patch, they need you in the booth, like, *right now*. And here's a list of music. The first list is 'Must Play.' The second list is 'Do Not Play.' My mom doesn't want anything with profanity in it, or you know, implications of sexual activity or stuff like that. You know, keep it clean."

"Sure, Claire, whatever," Patch said, rolling his eyes. "This should be fun," he muttered to Nick, loud enough so his friends could hear.

"Okay, we need you there now," Claire said. "And the rest of you, I want to see you dancing!"

She clicked off in her heels, which looked uncomfortable.

"I guess I'm a DJ widow," Lia said.

Phoebe grabbed her hand and motioned to a trio of performers. "Don't worry, we'll take care of you. Come on, let's go check out those fire-eaters."

CHAPTER THIRTY-FOUR

Nick wasn't particularly enjoying himself at the ball, but he wanted to keep Phoebe and the other girls happy and not be a bore. The key from his grandfather's house, still hanging on a string around his neck, felt like it was searing a brand in his chest. When would he learn what it actually opened? It had been a week since he and Phoebe were in Southampton, and they still hadn't gotten anywhere.

Nick's parents were seated at a prominent table, and his two brothers were at another table with their dates and friends. Nick had wanted to ask his brothers, Benjamin specifically, about Palmer's challenge, but he didn't feel like he could without the risk of their father hearing about it.

As he sat down, he felt a headache coming on, though it wasn't from the champagne. When he had picked up his escort card containing his table assignment, the black stock calligraphed in gold read "Table 1603." There was no table numbered 1603; there were only about forty tables, designated as One through Forty. He showed it to Phoebe, and found that he was actually seated at Table Fourteen with her.

Still, as he pocketed the card, it left him with an unsettled feeling.

After the salad course had been cleared, Letty Chilton, the chair of the Ball Committee, stood up to make a speech, her husband, Martin, sitting nearby. She was wearing a turquoise dress that made her look like she was dressed in one of the tablecloths. As she welcomed everyone from her position on the dais in front of the temple, the lighting created ghostly shadows on her face. Nick spaced out during most of the speech, as it was all about boring stuff like how proud she was of all the donors, how much work they had all done, and how much the Egyptian wing was a vital part of this city. Nick loved the Egyptian wing—it was a stone's throw from his bedroom window—but he felt like Mrs. Chilton was using it as her own personal triumph, as if she were responsible for all the hard work that had been done by the curators, the scholars, the archaeologists, and the art historians.

Letty Chilton probably wouldn't know an Egyptian artifact if she tripped over one in Central Park.

"In closing," she said, "I'd like to say how grateful we are to our friends in Cairo for loaning us these glorious objects, here now at the Met for all the world to see. You have truly brought Egypt to those who might never experience it. Thank you."

There was thunderous applause as Mrs. Chilton beamed at the crowd and then carefully stepped off the small platform.

At that moment, the power went out.

Patch had cued up the next song that was to play after Letty Chilton's speech, as she had informed him that she loathed nothing more than the awkward silence that occurs after applause has died down but before conversation resumes. Patch was to fill this gap by starting up the music immediately—almost, she had implied, under penalty of death. (Letty Chilton had been victim to a terrible incident at the Metropolitan Club the previous year when she had given a toast and then there was no music for a full ninety seconds after it had concluded. The memory, clearly, had stayed with her.)

Now there wasn't silence, but there wasn't music, either. As the museum went dark, there was shouting and commotion. With all the candlelight, it wasn't pitch-black exactly, but startling nonetheless.

Claire Chilton ran up to him, in a near hysterical fit. "Patch! What is going on? Why is all the lighting going out? Did you do something? All these cables! Did you knock something over?"

"Claire, I play the music. The lighting booth is over there," he said, motioning to the other side of the room.

She scowled and ran across the room, though she was intercepted by her mother, who was equally hysterical.

Just relax, Patch thought. What were they all so crazy about? The lights would come back on when they came on. It was probably just a temporary outage caused by a surge in the power grid. All the extra lighting for the party was taking up an awful lot of juice, not to mention the klieg lights outside, which had been on since six P.M.

Then Patch heard something else: the sound of smashing glass from the west side of the room, followed by a few loud screams. Patch looked up, trying to determine through the crowd what was going on. The bodies crowded around the artifacts, as people made their way toward the exits. Patch wondered why everyone didn't stay in their seats. With all the events that had taken place in the last ten years in New York City, even a mere power outage was enough to get people to panic.

As the crowd cleared around the west side of the room, the source of the smashing glass became clear: one of the display cases had been broken into from the side and was now empty. Patch felt a lump rising in his throat.

He had heard the museum's head of security speaking with his guards earlier that day when he had come in for the sound check.

Because of all the extra power that would be required by the caterers, the lighting, and the sound—and because the museum would be doubly staffed with guards during the party—the museum had made an executive decision, that now, in retrospect, didn't seem terribly smart.

To save power and try to prevent an outage, they had turned off the security alarms on all the cases.

CHAPTER THIRTY-FIVE

Phoebe had stayed with her group of Nick, Lauren, Thad, and Lia at their table near the glass wall that faced Fifth Avenue. It wasn't a prime table at all—they could probably thank Claire for that—but their champagne glasses were full, they were having a good time, and there didn't seem any reason to get caught up in the pandemonium around them.

Five minutes later, the lights came up again. It wasn't the ambient lighting on the temple, though: it was full-on, bright-as-day museum lighting. Everyone looked around in shock, as if the sun had risen and they could now see every blemish and imperfection around them. A few women pulled out their compacts and started frantically checking their makeup.

Phoebe glanced over to Patch, who was still in the DJ

booth. He seemed to be waiting for a cue from the powers that be, and wasn't going to start the music until he got one. He also seemed to be listening in on his headset, which was wired in with the event planner and the head of security.

There was no music, and the lights stayed bright as ever. It was as if the party had been abruptly killed, shot dead, and its corpse now strung up for all to see.

About half a minute later, the sound of crackling radios and heavy footsteps came from the entrance to the museum. Lauren stood up and pointed to the museum's west wall of display cases.

"Phoebe!" she hissed. "The necklace! It's gone!"

Phoebe looked as other guests started to notice. While the lights had been out, it was difficult to see that part of the room; for safety reasons, there weren't any candles near the artifacts, so they had been in darkness after the power went out. Now everyone started whispering in shock and horror. Those who were standing near the case moved away from it, as if mere proximity might implicate them in the crime. More people started shuffling toward the exits.

A row of a dozen policemen formed at the entrance to the Egyptian wing, creating a human wall that blocked anyone from leaving the museum. A team of detectives pushed through the crowds.

"Step away from the case, ladies and gentlemen," one of them said.

A roll of police tape was unfurled in a twenty-foot perimeter around the case.

"No one touches anything. No one moves anything," a detective instructed. "We're sorry to do this, but it's necessary if we want to find the necklace."

Letty Chilton came up to them. "Officer, you can't possibly detain our guests like this. For some of them, this has been a huge shock. . . ."

He brushed her off as if swatting away a fly. "Ma'am, I need you to step aside."

There was shouting from the north side of the temple. "This girl is wearing the necklace!"

Another officer spoke up. "This one, too!"

"No, no, you must understand!" Mrs. Chilton cried. "Those are reproductions! They're not the real thing!"

There were gasps, and then nervous laughter from the crowd.

"How close do they look to the real thing?" the detective asked.

"Lauren?" Mrs. Chilton looked around as Lauren stood up. There was silence in the room. Phoebe admired how composed Lauren was, given the situation.

"Well, Mrs. Chilton, you asked me to make them look as real as possible."

The crowd laughed again, and Phoebe thought she saw Mrs. Chilton blushing underneath all her makeup.

The detective spoke into a bullhorn. "I'm going to need anyone wearing a reproduction of the Scarab of Isis necklace to surrender them to my officers. Line up over there." He pointed to an officer who had commandeered one of the tables. "They will be tagged and returned to you in due time."

"Shouldn't you be looking for the real one?" Mrs. Chilton asked.

"Ma'am, we have no proof that one of these ladies isn't wearing the real one," the officer said. "Would be pretty handy, wouldn't it? How many are there?"

"Fourteen," Lauren said.

By this time, at least three dozen more officers had entered and started taking statements. A bag check was set up at the exit to the museum, and after each guest had been questioned and their purses and pockets had been checked, they were free to leave.

There was an interminable wait, and the bartenders had been instructed to close down the bars. They, too, were to be questioned before the evening's end.

Phoebe and her friends sat and nursed their glasses of champagne, now joined by Patch. Bradley Winston came by with a flask, but most of the table declined.

A little after one A.M., Phoebe finally got into a cab. As it sped down Fifth Avenue, she felt herself nodding off, drifting into dreams, wondering who could have pulled off the theft of the Scarab of Isis necklace.

Lauren decided that she would walk home from the ball, as it was only a few blocks, and she loved the snow that had started falling. She glanced behind her at the Temple of Dendur, lit brightly behind the glass wall of the Sackler Wing that faced Fifth Avenue. A sense of nostalgia hit her suddenly. It had been such a beautiful night, even with the drama, and she longed to share it with someone. But perhaps she was better off alone with her thoughts.

She heard some footsteps and turned to see Thad running down the steps toward her. Behind him was a handsome guy with olive skin and dark, piercing eyes.

"You're not going to believe what happened," Thad whispered. "I think I met someone."

Did everyone in the world have a date? It had started to seem that way.

"This is Kurt," Thad said, introducing the cute guy. "His parents are professors at Princeton. He's just in the city for the night. We're going to grab a nightcap somewhere. You want to join us?"

Lauren shook her head. "I think I'd better be getting home."

"Let us walk you home," Thad said.

"I'm fine," Lauren said. "I think I just want to enjoy the evening. Being out in the snow reminds me of when I was a little kid."

Thad nodded. "You sure?"

"You go ahead."

As Lauren bundled her coat and scarf around her, Claire walked by her. "Lauren, you can't possibly be going home alone."

Lauren looked up. "Yes, Claire, I am. Do you have a problem with that?"

"Oh, no," Claire said as she surreptitiously plucked a cigarette from the pocket of her coat while nervously watching the steps, probably to make sure her parents couldn't see her. "I just always imagine you surrounded by tons of boys. Like last semester."

Lauren paused. Claire was so annoying, and so rude, and it stung, hurt like a fall on the icy sidewalk. She knew it shouldn't affect her, as Claire was everything she didn't want to be. Lauren composed herself after a moment, cinching the belt on her overcoat and facing in the direction of Park Avenue. She knew she shouldn't say what she was about to say, but she had taken enough from Claire, and she didn't care if her mother was their decorator.

"That's funny, Claire," she said over her shoulder. "Because I always imagine you rotting and alone."

CHAPTER THIRTY-SIX

The next morning was Valentine's Day, and Patch woke up early. Unlike the others, he hadn't been drinking champagne the night before, since he was working, at least until the necklace debacle. He had been excited about the DJ gig, and even though Claire had been a complete pill, he was disappointed he hadn't been given the chance to finish off his set list. He'd also wanted to impress Lia with his taste and skill.

Patch padded into the kitchen, and as usual, Genie was already up, doing the Sunday *Times* crossword puzzle.

"I hear you had quite a night," she said.

"How do you know that?"

She held up a copy of the *Daily News*. "Freddy downstairs gave me his," she said, referring to the doorman on the early Sunday morning shift.

The headline on the cover read: "Oh, Goddess! Ancient Jewels Heisted at Socialite Ball." Inside, the story recounted all the facts that Patch already knew from having been there himself. There hadn't been much time for actual analysis; that would come online and in the later editions of the paper.

In the *Daily News* spread, there was a close-up of the original necklace, a file photo provided by the museum.

"I think you should see this," Genie said. She held up an old, yellowed news clipping from *W* magazine, one Patch hadn't seen before. It was similar to the photo that had been in the *Times* nearly twenty years ago, of his mother at the last Dendur Ball, but this one was a close-up.

His mother was wearing a necklace that looked like the Scarab of Isis. The caption noted that she was wearing a rare replica of the necklace. The original had been on loan to the museum and was being shown in New York for the very first time.

"They made replicas for everyone twenty years ago as well?" Patch asked.

"No, no, that wasn't it," Genie said. "Far be it from Esmé to do something that wasn't unique. She's wearing something that someone gave to me. Well, I suppose you can know. She's wearing something that Palmer gave to me."

"Palmer Bell?"

"Yes, while we were engaged. He had been on a trip to

Cairo, and he was very taken with the necklace when he viewed it at the Museum of Egyptian Antiquities. He had a copy made, based on photographs. He gave it to me on the night of our engagement. It may have been a copy, but it was one of a kind."

"And you gave it to my mom?"

"Yes. I had no attachment to it anymore."

Patch wanted to learn more, but he knew better than to pry. Genie would sometimes clam up completely if she thought he was getting too nosy about the past.

"Where is the copy now?" Patch didn't even know why he was asking this, but somehow it seemed important to know about something that belonged, ever so briefly, to his mother.

"Esmé smashed it during one of her fits. She said she dumped it in the park."

"Genie, why are you showing this to me? I'm not sure I understand."

She frowned. "There's something suspicious about all of this. All you kids serving on that committee. They make replicas for the girls to wear. And then it's stolen?"

"Are you sure you're not drawing too many conclusions?"

"Do you know anything about that necklace? Do you know what they say about the goddess Isis?"

Patch shook his head.

"She was one of the most important Egyptian goddesses,

the goddess of magic, motherhood, and fertility. The ancient Egyptians believed the Nile flooded each year with tears of sorrow for her husband who died, the god Osiris."

"What does this have to do with the necklace?"

"Only that it's a terribly important artifact. It would be a shame if it were never recovered." She paused. "And that, to me, the necklace is a symbol of grief."

Patch nodded. "Do you think the Society has anything to do with this? I mean, the event last night was overrun with Society members."

"I can't say." She glanced down at her newspaper. "I really should be getting back to my puzzle. If I don't finish it in one go, I never get it done."

Leave it to his grandmother to muddle up his Valentine's Day with a mystery. And Isis? Osiris? Tears of sorrow? What did that have to do with anything?

His phone buzzed with a joking text from Lia:

HAPPY V-DAY, SEXY. IF YOU'RE GIVING ME THAT NECKLACE TONIGHT, YOU KNOW I DON'T REALLY LIKE JEWELRY.

Patch smiled. He had a big evening planned for the two of them, but first he wanted to try to figure out what had happened last night at the Met.

CHAPTER THIRTY-SEVEN

At Nick's apartment, no one could talk of anything but the jewelry heist. The theft was all over the papers, and more information and reports emerged gradually during the day. Upper East Side gossip circles, of which Nick's mother was an integral part, were relishing the scandal, and different and often conflicting accounts of what happened to each guest were traded back and forth like war stories. Some speculated about various guests who were present at the ball; among the suspicious parties were a pair of too-slick, oft-photographed socialites rumored to be the daughters of a Moscow crime boss. Others said the necklace theft could only be the work of Middle Eastern terrorists. One woman claimed that she had spotted a woman walking her pugs down Fifth Avenue and wearing the necklace that morning.

Nick was relieved when he got a text from Patch asking to meet him across the street. They took a walk around the back of the museum, avoiding the police cars that were barricading the institution, which had been closed down for the day. The theft was a major one, as the necklace was valued at nine hundred thousand dollars, and the police, museum officials, and insurance investigators had an interest in making sure it was found. The entire incident was also an embarrassment for the museum, which prided itself on its security. In one of the articles Nick had read, the museum's director of security was quoted as saying, "When we as an institution start to feel too safe, we're actually the most vulnerable."

As they walked, Patch's breath was visible in the cold air.

"I need to show you something," Nick said. He pulled out the card from the previous night, and Patch read it.

"'Table 1603.' Where'd you get this?"

"It was my escort card from last night. What do you think that means? Do you think it's a clue?"

Patch shrugged. "I don't know what to think anymore. My grandmother has this idea that the whole necklace thing is connected to your grandfather." He told Nick about everything that Genie had said that morning about Palmer's obsession with the necklace, and how he had made a copy of it for Genie.

"That's crazy," Nick said. "My grandfather's still in the hospital. How could he have anything to do with the theft?"

Walking with Patch, in this rare moment of privacy, Nick felt a chill. He had been hiding something from Patch for more than a month now, the secret his father had told him on New Year's Eve. Every day he didn't reveal what he knew, it became more and more awkward to tell his best friend.

That was the thing about secrets: they ate you up inside until there was nothing left, a hollow cadaver of a person. Nick tried to ignore his feelings and not let on what he was thinking, his fear that once again, he would lose Patch's trust. Nick had to believe the information would be revealed at the right time, in a way that wouldn't jeopardize their relationship. But now was definitely not the right time. Nick tried to focus on what was in front of them.

Patch nodded. "I think we should focus on the clue you got last night. I don't think it was a mistake. I mean, it's so far off in terms of numbers; the tables only went to forty or so. There's no way it wasn't meant for you." Patch paused. "Let me try something." Patch pulled out his iPhone.

"What are you doing?" Nick said.

"Well, it might be a combination—which, like your key, really doesn't help us, but it also could be an address."

Patch punched in the numbers 1603 to the map feature on his phone.

"You think it's just going to pop up an address?" Nick asked.

Patch waited until the page had loaded. "It is an address. In Copenhagen."

"Copenhagen?"

"Yup." Patch grinned. "In Denmark."

"Why are you smiling?"

"This is so insane. I mean, Palm Beach is one thing, but they expect us to go to Denmark? Forget about it. We don't even know what we're looking for!"

They had circled around to the south side of the museum, exiting near the Three Bears Playground.

"So you're just going to give up?" Nick asked as they paused on the sidewalk.

"It's not giving up," Patch said. "I think we need to know that some leads are worth following, and others aren't."

"And you've deemed this one to be worthless."

"Keep the numbers, Nick. The answer will come. I have a feeling it's closer than we think."

The police cars were still swarmed in front of the Met, and the two boys kept a wide berth to avoid getting caught up in the melee.

"I've got to go," Patch said. "Date tonight."

Nick nodded. He would be seeing Phoebe, too, but something about trying to celebrate a trivial holiday with her felt lifeless and dull. Until he could figure out what his grandfather had been trying to tell them, that would be his real passion.

Nick touched the key that was around his neck, the key he had been guarding. Never before had he felt so close to an answer, yet also so far away.

CHAPTER THIRTY-EIGHT

That evening Patch rushed to the corner of 59th Street and Fifth Avenue, where he had asked Lia to meet him for the Valentine's Day he had planned. He cursed himself for running late when he saw her standing at the corner where all the horse-drawn carriages and their drivers congregated. She was ignoring the tourists and tacky souvenir stands and looked mildly annoyed, as if she had expected something more exotic from Patch on Valentine's Day, like a concert downtown or passes to a speakeasy club on the Bowery.

After greeting Lia with a kiss, Patch walked up to one of the drivers, a scruffy guy in a thick flannel coat, whom he recognized from a ride he had taken a few days ago. On Thursday afternoon, he had talked to a few different drivers, finally meeting one who agreed to help him out.

"Come on," Patch said to Lia, motioning her over. "Meet Chester."

Lia looked up at the horse, a gold and cream palomino. "You're joking," she said. "Are we really?"

Patch nodded. "Yup. Get on up."

Lia laughed. "I can't believe this."

"Oh, it gets better."

He handed an envelope to the driver. In it was two hundred dollars in cash, much more than the cost of a ride through Central Park.

"Kid, if anyone says anything, you're taking the blame for this, you got it?" the driver said.

"I understand," Patch said.

"Wait, *I* don't get it," Lia said. "What's going on?"

Patch climbed up into the driver's seat and motioned for Lia to sit next to him. The driver got out of the carriage and gestured for Patch to get going before anyone noticed.

"Where are we headed?" Lia asked.

"We're going to see a bit of the city," Patch said.

Lia smiled. "Okay—but you know that if we get arrested for this, we're ending up on the cover of the *Post*, right?"

"Maybe that's a risk worth taking."

Instead of heading into the park, as the horses usually did, Patch maneuvered the carriage down Fifth Avenue. For once, he was grateful for the riding lessons he had taken with Nick when he was younger, as driving a carriage wasn't all that different from riding a horse. The driver had also given him a short primer a few days ago.

It was Valentine's Day, the shops on Fifth Avenue were all lit up, and no one paid them any mind. If they did, it was only to tip their hat or whistle at his romantic gesture.

Not many New Yorkers realized that taking a carriage ride out of the park, particularly when you didn't have a license, was completely illegal.

They reached 42nd Street, and Patch started to turn right so they could go back up Sixth Avenue.

"Hey, what are you doing?" Lia asked.

"What do you mean? You want to go downtown?" He was surprised at her audacity, but they had made it to 42nd Street without anyone stopping them. Maybe they should go all the way downtown.

Lia grinned. "You're always saying how you want to get out of your little world, aren't you? Now's your chance. In a horse-drawn carriage!"

Patch nodded. It was true. Everything with the Society had felt so suffocating. As he looked up at the lights of Fifth Avenue, this little adventure was a welcome dive into the dark, dazzling unknown.

"Are you serious?" he asked.

"Yup."

The light turned green, and Patch continued directing Chester to keep walking. He broke into a trot, and Patch held the reins tightly.

"He's trying to keep up with traffic!" Lia said, laughing. He was a good horse, and Patch wanted to make sure that he was okay. But he didn't seem to mind at all—he seemed rather pleased at breaking out of the usual *clomp-clomp-clomp* routine of rides around Central Park.

"You are totally ruining my plan!" Patch said in mock annoyance. He was actually grateful. Fifteen minutes out of the park was one thing, but an hour or more—now *that* was romantic.

Twenty minutes later, they were down in the Village on a quiet side street. They parked Chester in an empty space and then grabbed some falafel sandwiches and fries at a shop Lia liked. As they ate them in the carriage, Chester craned his neck and sniffed the air curiously.

"It's certainly a whole different world from the Dendur Ball, right?" Lia said.

"Yeah, that's an understatement," Patch said.

"Do they know anything more about who stole the necklace?"

Patch shook his head. "I don't think so. I have a suspicion that, you know, the Society had something to do with it. Nick got a weird escort card last night at the ball. It had a series of numbers on it. And my grandmother thinks that Nick's grandfather has something to do with it."

"What do you think?"

"Hell if I know," Patch said. "I just want life to go back to the way it was before all this happened. When I had my vlog."

"Oh, I almost forgot—" Lia said. "My parents have a producer friend who I would really like you to show your DVD to."

"I don't know if I can do it—the Society has control over all the footage."

"No, I mean, we could explain that this was just a sample. That the real show would focus on different people. Do you think you could give me something to send to him?"

"Sure, I guess. I mean, you know that I don't technically own the option on the material for another six months, right?"

"I think he should see it now. He's an old family friend. He'll understand that you can't officially start working on it before June."

Patch figured it was unlikely that he could get in any more trouble than he already had been in. He would have to ask Eliot Walker to send him the contents of the safe-deposit box. If he and his four friends were close to getting out of the Society, maybe that was a risk worth taking.

"Let me treat you to something," Lia said. She hopped out of the carriage before Patch could say anything.

She returned a few minutes later with two cups of gelato.

"Only you would get gelato in the middle of February, outside," Patch said.

"You don't like it? I got pistachio and butterscotch."

"No, no, I love it." He smiled.

Patch grabbed one of the heavy blankets that was on their laps and pulled it closer.

"This stuff is the best," Lia said. "I like to go here whenever I can. Of course, for me, it's uptown."

They enjoyed their gelato quietly. The city was silent that night, as if most of Manhattan had been divided up into two's, lovers sharing intimacies. Gone were the frat boys, the tourists, the rowdy barhoppers who usually roamed these streets.

Patch looked at his watch. Genie was always upset with him if he was out too late on a school night. "Okay, eat up, we need to get back uptown."

Just as they were pulling out, they got a strange look from some traffic cops. Patch gamely gave them a salute and continued on up Sixth Avenue. Lia smirked as the two cops shook their heads.

When they reached the park, they rode back in, parking the carriage in an empty lot behind the zoo. Lia pulled the blanket around them and gave Patch a kiss on the lips. Her lips felt like they had frozen over; surely, the gelato hadn't helped.

"You're like ice," he said. "We should go warm up."

She smiled. "I don't care. When else do you get to hang out in the park, under the stars, in a carriage, with no driver watching over you?"

He remembered that he had packed a thermos of hot chocolate in his backpack, and now he poured out a cup. "This should help."

Lia nodded appreciatively, and after taking a sip, kissed him again.

The next morning, Patch woke up with a smile. Every element of his date with Lia had come together perfectly.

Now he threw on a bathrobe and padded outside to get the newspaper. He picked up the copy of the *Times* that he and Genie shared every morning and felt something heavy in it.

There was a padded envelope tucked inside the paper, addressed to Genie, with only her name, typewritten on a label: "Eugenia Rogers Madison—by hand."

Though he was eager to learn what was in it, he suppressed his curiosity. Genie was in the kitchen making coffee, and she looked surprised when he handed it to her. She sat down at the kitchen table and opened the envelope.

Inside, there was a note that read:

For Eugenia,
Who deserves only the original.
P.B.

And then, to both of their amazement, out slid the original Scarab of Isis necklace.

CHAPTER THIRTY-NINE

T hat bastard!"

Nick entered the apartment just as Genie was muttering this epithet in Patch's general direction. It was seven A.M., and Nick and Patch had school that day, but Genie had demanded that Nick rush right down as soon as the necklace arrived.

The Scarab of Isis sat on the kitchen table, on top of its padded envelope. As if it were kryptonite, no one dared touch it.

"Nicholas, what on earth am I supposed to do with this? You take this right back to your grandfather and tell him I don't want it. No, better yet, I'm going to take it to the police. I'm sure they'll be very interested in the fact that it's been in his possession for the past two days!"

"No," Nick said. "Genie, I don't think that's a good idea. I mean, we don't know what the circumstances were—"

"The circumstances! The circumstances were that he stole it from the museum!"

"Genie, he's still in the hospital. There's no way he could have stolen it." Nick looked to Patch for support, but his friend seemed confused as to what to say.

"Oh, hell, I don't know what the right thing is to do!" Genie plunked herself down at the kitchen table in exasperation. "He always joked that one day, he would give me the original. That good-for-nothing miscreant! Now I'm stuck with it!" She paused, and a look of sadness crossed her face. "Just like I was stuck with the memories for all those years."

She looked plaintively at the two boys, and it was as if years were suddenly erased from her face, as if she was becoming a twenty-one-year-old girl again. "One has such mixed feelings, you know, about these things. I loved your grandfather, Nick. Loved him, I think, as I have never loved anyone else since then. My husband was a good man, a sweet man, warm and generous and kind. But he and I never had the same feelings that your grandfather and I had."

"Why then?" Nick asked. "Why didn't it work out? You never told us."

Genie straightened up and composed herself. "Palmer was a member of the Society, as you know. I couldn't be, as I was a woman, and they didn't admit women formally until the

1970s. But I didn't approve of their methods—I still don't, as you know—and I made that very clear to him. I urged him to defect from the group. I had no idea the hold that they could maintain on a person. We continued planning the wedding, but it remained a sticking point with us."

Nick's phone rang, and he quickly silenced it.

"The night of our rehearsal dinner at the Yale Club, Palmer never showed up. I had bought a new dress and was wearing the necklace that he had given me on our engagement: the copy of the Scarab of Isis. My mother thought I looked foolish. I fancied myself as glamorous, as exotic. That was how he liked me to be, even if I really wasn't. You can imagine how silly I felt when he stood me up."

"Where did he go?" Patch asked.

"His father packed him on an ocean liner that was headed for Italy. He was going to do his version of the Grand Tour. It was unconscionable, really, what they did. You don't do that to a young woman."

"And it was all because you wanted him to leave the Society?"

Genie nodded. "I believe so. That's the only logical explanation for it. Nick, your grandfather could be a wonderful man, but he only recently developed a backbone. He was a spineless creature back then, in his twenties. He was nothing more than a pawn of his family." She paused. "You can understand why I am so protective of both of you."

Nick's phone rang again, and once again he silenced it.

"I have always blamed the Society for what happened," Genie said. "I know that perhaps it's foolish, for me to hold such a petty thing against such a complicated organization. I have no idea what kind of forces were at play. Perhaps I will never know."

"He loved you," Nick said. "From this note, I mean—I know it's bizarre, but he clearly still has feelings for you."

"Nick, feelings die. You must understand that. They seem so fresh, so eternal, at your age, but at a certain point, one simply stops caring. Palmer's note is nothing more than a boyish memory. You can't take that kind of thing seriously. He had a life, with his wife. I was not part of that."

Nick looked down at his phone, which had a message.

"You should get that," Patch said. "It looks like your mom is trying to reach you."

Nick called his mother back. She answered quickly and delivered her news with little emotion.

"Oh my God," he said. His fingers felt numb as he held the phone.

"What is it?" Patch asked, after Nick hung up.

"It's my grandfather," Nick said. "He died this morning, in the hospital."

"Oh my dear," Genie said. "I'm so sorry. I feel like such a fool! I shouldn't have said those things about him. This must be such a shock. Does your family expect you back? We shouldn't be keeping you here."

"No, it's okay," Nick said quietly. "Could I stay here for a few more minutes?"

"Of course," Genie said. "Let me get you a cup of coffee." She busied herself around the kitchen.

Nick needed a refuge from the craziness that was sure to ensue in his family's apartment. Not only was there the issue of what to do with the necklace, but there would be funeral arrangements and an obituary and condolence cards and more flowers than he could imagine.

The last time he had seen his grandfather, he had asked Nick to solve that riddle, the one that would help him get out of the Society.

Now that Palmer was gone, Nick didn't know if they had lost their chance. But he knew they still had to try.

More than anything, his grandfather's last words to him rang through his head: "Nicholas, you have always had everything you need."

After learning the news of his grandfather's death, Nick was even less sure what to do about the necklace. As his family name was at stake, Genie had allowed Nick to make the decision about what to do with the stolen necklace. She said she didn't want any part in it and had given it to him in the padded envelope. By the time Nick headed upstairs to face the chaos in his apartment and finish getting ready for school, his parents had already left for the hospital.

Nick carefully placed the scarab amulet in an empty desk drawer in his room. Several hours earlier, before hearing the news about Palmer, Nick would have brought the necklace to the police and told them the story of how it had arrived, but now that didn't seem right. Nick didn't want the story of the necklace overshadowing his grandfather's death. And Patch didn't want his grandmother brought into the scandal of the theft. Nick felt an obligation to protect Genie.

Going to school that day was a dose of much-needed reality, time to reflect on the right course of action. Nick didn't tell anyone about the necklace, not even Phoebe. He needed to think it all through. If he went to the police, they would want the whole story. If he appeared at the museum, they would want an explanation as well. But it wouldn't be right to keep the necklace, either.

He would have to return it, anonymously.

When Nick arrived home to the apartment that afternoon, he carefully closed and locked his bedroom door. He put the necklace back into a new, heavily padded envelope, closing and sealing it tightly while wearing gloves to avoid fingerprints. He was able to find a return address from a Metropolitan Museum mailing that read "1000 Fifth Avenue," which he pasted onto the front of the envelope. That evening, he walked outside and placed the envelope in a mailbox right across the street from the museum. He would have taken it directly there, but he didn't want to risk being caught by a security camera.

By the next afternoon, the news was all over town. The museum revealed that the necklace had been returned by an unidentified party and they were grateful for its swift delivery. His plan had worked.

CHAPTER FORTY

Lauren hadn't wanted to attend Palmer Bell's memorial service, but she did it for Nick and Phoebe. If Alejandro's funeral had been like a carnival, then Palmer's, at St. Thomas, also on Fifth Avenue, was an austere, black-clad mass. Lauren had taken Phoebe to Saks the day before in order to find something appropriately respectful and colorless. Phoebe was sitting in the first row with Nick and his family, including his two brothers, while Lauren sat behind them with Patch, Thad, and the other Society members. Lauren knew her friends understood the hypocrisy of honoring a man who was responsible for so much damage. But no one wanted to cause trouble, particularly since it might jeopardize the chances of the five of them getting out of the Society.

The service was completely impersonal, a series of hymns

and readings about service and justice and truth. Lauren was glad that, unlike Alejandro's, it was relatively short, less than forty-five minutes. Afterward, Lauren joined Phoebe, who was standing with Genie and Patch outside the church.

Phoebe gave Genie a hug on the icy sidewalk. "I'm so sorry," she said.

Genie swatted her away with a folded program. "Oh, don't you be sorry, dear. I still curse that man's name for everything he was responsible for. I'm only here because it's the right thing to do."

Patch merely shrugged at the girls, and there was an awkward pause.

"Well, I need to go downtown, actually," Lauren said. "I figured that I might as well take the rest of the day off, since they're not expecting us back at school. I have to stop by Giroux. Phoebe, do you want to come with me?"

Phoebe shook her head. "I think I'd better stay with Nick, you know, make sure he's okay."

"Of course," Lauren said. "I understand."

Lauren parted ways with the rest of the group and took the subway downtown. When she arrived at Giroux, she headed to Sebastian's office. She had sent over a portfolio earlier of her new designs for the Colette store in Paris, and she was eager to hear what he thought.

He was in his office. Lauren knocked on the door and then popped her head in.

"Lauren! Come, sit!"

Lauren sat down on one of the two Eames chairs in his office. Sebastian had given her this new opportunity that she needed, and yet she wondered if she really deserved it. She was encouraged by the fact that her designs were selling, both nationally and in Europe. Was that proof enough that she had talent?

"I'm curious to know what you think about the Colette line," she said. "I decided to go in an Egyptian direction this time, as I was inspired by the Dendur Ball. But these are reinterpretations, more like the pieces that became popular in the 1920s and beyond."

Sebastian flipped through Lauren's black portfolio. "These are beautiful. I think we're all set with this. Colette will love these."

"I hope so," Lauren said. "Will you let me know what they say?"

"I'll do even better. I want you to come to Paris next month, for a week during spring break, to view the unveiling of their new collection. It will be *huge* to have the actual designer in their midst."

"Really?" Lauren asked. "To Paris?"

"Absolutely," Sebastian said. "I want to introduce you to some other European buyers, and I'd like you to accompany me on visits to several ateliers. I probably shouldn't mention this, but a few designers have also expressed interest in using your pieces as accessories in their upcoming runway shows."

"Oh my God—can you say who?"

"I'd rather not. I don't want to get your hopes up. But I can assure you that if any one of them picked your line, you'd be extremely pleased."

Lauren blushed. "Thank you. I don't know what to—this is just so exciting!"

"Well, you deserve it." Sebastian leaned forward. "There's something else I wanted to mention to you. That little incident that we had last month?"

"Oh, please, I'd rather not think about that," Lauren said, groaning. He was referring to the awful episode with the stolen earrings.

"We've learned who was responsible for it," Sebastian said. "One of the security guards, not Danny, but the other one that week, a temp from the agency, was paid off to place the earrings in your bag. I don't know who arranged it, but I'm glad that it was cleared up. Of course, I never believed that you had done it."

"Thank you," Lauren said. "I appreciate that." She wasn't really sure what to say, as she felt such mixed emotions. Clearly, the Society had been responsible, but did Sebastian not know that? Were all these orders coming from a higher place? Maybe she had achieved the connection with Sebastian on her own merits, and his affiliation with the Society was purely coincidental. In that case, perhaps she could still work for Sebastian and not be a member of the Society, if the five of them could manage to get out. But was that right? She wanted to go to Paris, to have that opportunity, to be mentored by famous designers, to meet people in the fashion industry. But what were the strings that were attached to it all? What price would she have to pay?

CHAPTER FORTY-ONE

The next day, the Bell family was called together for a reading of Palmer Bell's will. Nick's father had assisted in its preparation, so most of it was perfunctory, but it was a formality that Palmer's last wishes be read to the group of interested parties.

The Bell family's lawyers were in a landmarked midtown office building with a beautiful WPA-era mural in its lobby. It was the type of space that, to Nick, spoke of tradition and legacy, of one's place in the history of the city. The meeting had been set for ten A.M., and he had arrived separately from the rest of his family. As Nick was about to enter the elevator bank, he was surprised to see Patch talking to a security guard. His friend was given a badge and he started walking toward Nick.

"Patch? What are you doing here?" Nick called.

Patch caught up to him, slightly out of breath. "I'm not really sure. I got a call yesterday that I was supposed to attend a meeting at your father's lawyer's offices."

"Why didn't you tell me?"

"I thought you knew about it already."

Nick looked at his watch. "We'd better be getting up there. They're going to be starting soon."

In preparation for the meeting, Nick had slicked back his dark hair and was wearing a suit, Italian loafers, and a wool winter coat. He examined Patch's outfit: khakis, a button-down, Converse sneakers, and a huge parka.

"You look nice," Patch said. "I sort of wish I had dressed up a little more."

"Don't worry about it," Nick said. "It's a lawyer's office. They work for us, remember? But who called you about this, anyway?"

The elevator was nearing the twenty-first floor.

"I didn't catch her name. Someone's assistant, I think. She just said it was important and it had to do with your family."

Nick didn't have time to think about what it meant as they were ushered in, though he sensed that something important, maybe even life-changing, was about to be revealed. He sat down at the large polished conference table with the rest of his family, while Patch took a seat along the far wall of the room.

Nick was sitting next to his two brothers, Henry and Benjamin, and directly across from his mother and father. Farther down the table was Nick's uncle, Philip, and his wife, Eleanor, who had left the Upper East Side for the suburbs of Westchester; their children, Maggie, twelve, and Caroline, ten, were presumably at school. Philip and Eleanor had distanced themselves from the family in recent years, and Nick hadn't seen them at any of the Society functions. He wasn't sure if they were members or not.

Nick had noticed his father flinch when Patch entered the room and his mother whisper something to his father.

Oh, God, Nick thought, *here it comes.*

Aldon Story, the Bell family lawyer, started by reading through what seemed like an interminable list of assets. There were all of Palmer's investments, including businesses and real estate that Nick had never even known about.

Finally, they got to the financial assets. Parker Bell was stoic, but Nick could see Henry and Benjamin shifting in their seats. Nick's mother, Gigi, kept wetting her lips. Eleanor whispered something to Philip.

Sharks circling around a bleeding carcass, Nick thought. They had all known this day would come; some of them might have already been aware of their inheritance. And yet still, there was a finality in having it all read aloud.

Parker and Georgiana Bell would be receiving a significant amount, as would Philip and Eleanor, well over a quarter of a billion dollars. Then the lawyer began to read off the list of grandchildren: Maggie, Caroline, Nick, Ben, and Henry.

Each of them would be the beneficiary of a trust valued at thirty million dollars. For the three boys, the trustee, until they reached the age of twenty-five, would be their father, Parker Bell. From what Nick understood about trusts, this meant that his father could give each beneficiary access to each trust at his discretion.

As expected, the remainder of Palmer Bell's estate would go to the Bradford Trust, to be used for whatever endeavors, charitable and otherwise, that it saw fit.

Nick's shoulders relaxed and then tightened again. It was good news—wonderful news, actually—that the trust was so generous, but it wasn't exactly good news that his father would remain the trustee for so long.

Mr. Story cleared his throat. "There is one more beneficiary in Mr. Bell's will."

Everyone looked around in confusion. Was there someone who had been missed? A long lost cousin whom Palmer had decided to include?

"I believe he is here today," Mr. Story said. "The last beneficiary is Patchfield Evans the third, Palmer Bell's grandson."

Nick sat back in his seat, simultaneously stunned and fascinated at this development. This confirmed what he had known. Confirmed the truth he had been hiding from his friend for the past two months, the truth Nick had tried to ignore.

This would change everything.

Did his father know Patch was to be a part of the will? Would Patch himself have any clue about what this meant?

Nick looked over to Patch, who was still sitting at the edge of the room, awestruck.

Nick's brothers were even more perplexed.

"What—Mr. Story, what does this mean?" Henry asked. "How is Patch related—"

"Henry, settle down!" Parker Bell said.

The lawyer spoke. "I believe it will all become clear soon," he said. "As for each of your trusts, you should contact our office individually to make arrangements regarding its disbursement. There are certain parameters that have been put in place, which your specific trustee—in each case, the father in each family—can change at any time. We will discuss how that works individually with each one of you."

"But what about . . ." Ben asked, his voice trailing off.

"Ben, Henry, Nick, I'll discuss it with you at home," Parker said.

Patch looked as if he might be ill. He made a motion to Nick that they should leave, and Nick nodded to him, getting up. Nick had no idea how he was going to explain the little that he knew.

"Nicholas, where are you going? We're not finished yet!" Parker Bell said.

"I think we're finished, Dad. I'll see you back at home."

Nick pushed open the door to the conference room, and Patch followed him.

Once they were out on the sidewalk, the chilly air was like a wake-up call.

"What just happened there?" Patch said.

"Well, you're thirty million dollars richer," Nick said, laughing.

"Wow, um, okay—it may take me a few days to process this. And what's this about your father being the trustee?"

"That's just the way trusts work. Until we turn twenty-five. They don't want you to blow the whole thing."

"But more importantly," Patch said, "why? What did I do to deserve this? Your grandfather never really cared for me, as far as I could tell. I don't even know if your father likes me. The lawyer said I was a grandchild of Palmer's. How could that be the case?"

Nick thought back to everything he knew. He decided to speak carefully.

"Is it possible," Nick said, "that your father, Patch, Jr., wasn't really your father?"

"Then who was my father?"

Nick paused before answering. "My dad?"

The two of them stood in stunned silence on the sidewalk

236

as people passed them, cars honked, everyone went about their daily life on a mid-morning in February.

"So that makes us . . . brothers?" Nick asked.

"Half brothers, to be precise," Patch said. "So my mother and your father—our father—had a—I don't know, an affair of some kind?" Patch seemed truly confounded by the news.

Nick stood there with Patch for a moment, in amazement that this moment had finally come. He wiped away a tear from his eye and then put one arm around Patch, squeezing him tightly.

"Come on," Nick said. "Let's get out of the cold."

CHAPTER FORTY-TWO

They decided on the bar at the Algonquin Hotel, which was a slightly shopworn, pretzels-and-peanuts kind of place with leather banquettes and sketches of Broadway shows on its wood-paneled walls. Nick said he had agreed to meet up with Phoebe after the reading of the will, and he texted her their location. The bar was open for lunch, and they pretended that they were there to eat, but neither Patch nor Nick expressed much interest in food. Nick ordered some fries for the table and three Cokes.

Phoebe arrived a moment later. She looked at Nick, then at Patch. "What's going on here?"

"We'll explain in a second," Nick said.

"I might need something stronger," Patch said, only half-joking as he motioned to his Coke. He was still in shock from the news and wasn't really sure how to process it. "Can I get a dirty martini?" he mock called to the waitress.

"Hold on there, *Lost Weekend*, let's keep our heads on, okay?" Nick said.

Nick explained to Phoebe, as quickly as he could, what had been revealed. Phoebe nodded in amazement.

"I should call Genie," Patch said, interrupting Nick's story. "I don't know if I can reach her, though." Genie was in the Catskills with a friend for a few days, at an old mountain retreat where she could curl up by the fireplace, play backgammon, and read paperback mysteries. She had decided she needed to get out of town after all the excitement of Palmer's death and the necklace heist. The problem was that this made her annoyingly unreachable. "She never has her phone turned on, unless it's in the charger," Patch said. "It has somehow escaped her that the purpose of a cell phone is to keep it with you."

He tried her, but it went directly to voice mail. She wouldn't be returning home until the weekend.

Patch decided he would call the next best person who might be able to explain it to him. His mother's number at the hospital was programmed into his phone, and he dialed it. It was a snap decision to call her, and as he heard the line ringing, he started to think better of it. What would he say to her? Was this really a conversation he wanted to have in front of Nick and Phoebe? A nurse answered the main line at the

Stoney River Psychiatric Hospital in Ossining, and he asked for his mom. After a moment, the nurse said she was unavailable, but they would give her the message. He was almost relieved she hadn't been there.

Nick and Phoebe looked at him plaintively. He felt like someone they had to feel sorry for.

"What's up, you guys?" Patch asked.

"It's so odd," Nick said. "Like, I feel like we should be celebrating about the trust funds, but that doesn't feel right. My grandfather could be an ass, but clearly he was looking out for you—for us—in some way."

"Except that now he's left us with an even bigger mystery to solve," Phoebe said.

"God, where is my grandmother when we need her?" Patch said.

Nick took a sip of his Coke. "Okay, let's figure this out. I'm going to speak openly here. Your mother and my father clearly had something going on. Our fathers were friends, so that can't have sat well between them."

"Unless my father—well, who I thought was my father— unless he didn't know."

"He had to have found out," Phoebe said. "How could he not?"

"I don't know," Nick said. "It's possible he never knew about it. What I don't get is, if my grandfather—our grandfather—was going to include you in his will, why did he have such strong feelings about you being in the Society? Why were they so upset when you taped the Night of Rebirth?"

The three of them were silent for a moment. "I have an idea," Phoebe said. "Just from what I know about your grandmother, Patch."

"What's that?" Nick said.

"Forgive me if I'm out of line here." She stirred her soda with a straw.

"Go on," Patch said.

"I think that if Palmer and Genie were once engaged, then Patch was a symbol of everything that he couldn't have, of something forbidden. He couldn't marry Genie because of family pressures to marry someone who approved of the Society. But Parker could have your mother in his life, Patch, at least by having an affair with her."

"I've been pretty sure, since the fall, that both of my parents were Society members," Patch said. "So how does that make my mother something forbidden?"

Phoebe spoke up. "What was forbidden about her was that she wasn't his wife." She looked sheepishly at the two boys.

"I think Phoebe's right," Patch said. "Palmer resented me because I reminded him of what his son had done."

"But then he came around in the end," Nick said, shaking his head in amazement. "Phoebe, do you remember what he told us in his hospital room? He said something about how he didn't want us to live the life set up for us by our families.

How destructive that could be."

"So maybe this is your ticket out?" Phoebe asked. "Is this his own way of helping you out of the Society?"

"We're not out yet," Nick said. "But this certainly doesn't hurt."

"No, I'd say thirty million dollars doesn't hurt," Patch said sarcastically. "Except that we still have no idea what the real story is." He still couldn't wrap his head around the trust. It seemed imaginary, like Monopoly money.

"I think we should take it from the beginning," Phoebe said. "Don't you think that figuring out Palmer's whole mystery, whatever he was trying to tell you in his room at the hospital, is the first step to all this?" She finished her Coke and nervously stabbed at the ice with a straw. "You've tried the key everywhere. But what about those numbers you mentioned? What were they again?"

"1603," Nick said.

"And you've tried addresses already, right? Give me your phone for a sec."

Nick handed over his iPhone, and Phoebe punched in the numbers. She scrolled through a few entries on Google and frowned.

"Have you ever thought it might be a year?" she asked.

Patch and Nick shrugged. "How would a year help us? Usually these things are an address. Like the chess tables last semester."

"Right, but maybe it's a year that leads us to an address."

"What are you showing up?" Nick asked.

"Nothing significant. Except that 1603 is mentioned in several entries as the last year of the Tudor dynasty."

"Oh, great, so we have to go to England," Patch said. "I said no to Denmark, and I say no to England, too."

"We don't have to go to England," Phoebe said. "We just have to go to a place that *looks* like England."

CHAPTER FORTY-THREE

Phoebe had some crazy idea about where they should go in the quest to solve Palmer's riddle, but Patch's attention was diverted. He would be joining them on their journey the next day, which, thankfully, was a Saturday, but for now, he was more concerned with solving the mystery of his own parentage. Could he really be Parker Bell's son? Or was it something else? And what did it mean to be someone's biological son, anyway, especially when you had never been treated as that person's child? Was your father the person whom your mother slept with to conceive you, or was your real father the man who raised you?

Even if that was a man who had disappeared from his life, had drowned in the Atlantic Ocean, when he was five years old.

For all the time that Patch had spent with the Bells—good, bad, indifferent—Parker Bell could very well be his father.

Except that fathers didn't keep their sons hostage. Fathers didn't execute nefarious plans to harm their sons.

But maybe Parker Bell didn't know that Patch was his son until today? And how was Nick so sure that Parker really was Patch's father? Nick hadn't let on anything about it before. What if it were something that went back even further, to Palmer and Genie? What if Esmé was actually Palmer's daughter, and Patch, Jr., really *was* his father? Was that even possible? It hadn't even occurred to Nick and Phoebe, but how did they know it wasn't true?

All these thoughts were spiraling around in his head like an insane kaleidoscope as Patch entered his building. As he waited for the elevator at the end of the lobby, he saw Parker Bell talking to the doorman.

He needed to know. He didn't particularly want to talk to him, but he needed to know.

Patch strode right up to Mr. Bell and tapped him on the shoulder.

Mr. Bell turned around and looked at Patch, first with annoyance, then with something resembling tenderness. "Patch," he said. "All this must be a surprise for you. Why don't you come upstairs?"

Patch nodded. He followed Mr. Bell into the elevator, and for the first few floors, they were silent. Mr. Bell finally spoke.

"I never intended for you to find out this way. I thought the lawyers were going to set up a private meeting. But once you were there at Mr. Story's invitation, I realized that you deserved to be there as much as anyone else."

"I'm not exactly sure why, sir. I wish you'd tell me."

Mr. Bell looked Patch up and down, his eyes lingering, Patch was sure, at his dirty sneakers and frayed khakis.

"Let's go into my study."

Patch followed Mr. Bell through the apartment that he knew so well, though he had spent little time there lately. Even though he and Nick had resumed their friendship, he still felt like he wasn't welcome in the Bells' inner sanctum. He also suspected that Gigi, Nick's mother, didn't like him very much, and so he had stayed away.

Mr. Bell's study was wood-paneled, with floor-to-ceiling bookshelves and windows that faced Fifth Avenue. Two burgundy leather chesterfield sofas sat facing each other. Patch sat down on one and Mr. Bell on another.

"Well, I imagine you and Nick have figured out what this is all about," Parker said.

"Not really."

"I cared for your mother very much," Parker said. "We had

some very nice times together. It was a mistake, though." He paused. "I'm sorry, I don't mean to suggest—"

"I understand," Patch said.

"What I am trying to say is that I should have remained faithful to my wife. Your mother and your father—or at least, the man you knew as your father—were having trouble conceiving. And so when your mother became pregnant, she was happy. For Esmé, it seemed like the solution. We were a perfect foursome. Of course, only she and I knew about it."

"My father never knew?" Patch found this hard to believe.

"No, that's not entirely true. He found out, which was difficult, to say the least. And my wife, Nick's mother, found out as well. It split up our little group. It was a sad, sad time. Particularly when your mother had her difficulty. I wanted you to be close, and so I arranged to help subsidize the apartment that you and your grandmother live in now, as Eugenia was having trouble paying the maintenance fees. Your grandmother, by the way, doesn't know that; she believes that her fees were simply lowered on account of her age. My wife, needless to say, was not pleased about any of it."

"So that's why she's disliked me all these years," Patch said.

"I wouldn't say that, Patch. She's just worried about Nick."

"Oh, you mean, she doesn't like him hanging out with the kid from the wrong side of the tracks?"

"You're hardly from the wrong side of the tracks!" Parker laughed. "You come from one of the most distinguished families in New York. George Madison and your grandmother made a fine pair. As did your mother and father—well, you know, Patch, Jr.—oh, dear, this is complicated. Anyway, you have nothing to be ashamed of."

"I'm not *ashamed* of anything," Patch said.

"That's good." He paused and pulled out a cigar. "Would you like one?"

Patch shook his head. Why was he trying to act like he could suddenly be his dad? Patch had seen how Parker treated Nick through the years, and he knew that the man could turn his charm on and off in an instant.

Parker cut the tip from his cigar and then lit it, blowing puffs of smoke into the air.

"How did it all happen?" Patch asked. "I mean, how did it go down?"

"I'm not sure I can get into all that," Parker said. "Dendur was a complicated matter."

"I'm sorry, 'Dendur'?"

"We called it 'Dendur,' as Esmé and I believed that you were conceived on the last night we were together, the evening of the last Dendur Ball. After that, the lawyers all called it the 'Dendur situation.'"

"What involvement did they have?"

"Helping your family out, making sure your grandmother could stay in the building even after your mother and father no longer had their apartment. And setting up the trust for you with your grandfather. I had promised all that to your mother. Palmer didn't understand it at first, but once I explained it to him, he acquiesced. I think he was jealous. The Bells and the Evanses. We've always liked your family. You know about his feelings for your grandmother."

"I'm so glad we could be a source of amusement to you," Patch said. The cigar smoke was making him nauseous.

"Don't be so flip," Parker said. "You have always had something special, Patch."

"What's that?"

"Do you know what a caul bearer is?" Parker stood up and went to his copy of *Webster's*, flipping it open. "You are a child who was born in the caul, which, not to mince words, is the amniotic sac. It is very rare, unlike anyone else in our family. Traditionally, it has marked a child for greatness. In ancient Egypt, it actually meant that a baby was fated for the cult of Isis, an order that some say still exists today."

"Oh, let me guess," Patch scoffed. "You're the head of the cult of Isis, too?" He may have been sarcastic on the surface, but he had to admit that he was intrigued.

"Not exactly," Parker said, laughing. "You'll have to discover that one for yourself."

"Okay, I guess I'll add that to my to-do list," Patch said.

"It is a shame that your greatness has not truly emerged yet," Parker said. "Thus far, you have been nothing but a weak link in the Society, a link that has threatened to bring it all down. In December, when you were initiated, I thought we might begin to see some of that greatness from you. Instead of fulfilling that mission, you and your friends have been Infidels. I would expect more from my sons. Of course, in many ways, you have completed exactly the pattern we see in all our future leaders: you start out as rebels, and eventually you find yourselves in charge."

Patch felt an anger welling up inside of him as he stood up. Almost out of nowhere, he found himself yelling at Parker. "For *seventeen* years you keep this secret from me, and now you want to call me your son? I don't think so! You're not my father, and I'm not your son. You don't get that privilege automatically. It's something that you have to *earn*. My father was the man who drowned twelve years ago. Don't ever forget that." Patch was shaking as he said these words, but he had never felt so strong in his convictions.

Parker looked as if Patch had upturned an ashtray in his face, but he did nothing as Patch left the room.

As Patch stormed through the Bell foyer and into the

elevator, he thought about the greatness that Parker had mentioned. He wondered whether this greatness was really intended for him, or if he had merely been born in the wrong place, at the wrong time.

CHAPTER FORTY-FOUR

The year 1603, according to Phoebe, was the last year of the Tudor dynasty, ending with the death of Queen Elizabeth I. Phoebe was convinced that the salient piece of information in all this was one word: *Tudor*.

"Come on, Nick," she prodded him after they had said good-bye to Patch in front of the Algonquin. "What have we seen recently that's Tudor?"

Nick shrugged as they walked east. "Beats me." It seemed like another one of his grandfather's mind games, even if it had been administered from the grave.

"I can't believe it—I was hopped up on tranquilizers and I remember the Tudor-style house that we all met at, the day after Thanksgiving. It was the day that—well, you know."

It was the day that Jared's death had been announced.

It had been a traumatic day for everyone. Phoebe had been driven in a town car from the city after nearly having a nervous breakdown. It wasn't a day in which Nick had been focusing on local architecture.

"I don't know much about houses," Phoebe continued, "but I do know what a Tudor revival looks like. We had them all over Los Angeles. It was what rich people lived in to make it look like they were descended from British royalty or something."

Nick nodded dumbly. Why hadn't he thought of that himself? Four digits. A year. Now it seemed so obvious.

"Okay," he said. "Then we go to Southampton."

Phoebe, Nick, and Patch arrived at the Southampton property, which Nick said was known as Eaton House, after the *Mayflower*-era family who had farmed the land, the next day around noon. While his father had mentioned the name of the house before, none of them knew who owned the house or what went on there, only that they had been summoned to it for that Society meeting in the fall. Thankfully, Nick's map-like memory of Southampton's back roads had come in handy, as he remembered where the house was without even having an address. It all started coming back to him: the grand house, greeting Phoebe at the door, everything he had felt being separated from her and then seeing her again. How he knew then, without a doubt, that she was the one. He remembered leaving the house that day and spending the night at his parents', the first night they had spent together.

Nick chided himself. This wasn't the time for fond memories. They had a job to do.

The gate was open, and Nick drove his beat-up Jeep Cherokee up the gravel driveway. The estate was the same as Nick had remembered it, though in the dead of winter it seemed more desolate, with barely any leaves on the trees, ground cover that was frozen a dull green, and muddy portions of the sod and landscaping that would only come back to life in the spring. Nick remembered how lavish the grounds had been, though they hadn't gotten to enjoy them: there was a croquet court, an English garden, a reflecting pool, tennis courts.

"So you're still telling me that we have no idea who owns all this?" Phoebe asked. "I mean, it's a house. Someone must live here, right?"

"I have no idea," Nick said. "The Bradford Trust must own it, I guess? Far be it from them to tell us that."

"Far be it from your father to tell us that," Patch said sarcastically.

"Um, *our* father, bro," Nick said.

Patch was silent for a moment. "Right," he finally said.

The tone in Patch's voice stung Nick. They were supposed to be friends, best friends; now they were supposed to be brothers, or half brothers, at least. And yet everything they had been through had only alienated them from each other.

Nick knew it wasn't permanent, but it felt like he and Patch were walking this delicate line between trust and betrayal. Now, after yesterday's revelation, Nick was nervous about talking to Patch. Nick was supposed to tell his best friend everything, and once again, he had failed.

Nick turned around to look at Patch in the backseat. "You haven't been here before, have you?"

Patch shook his head. "Nope. I mean, I've driven by while staying with you, but I always assumed it belonged to some banker or something."

The three of them walked up to the front door and stood there, unsure of what to do.

"We can't just ring the doorbell," Nick said. "'Um, hi, we're here to try out a key on a few locks.'"

"Should we go to a back door or something?" Patch asked. "This house looks like it has about ten different entrances on the first floor."

At that moment, the giant oak door opened, its knocker clattering ominously. The three of them were startled, and Phoebe grabbed Nick's arm.

They stared in amazement. It couldn't be, but it was.

"*Horatio?*" Nick finally asked. "What on earth are you doing here?"

CHAPTER FORTY-FIVE

Ten minutes later, they were sitting in the library of Eaton House, which was almost cozy, considering that it was an estate with no personal effects in it whatsoever. The room they were in was filled with books, objects, and paintings, but it lacked any specific touches: no family photos, no albums, no libraries of worn-out paperbacks. Horatio had lit a fire and was serving the three of them hot apple cider.

"There was a stipulation in your grandfather's will," he explained. "A private agreement that he and I had together. Not something the lawyers would have read to you yesterday."

Nick was amazed at how much of the Bell family business Horatio was aware of. He warned himself to be on guard. As they sat there drinking cider, Nick was reminded for a moment of their time at the Great Cottage on Isis Island. He and all the other Initiates were dulled into submission with a steady dose of mouthwatering food, the best drinks, music, and good conversation. It had all concealed the fact that the Society was responsible for some truly evil deeds.

Was Horatio a member? An employee of the Bradford Trust Association? Nick had no idea.

"The stipulation was that your grandfather asked that if you did not reach your goal by the time of his death, I was to help you. I was about to visit you in Manhattan and bring you here, but I was informed this morning that you had already left. I think your grandfather would have been very pleased."

"What is this goal exactly?" Nick asked. "It would help if you could be a bit more specific."

"I can't be any more specific than your grandfather was," Horatio said. "I am an employee of his estate."

"Come on, can't you just give it up and tell us what's going on?" Patch said.

Horatio looked at them blankly. "Gentlemen, my life's purpose was to serve your grandfather. I can't leave him now, particularly when he has no say in the matter."

"But that's exactly the point!" Nick said. "He has no say in the matter. Can you at least tell us what we're looking for? What's he going to do? Fire you from the grave?"

"Master Bell, I can't bear to hear your grandfather spoken of that way. I am sorry if my vocation doesn't agree with you.

I am only here to serve."

Nick sighed. The guy was like a robot.

Phoebe stepped in, and Nick was grateful.

"Horatio, why don't you show us what Mr. Bell wanted us to see? I think that's what he would have liked, right?"

Horatio pulled a piece of paper from his jacket pocket. He unfolded it carefully, and read it as if declaiming poetry: "'You must go to the beach, you must go down below. Below the surface of things.'"

"That's what my grandfather told us," Nick said.

"Wait a second," Phoebe said. "It's obvious."

"What's obvious?" Nick asked. "Do we have to start digging or something?"

"No," Phoebe said. "The key will open up a door in the basement."

CHAPTER FORTY-SIX

Horatio led the three of them to the basement. They walked down a narrow staircase and through a series of rooms that were partially finished with brick walls and exposed timbers and had a dank, musty smell. It was an old-school basement, with a no-frills wine cellar, a root cellar for vegetables, and storage for furniture and odds and ends. All the clutter must have come with the house, Phoebe figured, since no one lived here, or so it seemed.

This was the type of basement where secrets were buried.

"I am to leave you here," Horatio said, a little too smoothly.

"Wait a second," Phoebe said. "I don't think so. Patch, you go with him." Phoebe had seen enough of the Society's maneuvers to know that she wasn't going to step into a strange basement without anyone aboveground knowing where she was.

"As you wish," Horatio said.

Patch followed him. "This was all getting a bit too Edgar Allan Poe for me anyway," Patch said. He was right. It was very "Cask of Amontillado," the story where one man leaves another to die in a catacomb. Phoebe shivered.

"If you don't hear from us in twenty minutes, call the police," Phoebe said.

Nick laughed at her, though she wondered if it was for Horatio's benefit. "We'll be fine. Pheeb, your imagination is far too vivid."

Phoebe glared at Nick. How could he be so nonchalant about all this? Maybe it was merely a front for the terror he was feeling. Horatio and Patch were soon upstairs again; she could hear their footsteps above her.

After going through several more doors, all of which were unlocked with nothing behind them, they approached an old steel door.

"Do you think . . ." Nick's voice trailed off as he held up the key. It seemed like their last chance.

"Go ahead," Phoebe said. She bit her lip as Nick removed the tiny key from around his neck. He inserted it into the brass lock and gave it a turn. To their astonishment, the door opened, as if it were controlled electronically.

The two of them stepped inside.

Nick fumbled for a light switch and finally found one.

Just as the lights flickered on, the metal door closed behind them.

"Oh my God," Phoebe said. She fumbled frantically at the door. Were they trapped?

"Relax," Nick said. He pushed a button below the light switch, and the door opened again.

"We'd better get out of here," Phoebe said. "This is way too creepy. What if there's no oxygen in the room or something?"

"Come on, don't you want to find out what this is all about?"

He was right. Phoebe blinked as she looked around. The door closed again. She noticed one difference already, as the door closed. Not only were the walls of this enormous room a clean, pure white, with properly finished surfaces, but the humidity was much lower, not the dank moisture of the basement, but an even, steady level of cool air. Not too dry, not too wet. And the lights were not too bright, not too dark.

Like a museum.

Phoebe looked around and Nick followed her. There were at least a dozen enormous wooden packing crates. She was suddenly drawn back to her time at the Schrader Gallery, when she had been allowed to browse the artist collections that were stored in the back room. She now realized that this was the same thing.

Inside all of these boxes were artworks.

Three paintings were on easels at the back of the room. She didn't recognize the first two, but when she looked at the third, she realized it was the Pollock that belonged to Nick's parents. She pointed it out to Nick, and he shook his head in dismay.

She looked at some of the names on the crates. Each was meticulously labeled with the name of an artist: Vermeer, Rembrandt, Degas, Cézanne.

Phoebe gasped as she read the title of each piece. "Do you know what these are?" she asked Nick.

"No, I don't." He seemed frustrated with her.

"They are only some of the most famous stolen paintings in the world. I mean, holy crap, was your grandfather really part of this? Do you know how much jail time he could have done if he was ever caught?"

They looked around the room, walking by each boxed work, as well as the few that were on easels. There were more famous names: Brueghel, Watteau, Manet.

"Okay, this has got to be a joke." Nick pointed to one box.

Phoebe read aloud. "The *Mona Lisa*."

"You're kidding me," Nick said. "The *Mona Lisa* isn't a stolen artwork."

"No," Phoebe said. "It's not. But it was stolen from the Louvre in the early 1900s. My mom read a book about it. At that time, they actually made copies, and then thieves would return either the copy or the original back to the museum, depending on how they were playing it."

"So you're telling me that the *Mona Lisa* in the Louvre is a copy, and this is the original?"

"No," Phoebe shook her head. "The *Mona Lisa* in the Louvre has been authenticated. Your grandfather had a copy there."

"But he had to have known that. Why would he keep a copy?"

"I think he probably did. Maybe it thrilled him to have a little piece of the history of art. Or, rather, the history of art *theft*."

"Okay, this is all getting too weird," Nick said. "I say we go back up."

Phoebe followed Nick through the door and back through the dank basement passageway.

"What do you think we should do?" Phoebe said, her voice echoing slightly in the basement. "I mean, these pieces have to be returned, don't you think? Some of those works have been missing for decades!"

Did Nick realize the enormity of what they had uncovered? The discovery of these paintings would shake up not only the art world, but quite possibly, the global economy. It would be in the news for months. Books would be written about it, films would be made, the parties involved would be interviewed—

If the Society knew about their discovery, none of that would happen.

Nick and Phoebe reached the staircase leading up to the first floor and were grateful when they found themselves in the kitchen of the enormous house. Patch was waiting there, sitting at the antique farm table while Horatio read a copy of the *Financial Times*.

As Nick and Phoebe told Patch what they had seen, he shook his head in amazement.

"Give me your car service account number," Patch said to Nick. "There's only one person who can help us figure this out."

CHAPTER FORTY-SEVEN

It took Patch fifteen minutes on the phone before he could cajole Genie into joining them in Southampton. She had come back late that morning from her vacation in the Catskills, and it was everything he could do to convince her that traveling two hours out to the beach would be a worthwhile pursuit. He promised her that a town car would meet her outside the apartment in twenty minutes. She fussed and complained, but ultimately, Patch told her she didn't have a choice.

With those words, she joined them.

The next few hours passed strangely, as Horatio began to prepare an elaborate lunch for the three of them. Nick insisted that he not go to any trouble, but they were hungry after their trip and the anguish of trying to figure out what was going on.

The three of them roamed around the house, but there wasn't a single personal artifact, not even a single clue, that led them to know its story.

"I don't think anyone actually lives here," Phoebe said, as they poked around one of the bedrooms.

"Why do you say that?" Nick asked.

"I just looked at one of the bathrooms. There are no toiletries, no personal items. Even a guesthouse would have certain amenities."

"Maybe the Bradford Trust keeps it as an investment, and the Society uses it for meetings," Patch said.

Nick nodded. "I think you're probably right."

"What I want to know," Phoebe said, "is where does the money come from to pay for all this?"

"Maybe we just saw it all downstairs," Nick said. "Maybe they sell off the artwork, bit by bit."

"It's possible," Patch said. "But I think it's a bit more aboveground. If they started with a certain amount of capital and they invested it wisely, they would have hundreds of millions of dollars by now. I mean, the older members pay dues, right? Like, ten thousand a year or something?"

"I think so," Nick said.

"Think about it—that's more than enough to pay for it all.

Let's say they have two hundred dues-paying members—that would be two million dollars a year. Invest that, year after year, and you've got more than enough to finance all this."

Horatio rang a bell downstairs in the kitchen, which meant they were being summoned for lunch. The smells of cooking had already started wafting up to the second floor. Once they had started their meal, Patch had to admit that Horatio's cooking was even better than that of Gertie, Nick's family's cook in the city. Horatio had prepared them a lunch of tomato fennel soup, grilled cheese sandwiches with truffle oil, a winter salad of apples and pecans, and a steaming pot of tea to go along with fresh lemon-glazed scones for dessert.

The three of them ate cautiously in the breakfast area on the sunporch.

"Hey," Phoebe said as she picked at her food. "How do you know he's not going to poison us or something?"

"I don't think we need to worry," Nick said. "I'm pretty sure that isn't what this is about. His allegiance was to my grandfather."

"I wouldn't say for sure," Phoebe said. She made a motion to indicate that they couldn't trust him.

"Look, you guys, I'm hungry, okay?" Patch said. "Can we just relax a little bit?"

"If he's eating it, then it's probably okay," Nick said. Patch had, after all, been through more than he and Phoebe had—and had come out relatively intact on the other end.

As they were finishing lunch, they heard a car pull into the driveway. Genie arrived at the front door, bundled up as if she were headed on an arctic excursion. Patch desperately wanted to talk to her about the situation with Parker Bell and what he had learned yesterday, but he restrained himself.

"It's Southampton, Genie, not Alaska," Nick said, teasing her, as he gave her a hug around her puffy form.

"I'm an old lady, Nicholas! When you're my age, you'll understand what it feels like to be cold!"

Phoebe helped her remove several of her layers, and the four of them sat down in the library, which was down a long corridor in the east wing of the house. A set of picture windows looked out on the English parterre, though most of it was frozen over.

After Horatio served another round of drinks—this time, it was hot chocolate—he gave them some privacy.

"I'm not really sure where to begin," Nick said.

"Oh, Nicholas, you always think that whatever you have to tell me is going to surprise me in some way. It's a rather darling quality of yours. Come out with it. There's not much that can shock this old broad."

Phoebe laughed, and Patch blushed.

"Okay . . ." Nick said, glancing at the closed oak pocket doors to the library.

"Just spit it out, Nick," Genie said.

"Fine. We have just found what might possibly be the world's greatest undiscovered collection of stolen art. Right here. In the basement. And we think my grandfather may be responsible for it."

Genie's face twisted for a moment, as if she were considering the consequences. For a moment, Patch thought she might be truly upset.

Then she started laughing.

Nick and Phoebe looked at each other in confusion.

"What's so funny?" Nick asked.

"People never change. Oh my goodness, how people never change!"

"What do you mean?"

"Let me tell you a story," Genie said. "Nick, your grandfather, among his many qualities, had a rather peculiar one. He liked to steal. Not little things or money, but art. The more rare, the more spectacular, the better. It wasn't economic; he didn't want to sell the objects. When he was at Yale, he became obsessed with French ormolu, you know, gilt Asian porcelains and so forth? He stole a music box for me, but I told him I couldn't accept it. It must have been worth ten thousand dollars."

"How did he do it?"

"I'm not sure. I don't think he did it himself—I think he had some kind of network of thieves. There was something about it all that excited him; he said he got a thrill from having contraband artwork and antiques in his possession." Genie shook her head sadly. "Really, it was very strange. After the first time, I told him that he had to stop, and he said he had. Only later, after our engagement was broken off, did I learn that he had continued."

"How did you learn this?"

"One hears these things. It was all chitchat at the time, just a high-level form of kleptomania. The rare eccentricities of a wealthy man."

Palmer—Patch's grandfather—was a high-level *kleptomaniac*?

"It's bizarre," Genie continued. "Every time I read about a major art theft, I thought of Palmer. The Gardner Museum in Boston? That one kept me up for several nights."

"One of the greatest unsolved museum heists of our time," Phoebe said.

Nick looked dumbfounded. "And you really think my grandfather was behind all this? I just don't understand it."

"Your grandfather had an obsession. He had to win, he had to be the best. Unfortunately, he was also a bit of a skinflint."

"What do you mean?" Nick asked.

"Nick, your family has stayed wealthy for the reason that many people are wealthy: they spend their money wisely. Your grandfather never liked to spend more than he had to. And sometimes that meant that he couldn't have everything he wanted. Are you familiar with the famous George Stubbs painting of the zebra in the woods?"

"I think I know it," Phoebe said. "It's a beautiful painting. It's like the zebra is totally out of context—you expect it to be in Africa or something and it's in this very European-looking forest."

"It is now at the Yale Center for British Art. Palmer was obsessed with it, a few years after your father was born. Said he felt like the zebra—a striped creature in a forest, a creature that didn't belong."

"How do you know all this?"

"A girlfriend of mine still traveled in those circles. Palmer was quite indiscreet when it came to his obsessions. Of course, that was always his philosophy, it seems—he kept his petty activities on the surface in order to mask his darker impulses. Talking about an art obsession was fine, but speaking of the Society was not."

"So what happened?" Nick asked.

"The painting was auctioned at Harrods in London, and a number of buyers were interested. Paul Mellon ultimately got the painting for twenty-two thousand pounds. Somewhere north of two hundred thousand dollars on today's market."

"Genie, how do you know all this?" Nick asked.

She looked at him over her glasses. "Nick, if you read all day like I do, you learn a lot."

The conversation made Patch uncomfortable. It was as if Genie was still obsessed with Palmer. Patch had hoped that his death would have put those feelings to rest.

"Apparently, he tried to reform over the years, but I never believed that he did," Genie continued. "He would have a relapse every few years; it was as if he couldn't help himself. I would hear stories from your father, who, as you know, was friends with Patch's father—"

Patch interrupted her. "Wait a second, Genie—I think we'd better clear something up."

Nick and Phoebe were silent.

"What's that?" Genie asked innocently.

"I know about Parker. I know that he's my real father. Or rather, my biological father."

Genie paused before speaking slowly. "I'm so sorry, dear, that you had to find out from someone else. I would have preferred to tell you myself. I never knew when the right time was; I thought perhaps when you turned eighteen." Her voice choked up. "I should have told you earlier. I should have trusted that you could handle the truth. How did they tell you about this?"

Patch looked uncomfortably at Nick and then at Phoebe. It was such a strange thing to speak about aloud.

"I am a beneficiary in Palmer's will."

Genie looked genuinely surprised. "What, did he give you

a painting or something? I hope not a stolen one!" She laughed awkwardly.

"No, not exactly."

"Well, Patch, what did he give you?"

Patch took a deep breath, and then offered a strained smile. "He gave me thirty million dollars."

CHAPTER FORTY-EIGHT

P atch!" Genie said. "You can't accept that. No, I won't allow it. It isn't right."

Nick felt ashamed about the situation. He took a sip of his hot cocoa to find that it was tepid and a nasty film had formed on the surface.

"Genie, I have to make these decisions for myself," Patch said. "I understand that you have feelings about Nick's family, but don't you think they owe it to you—don't you think Palmer owes you after everything he put you through?"

"Patch, you don't know the half of it. But you can't buy people off for heartache. Not even with that kind of money." She shook her head and drew her cardigan closer. "No, it's not right."

Nick thought maybe they should take a different tack.

"Genie, it's not like Patch is going to get a check tomorrow. I won't either. The assets will be kept in trusts until we are twenty-five. My father—our father—is the trustee."

Genie shook her head. "It doesn't sit well with me. I'm sorry, boys. I'll support you, you know that, but I can't stay silent."

"I understand," Patch said. "It's been a bit of a shock to all of us. It's not every day that you learn both that you have a different biological father and that you're the beneficiary of a trust."

"And that your best friend is actually your brother," Nick said.

There was an awkward silence before Patch finally spoke.

"Right," he said. "Can we just not talk about that right now?"

Nick wondered if Patch was upset about the outcome. He seemed so stoic about it—it was strange news, of course, but if Patch had to discover that he had a brother, wasn't it easier for it to be his best friend?

Maybe Nick had to start acting like a brother before Patch could treat him as one.

Genie looked frustrated as she put down her hot cocoa on the coffee table. "All right, let's get on with this," she said. "Where's this hoard of artwork you've been telling me about?"

Nick led Genie, Patch, and Phoebe down to the basement,

urging them all to watch their step as they walked through the dank, mildew-smelling passageway. When they reached the metal door, Nick used the key again and the door opened. He flicked the light switch, and everything was just as it was. He did notice one new detail, however: at the far end of the room was a large metal sliding door, the kind you would see on a loading dock. Nick imagined that it led to the outside, as these artworks couldn't be delivered to this room through the main house.

Genie walked around the antiseptic space, examining the labels on the sixteen pieces that Nick had counted. She shook her head, clucking as she read each one.

"He certainly got around," she said, shaking her head. "Imagine that. Sixty-something years of doing this. I'd say he relapsed every five to ten years. Probably did multiple hauls. These two are from the same museum," she said, pointing at two crates. "I remember reading about it in the newspaper." She turned toward Nick and the others. "So, here's the question: What are you going to do about all this?"

Patch rested his hand on a crate that contained a Vermeer. "I feel like it's really up to Nick."

There was a sound behind them as the door opened. Horatio stood there.

"I was asked to deliver a message to you," he said. "Your grandfather gave a simple instruction. He said: 'You must do whatever you think is right.'"

"Typical cryptic answer," Nick muttered in frustration.

"Well, maybe it is, Nick, but actually he seems to suggest that it is in your hands," Genie said.

Horatio excused himself and went back upstairs.

"Can I weigh in here?" Phoebe asked.

"Sure," Nick said, nodding.

"This is just me, speaking as an artist, and as someone whose works have been stolen before. The emotional trauma that you endure when this happens—it's beyond belief."

"Most of these artists were already dead when the works were stolen," Patch said. "I know that doesn't change anything, but—"

"It doesn't matter," Phoebe said. "Collectors donated the pieces to these museums. People worked hard so that they could buy the pieces and then show them to the public. Or maybe they even still owned them outright, and they were on loan. Maybe they were family heirlooms. The point is, they don't belong in this basement, where no one can see them except for a select group of wealthy Society members. If Palmer even let anyone see them." Phoebe took a deep breath. "I feel like the only honest thing to do is to tell the world about what your grandfather has done."

Nick looked at her. How could she be so nonchalant about this? It wasn't her family they were talking about. Maybe she couldn't understand. Her family wasn't well known. No one had any expectations for them.

"Phoebe, you have no idea what this is like," Nick said. "I don't want people knowing this about my grandfather. I know it isn't right, but it's just—well, honestly, it's embarrassing. It was one thing to return that necklace anonymously, but to return all of these major paintings, and for the world to know about it? It would tarnish our entire family name if word got out that Palmer Bell was an art thief. I'm not proud of many of the things my family has done, but that doesn't mean that I want everyone to know about them. In fact, I'd appreciate it if we kept all this between us until I decide what to do."

"Nick, aren't you perpetuating the cycle?" Phoebe said. "Aren't you just making it okay for other people to do the same thing that your grandfather did? I mean, whoever actually took the artwork for him—I'm sure they're still alive. Do you really want them doing this for more rich people? More people who get off on owning stolen art?"

"No, of course I don't," Nick said. "But my question is, why would Palmer lead us to all this?"

"I think he wanted the art returned after his death. He didn't have any use for it anymore," Phoebe said. "There's no other reason he would have told you about it."

"Maybe he was looking for redemption of some sort," Genie mused. "Of course, it's just like Palmer not to do it himself. Never wanted to get his hands dirty."

"Okay, but now that my grandfather's gone, how is it supposed to get us out of the Society? Like Horatio's going to wave his magic wand and somehow get us out? I feel like we don't have any hope of getting out, at least not this time around."

"There's only one person who can get us out now," Patch said.

"Who's that?" Nick asked, turning to him.

"Our father."

CHAPTER FORTY-NINE

Phoebe was grateful when it was finally time to leave Eaton House and return to Nick's parents' house in Southampton. The two properties were so different in style; while Eaton House was cold and foreboding, the Bell compound was as warm as a house on twelve acres could get. It was a classic shingle-style house, and unlike Eaton House, which was anonymous in its furnishings, it actually seemed like a family lived there.

Genie sat in the front seat, once again bundled up in a dozen layers, while Nick drove. His old Jeep ground its wheels onto the gravel driveway.

The four of them got out, and Nick pulled out his monogrammed key ring, picking one and using it on the front door.

A persistent beeping started from somewhere in the house.

"What is that?" Phoebe asked. After everything they had been through, she didn't feel like she could take any more surprises.

"I don't know," Nick said. "Is it an alarm system? We never had one before."

Genie observed the situation with curiosity, and Phoebe gave her an awkward smile. After all these months of avoiding the truth, it was a relief finally to hear Genie be honest with them.

"Patch, is there something you can do?" Phoebe asked.

"Alarms aren't really my thing," Patch said. "Thad taught me the basics, but I don't really know enough—"

At that moment, a loud shrieking began, a whooping alert that resonated over the potato and cornfields and seemed to shake the walls of the house.

Nick was blushing furiously as he tried to figure out what was going on; he had located a panel in a coat closet to the right of the front door. "I can't believe they wouldn't mention this to me," he said. "I don't even know how to work one of these things!"

Within five minutes there was a patrol car parked in their driveway. Nick and Phoebe stood dumbly near the front door, while Patch sat nearby on an iron bench with his grandmother. Nick had his ID in hand, and he handed it to the officer who approached them.

"This is my parents' house," he said nervously. "We were just coming here for the weekend. I didn't know they had installed an alarm system."

"Don't worry about it, kid, we're not going to shoot you. Let me just turn this thing off." The two cops laughed as the officer went to a control panel in the foyer and punched in a few numbers. Phoebe imagined that Southampton in the winter was probably pretty slow when it came to crime.

The cop looked at Nick's ID. "He's on the list of approved residents. You're fine, kid. Just get the code from your parents so it doesn't happen again."

"Thanks. Sorry for the trouble."

"Don't worry about it. We'll send your parents the bill!" The officer laughed again, and the patrol car pulled away.

"Let's go inside," Nick said. "I'm freezing here."

Everyone scrambled inside, and Nick went to turn up the thermostat. The four of them sat down in the kitchen, which, being central to the house, heated up more quickly than the rest of the first floor.

"Nick, why do you think they put in an alarm system?" Phoebe asked as she threw her coat over one of the chairs in the kitchen. "Because the Pollock was stolen? Why wouldn't they have told you?" It didn't make any sense.

"I don't know," Nick said. "Maybe they were trying to

catch us off guard or something. Maybe they think *we* stole it."

"Okay, and another thing: why the Pollock?" Phoebe asked. "Why would your grandfather steal it from his own son?"

"He always hated it," Nick said.

"I don't think that's the reason," Patch said.

"I have an idea," Phoebe said. "Remember, the Pollock was our starting point. Or at least, it was our first real clue. He could have just left a note on the mantel for us saying 'Go to Eaton House, you'll find some stolen art there.' But instead he sent us all the way down to Florida to find a key, then we had to try that key on each property, then you got the clue at the Dendur Ball, which sent you back to Southampton. . . ."

"What's your point?" Nick asked impatiently as Phoebe flushed. Why was Nick being such an ass about this? Had all the pressure finally gotten to him?

He leaned forward to touch her arm. "I'm sorry," he said.

Phoebe nodded in resignation, but she was still annoyed. Just because it was Nick's family they were talking about didn't mean he was the only one who had a stake in the matter.

Genie interrupted. "What she's trying to say, Nick, is that Palmer was giving you a roundabout tour of your heritage. Boys, where did you find the key?"

"In his study in Palm Beach," Nick said. "Which was filled

with memorabilia from his life. There were also the family photos on the mantelpiece. And all the history that was part of the Dendur Ball. The photograph of your mother, Patch. The picture of my parents."

"So what does it all mean?" Patch asked.

"I think it's like Horatio said. He wants us to do what we think is right," Nick said.

"He sent you to a series of important places in your family's history," Phoebe said. "The question is whether he's saying you should do what's right for your family, or what's right for all of us." She thought of the memorial marker, the one Patch didn't even know about. It was another example of something the Bells had covered up, another thing that wasn't talked about.

Nick frowned. "We need to do what's right for us. It's just that—well, we can't just let everyone know about the art—can we?"

"Perhaps he wants you to weigh out all the options," Genie said. "Considering that you are both technically members of the Bell family."

"Nick, I think you need to call your father," Phoebe said. "I hate to admit it, but he's the only person who can help us. Why don't you leverage your knowledge of the stolen art and try to get us out of the Society? Isn't that what Palmer wanted us to do?"

Nick nodded slowly. "I can make the call in the library.

Patch, I think you should listen in."

Phoebe bit her lip as Nick and Patch left the kitchen. Would Nick be able to stand up to his father?

It scared her that she didn't know.

CHAPTER FIFTY

In the library Nick called his father on every one of his numbers and finally was able to reach him on his private number that only rang in his study. He explained to his dad what they had found, about the trove of art in the basement of Eaton House. Patch listened in on an extension at the other side of the room.

"Well, you've done it," Parker said. "Your grandfather's been trying to reveal this to your brothers for the past year, and neither of them have picked up on his clues. I guess he finally had to be more blunt about it."

"I wouldn't exactly call sending us down to Florida, and then three times to Southampton *blunt*," Nick said.

"I suppose not."

"We've made a decision," Nick said. "We want the art

returned. I don't care how you do it, but we want it returned. I'm sure, for one thing, that you'd like your Pollock back."

"Don't you worry about that—we've made back more than its value in insurance. As for the rest of the pieces, Nicholas, I don't think that's a good idea. Those cases have all been abandoned long ago. No one is interested anymore. It's best just to let it go."

"Dad, we were led to it because he wanted us to find out. Palmer wanted us to return the art."

Nick's father sighed. "I would prefer that weren't the case."

"And I want it to happen publicly. People need to know what happened. So that it can't happen again. So the people he worked with will think twice the next time they get an offer to do something like this."

Nick looked at Patch, who was sitting on an ottoman, his brows furrowed in concentration. Nick couldn't blame Patch for wishing they didn't have the same father.

"I will facilitate the return of the art," Parker said firmly. "But it will happen anonymously."

Nick steeled himself. "Dad, I want it to be known what happened. I know you think it's embarrassing, but I'm tired of living under the weight of so many secrets."

"Do you have any idea of the sort of publicity this would create? Our lives would never be the same."

"Maybe that's a good thing."

"Nicholas, I will release the art, but I won't do it publicly. The world doesn't need to know about your grandfather's little hobby. It's a private family matter. You need to trust me on this."

"What about what Palmer promised us?" Nick asked. "That we would all be released from the Society?"

Parker laughed. "You really thought it would be that easy?"

Across the room, Patch winced.

"Easy?" Nick asked. "It wasn't *easy*."

"Nick, you don't even know what difficult is. When you're older, you'll understand the concept of difficult. Going to war is difficult. Starting a business is difficult. Your life isn't anything close to difficult."

Nick wasn't really sure what to say to this. "Dad, I—"

Across the room, Patch held up a hand, signaling Nick to stop speaking. Nick desperately hoped Patch had a better idea for how they were going to get out. Had he just ruined their chances by giving up the one piece of information that they had against the group?

"I think we're done here," Parker said. "Don't you worry. I'll take care of everything."

CHAPTER FIFTY-ONE

Y ou're joking," Phoebe said after Nick had filled her in on the conversation. "All this art is going to be returned, and your grandfather is going to go down in New York history as this wonderful, philanthropically minded man who never did anything wrong?"

Phoebe, Nick, and Patch were standing in the kitchen. Genie had gone out to the enclosed sunporch to rest.

"Look, I don't agree with it," Nick said. "But we don't have a choice. He said—"

Phoebe interrupted him. "You keep saying that we don't have a choice. But maybe it's up to us. Maybe we're the ones who have to break free. As long as you keep believing your father, then you're right, you don't have a choice." She was angry, but she needed Nick to know how she felt.

"Phoebe, he's threatened us in the past. The Society has done things, appalling things. I just don't know if we can—"

"Face it, Nick, you don't want anyone knowing about your grandfather. It's embarrassing. It would be in the papers for months. You and your family would face so much public scrutiny. And you can't handle that." She took a breath and looked at Patch. "What do you think?"

"Leave me out of it," Patch said. "I don't—I don't really know."

"You've got to have an opinion," Phoebe said. "It's your family, too."

Patch gave her an angry look. "I don't have to have an opinion," he snapped. "I didn't choose this. I'll be on the sunporch with my grandmother. The one who raised me."

Phoebe sighed as Patch left the room.

"Great," Nick said. "Now you've gone and made him feel bad. As if he's not feeling strange enough already, with everything that's happened."

Phoebe decided to ignore this. But she couldn't deny how frustrated she was. "Nick, I'm so sick of all this. And let me guess: this gets us no closer to being free of the Society than we were in the beginning of January."

"I'm not sure," Nick said. "I think it may have been . . ."
His voice trailed off.

"A setup? Admit it, Nick, we've played their little game

once again. We're too trusting, that's our problem. We can't believe them, any of them. I'm so tired of this!" She was getting hysterical, and she felt badly about yelling at Nick.

"Phoebe, calm down," Nick said.

"You know something else?" she said. "We've never considered this, but I don't think there really is a Society."

"What?" Nick said. "What do you mean?" He gave her a sideways look, as if she were insane.

"What I mean is, sure, there's a group of people, and they've gotten together and they've done some good things and many bad things. But in terms of its meaning, remember how the scroll we got was written and adapted by each class? That's exactly how they've constructed it—none of it has meaning in and of itself. *We* are the ones who have given it meaning. It's all created to keep us in line, to keep us trapped. Initiation rituals, bonfires, Egyptian mythology, swimming parties, French philosophy, stories about drowning, people dying—"

"You're saying that people dying wasn't real?"

"No, it was real, but we were the ones who gave it meaning. We were the ones who decided that we couldn't go to the police. No one told us we couldn't. We came up with that idea, remember? We were the ones who decided to be so afraid all the time."

"But they threatened us—when we didn't attend

meetings—" Nick sputtered.

"Right, but we decided we couldn't handle it. I didn't tell my mom about the rats because I was scared. Thad couldn't tell the truth about who planted the gin bottle because he was embarrassed about his mother's past. Lauren couldn't say who she thought put the earrings in her bag, because they would have said she was nuts."

Nick shook his head. "I get what you're saying, but Phoebe, this is still as real as anything I've ever seen. There is stolen art in that basement, and my grandfather is responsible for it. No one can deny that. Do you really want the world to find out about that?"

"There you go again—you've put so much value in your family's privacy, you're ignoring what's better for the rest of us."

"Phoebe, you wouldn't understand," Nick said. He tapped the kitchen floor in frustration with his right foot. "And I think—I think you're being crazy. All this stuff does have meaning. You know that. You can't pretend it doesn't."

Phoebe regarded Nick. She had never been more upset with him. It was a horrible, empty feeling, as if a cavern had opened in her heart. She considered the idea that he wasn't the person she was meant to be with.

She grabbed Nick's shoulder and held it tightly. "Don't *ever* call me crazy."

"I'm sorry," he said. "That was stupid." He put his head on

the table, cradling it in his arms. When he lifted up his head a moment later, his eyes were red. "I'm so sorry. Phoebe, I love you. I really do."

As if her body had taken over from her mind, she found herself shaking her head. "I don't know if you do," she said quietly. "I feel like you love your life in New York more. Your family. Everything it affords you. And maybe you even love this. All the drama. All the mystery. I mean, really, would our lives be as interesting without all this? Would we even be together? If we could break free, where would that really leave us?"

"How can you say that?" He looked at her, his face streaked with tears. "How can you say such a horrible thing?"

"I don't know," Phoebe said. "I don't quite feel like myself. I've just . . ." Her voice trailed off. "I should probably stop talking." She sighed deeply, and only then did she realize how exhausted she was from everything. "Maybe we'd better get going. We have to get back to Manhattan for that damned cocktail party." Claire Chilton and her parents had invited them all to a cocktail party that evening to celebrate the success of the Dendur Ball.

"Do we have to go?" Nick said. "I'm not exactly in the mood."

"I would kill to skip it," Phoebe said. She felt horrible for the things she had said, and now it felt like she couldn't take them back. The worst part was that she didn't want to take back some of it. She really would have loved to skip the party, to have some time alone to figure things out.

"Maybe we go for twenty minutes," Nick said.

"Twenty minutes," Phoebe said. "And that's it."

CHAPTER FIFTY-TWO

Lauren had been dreading the Chilton cocktail party that night. A snow had started falling earlier that day in Manhattan, and by evening it had turned into a blizzard. The cars along Park Avenue were inching through the powdery banks, and it was the kind of night when you wanted to stay in and relax, not go to a cocktail party. Luckily for Lauren, Claire and her parents lived only a few blocks away. Thad would be picking Lauren up at seven.

When he arrived, Thad's cheeks were pink from the cold outside, and he still had a few snowflakes in his curly blond hair. Lauren knew that he had started something with that guy, Kurt, whom he had met at the ball, and she was eager to get the details from him.

"You getting excited for your Paris trip?" he asked her.

She had told him about the opportunity that Sebastian had offered her.

She shrugged as she buttoned her wool overcoat and stepped into the elevator. "To be perfectly honest, not really. I wish I were. Something doesn't feel right about it." She was supposed to leave in several weeks; the trip was scheduled for the second week of spring break. "I know it's an amazing opportunity, and I should be thrilled."

"Well, the question is, what exactly are the strings, right?" He looked thoughtfully at the numbers in the elevator as they descended.

"That's what I'm worried about. Is it right for me to be going on this trip alone?"

"Do you want me to come with you?" Thad asked. "I mean, I don't mean to invite myself along or anything, but it would be amazing. . . ."

She smiled. "I could tell them that you have to come with me. But are you sure I won't be keeping you from being with Kurt?"

Thad shrugged. "It's so new, I think I'm allowed to go away for a week, right?"

"How's it going, anyway?"

Thad blushed, and Lauren started tickling him in the elevator. "Stop, stop, I'll tell you!" he said, laughing. "It's going great. He's wonderful. He's, like, one of the smartest guys I've ever met. I didn't think they even made guys that smart in New York."

"Well, he's from New Jersey," Lauren said.

"And I like that about him—he's not all stuck-up like everyone around here." The elevator doors opened and they stepped out.

"Does he know about . . . you know." She was referring to the Society, but they were walking through the lobby and she wanted to be discreet.

"I don't think so," Thad said quietly. "I haven't told him. I haven't gotten a haircut recently, so he can't really see the tattoo. I keep wishing that by the time we have that conversation, we'll all be out of it."

"Here's hoping," Lauren said with a sigh as she stepped out from under her building's awning and through the five inches of snow that had already fallen on the sidewalk. "Well, I'm really happy you can come on the trip." She took Thad's arm as they walked. "With you along, I'm starting to think it might be fun."

The cocktail party was being thrown to celebrate the success of the Dendur Ball, though Lauren recognized it all as a sham. Letty Chilton—and probably Claire as well—felt awkward about the power outage and the jewelry theft and, more than anything, that the media coverage of the ball had focused more on its scandalous aftermath than on the new additions to the museum, the money that was raised, or all the hard work that Letty and her daughter had done.

When they got to the party, the first thing they noticed was the music. Mrs. Chilton had clearly made an attempt to keep the atmosphere "youthful" as opposed to the classical selections she usually would have played at an event like this. Lauren recognized the Rolling Stones's song "Play with Fire," a creepy, bizarre song about a woman with an heiress mother, beautiful clothes, diamonds, and a chauffeur. It seemed appropriate, somehow, for the evening: vapid and mysterious.

It also reminded Lauren of Alejandro, for it was one of the songs that had come on when they swam in that heated pool last November. Since that day, Lauren had found it on iTunes and would sometimes play it over and over again, as it reminded her of that moment. A moment she would never have again.

How would she ever get over his death, when she was reminded of him constantly? When every song, every movie, every novel was about love: finding it, having it, losing it?

"Hey—" Thad poked her. "You're totally zoning out. Phoebe's coming over here." Thad had graciously taken Lauren's coat and given it to the attendant.

Phoebe had just arrived at the party, separately from Nick, it seemed.

"I need to talk to you," she whispered after she and Lauren had embraced.

"Sure," Lauren said. "Let's find somewhere quiet." She left Thad at the bar and took Phoebe to a far corner of the living room. She surveyed the living room and noted that her mother would have her work cut out for her. The current arrangement was twenty years of chintz sofas and reproduction nineteenth-century furniture against faded yellow-and-white-striped wallpaper.

"I don't even know where to start," Phoebe said as they sat down on a couch near the window. "Nick and I had this terrible fight. I guess that should be the least of it. The important thing is that I think we had a chance to get out, and he totally blew it."

Lauren felt her spirits drop. "Oh my God. What do you mean?"

"I can't talk about it here. We might still have a chance. But the thing is, I completely screwed up, and now I feel like I can't take it back. I said some really terrible things to him, about how he only cares about his family, and how he loves the adventure of all this more than he loves me."

Lauren shook her head. "Love makes you do crazy things, right?"

"I guess so," Phoebe said. "I was so frustrated with him. I just want us to break free from—" She motioned out at the room, at the Society members who had started to trickle into the living room, clustering around the fireplace. "From all this."

"But how do we do that?" Lauren looked nervously out at the crowds that were gathering, at Anastasia and Jeremy and Bradley, all chatting excitably. Aside from the five of them—the "Infidels," as they were called—the older class had merged with the younger one perfectly, as if they had always been friends.

"I think we just do it, consequences be damned."

"Phoebe, I don't think we can do that. What about the message my sister got? What if they do something to our families?"

"We don't know that they would do anything," Phoebe said. "But I suppose there's no way of being certain."

"Lauren!" They heard a voice from across the room.

The two girls looked up. It was Emily van Piper, headed their way. She was wearing a pair of high heels that must have been impossible to walk in outside.

"Lauren, I heard about your Paris trip!" She gave Lauren a hug and kissed her on both cheeks. "Are you so thrilled?"

Lauren had told Phoebe otherwise, but thankfully, Phoebe was smart enough not to say anything in front of Emily.

"Um, sure," Lauren said. "It's going to be gorgeous. I love Paris." She hoped she was enthusiastic enough to sound convincing. With Thad, though, it would be fun. Still, something didn't feel quite right about it.

"I need to go talk to Charles about something," Emily

said, looking over the girls' shoulders. "But let me know if you need any tips about the city—I was just there a few weeks ago. I found the most darling little tea shop in the Marais."

Lauren nodded as Emily flitted off. At the entrance to the living room, Claire Chilton was greeting everyone. Lauren saw that she was wearing another outfit from Giroux, a black cocktail dress Sebastian had designed.

"Look at her, she thinks she's this grand hostess or something," Lauren said bitterly.

"Just ignore her," Phoebe said. "She's not worth our time. Okay, so you've got to tell me: What do I do about Nick? Do I talk to him?"

Lauren sighed. "I don't know, Phoebe, maybe you need to spend some time apart."

Phoebe looked surprised at this statement, and Lauren was even startled that she had said it. Was she jealous of Phoebe? She didn't want to date Nick herself, as they had known each other since they were in elementary school. But maybe she was jealous that Phoebe had someone at all. Was it better to have someone you were fighting with than to be completely alone? She immediately regretted being so underhanded. Phoebe had become her best friend over the past several months, and she should have been supportive.

"Maybe you're right," Phoebe said. "We do spend an incredible amount of time together. Maybe I should get out of town or something."

"No, Phoebe, I didn't mean—I don't think you should do that."

"Why not? You just said—"

Lauren sank back on the couch in resignation. "I don't know, Phoebe. I don't really know what you should do."

CHAPTER FIFTY-THREE

As Patch and Lia rode up together in the Chiltons' elevator, Patch examined himself in one of its panels of antiqued mirror. He was glad he had dressed up a little bit for the cocktail party, even if that had only meant trading his sneakers for loafers and jeans for wool slacks. Even after all these years, he still never felt like he knew what to wear to functions like this one.

"Stop primping," Lia said. "You look great."

"So do you," Patch said, drawing her close and giving her a kiss on her cold nose. He hoped it would be okay that he was bringing a non-Society member to the event, but he figured it probably was—and after all they had been through, a big part of him didn't care anymore about the Society's petty rules.

Lia had been running late, so they had decided to meet

in the Chiltons' lobby; he hadn't had a chance yet to tell her about everything that had happened. The previous day, when Patch had found out the news about his relationship to the Bell family, he had felt like he needed to process the information alone before sharing it with anyone else. Now he wanted to tell Lia about it, but he didn't know when he would be able to find the right time.

"Do you really want to go to this thing?" she asked.

"What do you think?" Patch grinned.

"So we can bust out early and grab burgers?"

"Absolutely," he said as the doors opened to the Chilton apartment.

Once inside, Patch made the necessary introductions before he and Lia grabbed drinks and retreated to a corner of the Chiltons' dining room.

"I have some good news for you," she said.

"What's that?"

She lowered her voice. "Remember that producer friend of my parents? He saw your DVD and he really liked it. He wants to meet with you."

"Cool." Patch smiled. "I appreciate it. But you know I can't officially start working on anything until June."

"I know. I just think it's a good sign. And who knows, maybe he's interested in working on something else with you. I mean, it's not like a show about Chadwick kids is the only thing that you can do, right?"

"No, of course not." He had tons of ideas for different shows and documentary projects. Besides, it would be good for him to get away from the whole Chadwick scene for a little bit. If he did a show about something that wasn't related to the school, then the Society couldn't claim that they had control of it.

Maybe he had never really needed the Society at all, not to provide an angle for the show, nor to help him get it produced.

"You look like something's bothering you," Lia said.

"It's just—" A few of the party guests were starting to walk by the dining room. "It's been an incredible two days." It all came spilling out: He told Lia about what he had learned yesterday morning, about Parker Bell being his real father, Nick being his half brother, and about his inheritance from Palmer. It felt strange to talk about money so openly with Lia, but he felt like he needed to give her the whole picture. "And then today, we found—well, we found something that we think might be able to get us out of the Society. Except that Nick might have messed it up. It's not really clear." Some of the other Society members had entered the dining room and were nibbling at the buffet that had been set up. "We probably shouldn't be talking about this here."

"Do you think we could sneak out?" Lia asked.

Patch thought about it for a moment. They had already said hello to Claire and to Mr. and Mrs. Chilton. "I think so.

You're going to have to grab our coats, though. If they see me out there, they'll notice and ask if we're leaving."

"No problem."

Lia went to find their coats. Patch waited for her in the dining room, and then motioned for her to follow him when she returned. The two of them discreetly slipped out of the dining room and across the hall into the kitchen. A team of caterers was busy putting canapés on trays and barely noticed them.

Patch opened the back service entrance next to the pantry. The service area was a gray-painted stairwell with a garbage chute and recycling bins.

"Had you been to this apartment before?" Lia asked.

"Nope. But most apartments like this have a back stair-case that goes off the kitchen." He looked down. "We're only on the sixth floor. I think it's worth it to walk."

They put their coats on and walked down the six flights to the lobby, where they were able to escape undetected. Ten minutes later, they were sitting in a booth at Genie's favorite coffee shop on Second Avenue.

They ordered two cheeseburgers, plus a coffee for Lia and a hot chocolate for Patch. After they were alone again, he explained about the trove of stolen art they had found. "You can't tell anyone about this, you understand?" he said. "It's up to Nick what happens with this information. We all promised him we wouldn't say anything."

"But I thought you were upset that he wasn't able to get you guys out of the . . . you know."

"I am. But this information is the last card we hold. And I think I have a plan for how we can use it."

Lia rolled her eyes. "You never stop, do you?"

He ignored her jab. He had some ideas, but his scheme wasn't fully developed yet.

"The story gets weirder," he said. "Have you ever heard of a caul bearer?"

Lia shook her head.

Patch explained what it was. "It's supposed to bring luck to the child who's born with it."

"You just said you inherited thirty million dollars. I'd say that's pretty lucky."

The waitress arrived with their drinks, and they lowered their voices.

"Parker gave me this big lecture about how I had disappointed him, how I was meant for greatness, but I hadn't exhibited it yet."

"How is he so sure that he's going to be the one who sees the greatness in you?" Lia asked. "Maybe your greatness isn't meant to emerge yet."

She was right. What did he care about Parker's opinion of him? Parker had little conscience about his own actions, so how was he fit to judge Patch?

"You'll do your own thing," Lia said. "But I have a feeling

it's not going to happen with these idiots."

"I guess you're right. I think what would make it all more clear for me would be if I could really understand what went on between him and my mother. Why would she get involved with him? Did my father not know about it? My grandmother won't tell me—and I'm not even sure if she knows exactly what happened herself."

Lia took a sip of her coffee. "I think there's only one way you're going to solve all this," she said. "I know you don't want to do it, and I know it's not going to be pleasant."

"What's that?"

"You need to go and see your mother."

CHAPTER FIFTY-FOUR

The Chilton party was exactly as Nick had expected: bad food and even worse company. Letty Chilton, in her attempt to save a penny, had hired a third-rate caterer, and it was evident in the dried-out hors d'oeuvres that were coming from the kitchen. The rock music was obnoxious and too loud. It wasn't even that Nick didn't like the selections; it was more that it seemed out of place in this environment. Nick ordered a martini at the bar and drank half of it in one gulp.

He was still upset about the fight in Southampton with Phoebe. The entire drive back, everyone had been silent in the car, save for the occasional comment or attempt at conversation from Genie. Phoebe had decided to go home and change, and would be arriving at the party separately. Nick looked out for Patch at the party, but couldn't find him.

A few minutes later, Claire walked by and greeted Nick with a kiss on the cheek, which was unusual.

"Hello, Nick," Claire said, and he nodded in return. "Come have a cigarette with me?"

This was odd. Nick didn't even know that Claire smoked.

"Uh, sure," he said.

She motioned for him to follow her down the hallway. "Let's go to the library. My dad smokes cigars in there."

Nick nodded and followed her into the library. He didn't smoke himself anymore, but he wondered what she had to tell him. There wasn't any reason for her to pull him aside. Maybe she knew something about what they had discovered in Southampton.

She shut the door behind them. The room was decorated in classic dark oak bookshelves and hunter green, though everything looked a bit shabby. Nick had heard that Lauren's mom had been hired to give the apartment a facelift, but clearly it hadn't happened yet.

Claire cracked open one of the windows and sat down on a leather sofa, placing a large crystal ashtray on the seat next to her.

"My parents don't know that I smoke," she said. "Obviously."

She lit up and then exhaled in the general direction of the window. Nick sat down in a leather club chair and she handed him her pack of cigarettes.

"I quit last year," he said, declining it. "So, what's up?"

"I wanted to talk to you about something," she said. "Nick, you know the Society is very important to me. Of all the people in our class, I would say I take it more seriously than anyone. But I haven't gotten a single advantage or privilege because of it. You have everything—you're Nick Bell. Lauren has a jewelry line. Phoebe gets a gallery show. Patch can do whatever he damn well pleases. Of all of you, all fourteen of you, I'm the only one who really cares about the group."

"Claire, I'm not really sure why you're telling me this."

"I know you're going to be offered a leadership position in our class very soon," she said.

"What do you mean?"

"You're the obvious choice. Your father is the Chairman. Your grandfather was Chairman Emeritus. You're the next in line."

"That's not technically true. What about Henry and Benjamin?"

"I think that your father is more interested in grooming you," she said. "Henry and Benjamin are easy. They've already fallen in with the group's rules, and besides, they're not Conscripts anymore. Your father wants to give you a leadership position so that you'll stay loyal, so you'll stop being the leader of the Infidels."

Nick looked at her incredulously. "You think I'm the leader? And that name—someone else came up with that name, not us! Besides, how do you know any of this?"

She exhaled another stream of smoke. "My parents tell me everything. I'm not like the rest of you—I don't see my parents as enemies. I trust them, and they trust me."

"I don't think they'd be too happy about you talking to me this way."

"Hear me out. I think you'll find that what I want makes sense. It's pretty simple: I want your position in the Society. I want you to cede it to me."

"Claire, I don't have any *position*. Honestly, you've taken more of a leadership role than I have, by heading up the Junior Committee for the ball."

Claire waved her hand at the suggestion, dispersing the smoke into the air. "That's such typical sexism. Women get to run things like party committees while men get to head up task forces, get to make decisions that affect the world? I want more than the Junior Committee. Stuffing envelopes won't exactly give me lessons in leadership."

"Okay," Nick said, "so what am I supposed to do?"

Claire looked surprised. "Wait, you're going to do it?"

"Claire, clearly there's so little that you understand about me and my friends."

"What do you mean? All I know is that your friends don't like me."

"Come on, that's not true." He wasn't really sure what to say to such an awkward statement.

She looked at him askance.

"Okay, so it's a little bit true. But you're not very nice to them."

"I don't really care. I'm not out to make friends."

"Claire, just tell me what you want me to do."

"Tell your father that I should be the next leader of the Conscripts. Charles has been fulfilling that role since the fall, and I know your father wants it to be you after him."

"Fine."

"Well, that was easy," she said, stubbing out her cigarette. "I thought it was going to be ugly."

"How would it be ugly?" He knew he probably shouldn't ask this question, but he was curious.

Claire paused for a moment before speaking slowly. "I know things about you, about your family, that I don't think you would want to be revealed. I know about Patch being your half brother. And I know that your father told you on New Year's Eve. And that you never told Patch. Your father told my mother, and my mother told me."

Claire was right. On the morning of New Year's Eve, after that horrible, dreadful series of days on Isis Island, his father had drawn him aside. Parker had relayed the story of how he had an affair with Patch's mother, Esmé, and that he was Patch's biological father. Nick had only started to heal his friendship with Patch the previous evening, and so he hadn't wanted to tell him. He had wanted to say something ever since that morning in the library of the Great Cottage, but it never seemed to be the right time. After that day, he had blocked it out. It had been easier not to deal with it, to pretend the information didn't exist. It was easier to believe it would become evident in due course, and he wasn't responsible for it.

More than anything, Nick wanted his friendship with Patch to go back to how it used to be, when Nick was a Bell and Patch was an Evans and the two of them were best friends.

Instead, he had done the worst thing, something that Patch might never forgive him for: he had kept the truth from his friend. But this time, he wasn't going to be afraid.

"So what about it?" Nick said.

"I thought I was going to have to tell Patch that you already knew," she said. "I don't exactly think you'd want him to find out, would you?"

Nick sighed. "Claire, has it ever occurred to you that it's a bit tiresome living under all these secrets? I'm going to tell Patch soon. And he'll take it for what it's worth. But I'm not going to let you pretend to blackmail me over some stupid position in the Society. What you don't realize is that you're doing me a favor."

"What do you mean?" She looked deflated for a moment.

"The last thing I would ever want is to head up the Conscripts. So you're not really taking anything from me at all."

"I really don't think—" She stood up, seemingly flustered.

"Good night, Claire. I'll tell my father about your wishes

in the next few days. Please thank your parents for the *lovely* party."

Nick turned around and left the library, walking down the hall to get his coat. He would have looked for Phoebe, but he sensed that he should give her some time to cool off. As he rode down in the elevator, he hoped he would never have to set foot in the Chilton apartment again.

IV
THE RETURN

CHAPTER FIFTY-FIVE

Six days later, starting after midnight, three enormous trucks arrived at Eaton House in Southampton. Eight workers dressed in black who billed themselves as a "white-glove delivery service" loaded the artworks out a back entrance of the estate's main house. The company was known for its discretion and didn't question why it was taking sixteen historically significant paintings to a warehouse near Islip Airport on Long Island, where the pieces would be repack-aged, addressed to their respective museums and owners, and sent via private air courier.

Two days later Nick saw that the story was on the front page of every major newspaper in the world. Because all the museums had issued amnesties on the return of each piece, no investigations would be started. Some of the museums wanted to identify the party who returned the artwork so that they could issue a reward, which, in at least one case amounted to five million dollars.

Not surprisingly, and much to the relief of the institutions, in the days that followed, no one came forward.

The day the story broke, Nick asked his father to meet him at the Society's town house on East 66th Street. He remembered when he and Phoebe and Lauren had asked to meet his father at the town house in December, and how their request had been rejected. Charles Lawrence, the leader of the Conscripts, had met with them instead, which had given them no answers.

This time, Nick had written his father a note, leaving it on the desk in his study. Taped to the bottom of the note was a clipping from the *New York Times* about the return of the paintings.

That would, he thought, make the message clear.

When Nick arrived at the town house at three o'clock, Parker was waiting for him. His father was sitting in the parlor on the first floor, drinking a cup of tea. The building was quiet, and Nick wondered if anyone ever used it during the day, apart from the Administrator. Perhaps the occasional member took advantage of it, but it seemed like the house was used mostly for parties.

"Nick."

Nick nodded at his father. "There's something you need to see." Nick pulled out his laptop, put it on the coffee table, and slid in a DVD.

"What is this? Nick, I have a very busy day. I don't have time to watch some little home movie of yours."

On the screen, an image flickered. Nick heard his father gasp.

First, there was an exterior shot of Eaton House, complete with its address in the frame. The camera led the viewer into the house, through the main entryway, down the hallway, into the kitchen, and down to the basement. A time code appeared on the footage, from two days ago.

"How on earth did you—"

"It gets better," Nick said. "Just watch."

The shot continued down into the basement. A team of men from the white-glove service were unpacking each of the artworks in order to inspect and record its condition. There were close-ups of each of the pieces: the Degas, the Rembrandt, the Vermeer, the Pollock, even the forged Leonardo da Vinci.

"You need to destroy this recording!" Parker said. "What were you thinking? How did you get access to this? Horatio was supposed to manage it all with the utmost discretion."

Horatio had been told by Nick and Patch, two days earlier, that the artworks needed to be filmed for insurance purposes, in case anything happened to them in transit. The butler, whose only desire was to do right by his late employer, accepted the explanation, and had allowed Nick and Patch to film the proceedings. Nick had barely believed that they had gotten away with it. But he still needed this next part of the plan to work.

The film continued, with a shot of the paintings being loaded onto the trucks, and the trucks pulling out of the front gate of the estate.

"Nick, this is absurd. I don't know why you would make such a film. What do you want?"

Nick leaned forward to stop the clip. His heart was pounding. "We have copies of this DVD, ready to be sent to every major news organization. The *Times*, CNN, Reuters, the Associated Press." What he didn't mention was that Patch had also sent a copy to Eliot Walker in Maine, who would put it in Patch's safe-deposit box. Patch had also already uploaded the footage to several remote servers. Among all of them, the footage was sure to stay intact.

Parker groaned. "Nick, I cannot believe that you did this! You need to destroy all those DVDs. This is absolutely absurd. Do you realize what damage you are potentially causing? I need you not to send those DVDs."

"We won't send them," Nick said, "if you grant us one thing."

"What's that? Do you want access to your trust fund early? I'd be happy to—"

"No, Dad. I think you know what we want. We want out of the Society. I want you to release me, Patch, Phoebe, Lauren, and Thad. You have to do it—you have no choice."

"This is not what your grandfather would have wanted."

"I'm not so sure about that," Nick said. "I don't think he was as enamored with the Society as you think."

"Well, you've certainly become very plucky lately," Parker said. "I would be impressed, if it didn't make me so angry. You do realize this will affect your inheritance, don't you? And as the guardian of the trusts that Palmer set up for you and Patch, I can make it very difficult for you to access them."

"Dad, we don't care. Money isn't important to us. The trusts aren't important to us. Not Palmer's trusts, nor the Bradford Trust. What's more important to us is our freedom."

"You are determined to be an Infidel to the end, aren't you?"

Nick shrugged off the comment. "You have to release us. How are you going to do it?"

Parker seemed stymied. "I don't know—we hardly ever . . . I suppose I'll have to consult the Council. There must be some kind of procedure for this." He looked at Nick. "Do you realize what a disappointment this is, Nick?"

"Only for you, Dad. It's only a disappointment for you."

Nick got up, taking his laptop with him.

"We want it to happen in the next twenty-four hours,"

Nick said. "If it doesn't, we will send out the film. Electronically as well as via courier. It will be in the news by this time tomorrow if you don't give us an answer."

"Will you leave a copy of the DVD?" Parker said. "How will I prove to them that this needs to be done?"

"I'm sure you'll find a way," Nick said.

He exited the town house, leaving his father behind. The first thing he wanted to do was to call Phoebe, to tell her that they had finally won, that they would be released. It was everything he knew she wanted.

He had left her a few messages over the past several days, but none of them were returned. He figured she was probably still angry with him over their fight, but he hoped that his actions today would make things right.

He called her, but it went to voice mail. He left her a short message to call him, and texted her as well with a simple note:

THINGS HAVE CHANGED.

CHAPTER FIFTY-SIX

On the third day of spring break, Phoebe was on an airplane headed for Los Angeles. She had put on her iPod and was trying to zone out, in the hopes that being a few thousand miles away from New York would solve some of her problems.

It had all started about a week earlier, after she had returned home from the Chilton cocktail party. Her mother had announced that she and Daniel were getting engaged. The two of them were drinking champagne in the living room, and they invited her to join them, but Phoebe had refused. Instead, she ran upstairs and locked her door. She was sensing the crazy feelings coming back—the panicked, suffocating emotions she had experienced last fall when the Society had started to close in on her. It wasn't only about Daniel. It was the art theft thing and the way Nick had handled it. Did her boyfriend not have any courage at all? When he had justified it to her, he sounded just as bad as his grandfather, the cowardly art thief. Nothing that any of them had done in the past few months—nearly all of which had been spearheaded by Nick—had gotten them any closer to getting out of the Society. He was as bad as the Elders: a player in an elaborate game set up for their own amusement.

A few days later, when the feelings hadn't abated, she booked herself a ticket for Los Angeles.

Now, having boarded the plane at JFK, almost no one knew where she was going. Not Nick, not her mother, not Daniel. Not even her father, whom she would be visiting.

The only person who knew where she was going was Lauren. Her friend hadn't encouraged her to go, but she had promised Phoebe she could keep a secret.

Nick had left her multiple messages, but Phoebe hadn't returned them. She loved Nick—for his humor, for his handsome smile, for his worldly perspective—but she had finally admitted to herself that perhaps they weren't meant to be together. Nick Bell, the shiny new boy she had met last fall, hadn't lived up to everything she had expected of him.

Phoebe checked the return address on the last letter her father had sent her, hoping it was still correct. It was an address in the Hollywood Hills, a desirable location. She was looking forward to the quiet, to time with her father, to walking the winding roads in his neighborhood, to hanging out by the pool, to immersing herself in a novel. Far away from everything in New York. As the plane was starting down the runway and everyone was asked to turn off their phones, a text message came through from Nick, along with a voice mail. She didn't bother listening to the voice mail, but she read the text:

THINGS HAVE CHANGED.

She doubted it.

Phoebe's plane touched down in Los Angeles, waking her from a restless sleep, her neck stiff and sore. She wished everything that had happened was merely a bad dream, but she knew it wasn't.

During the cab ride from the airport, she was grateful that she had packed sunglasses in her carry-on, for the Southern California light was blinding. It wasn't particularly warm, as it was only March, and the West Coast wasn't ever as warm in the spring as people thought it was, but the sunshine still felt good on her face.

Her cab pulled up at the house and she paid the driver. She buzzed the gate and waited for an answer. Finally she was let in by a housekeeper, who helped her with her rolling suitcase.

The house was stark and white, a modernist dream on a hill. She had never been there before, as her father had bought it after she and her mother had moved to New York. There was a Warhol *Jackie* in the entryway. Her father must have been doing well.

Phoebe's dad, Preston Dowling, came sauntering into the main foyer. He was wearing a sweater and jeans and looked like he had been working from home.

"Phoebe, it's so good to see you!" He gave her a hug. "I had no idea—are you okay? You don't look—"

"I know," she said. "I don't really look my best." She knew her hair was stringy, and that all the stress had been expressing itself in her body: she was breaking out, and she looked pale, with dark circles under her eyes.

"What's going on, honey?" He finally let go of her, and she realized she was about to start crying.

"Dad, I want to leave Chadwick," she said. "I want to move back to Los Angeles and live with you."

CHAPTER FIFTY-SEVEN

Phoebe's departure for Los Angeles had hit Lauren hard. While she knew there were other factors, she feared that her flippant comment at the Chilton cocktail party had encouraged Phoebe to leave town. Lauren kept playing that conversation over and over in her mind, wishing she could somehow change it. But no matter what she said to her friend, Phoebe was certain that a break from New York was what she needed.

And maybe the trip would be good for her. Lauren really didn't know what was best for her friend.

When spring break started, Lauren's little sister, Allison, had returned home from boarding school in Connecticut, filled with stories about school that she wanted to tell her older sister. When Lauren let her know that she would be leaving for Paris in just under week, Allison didn't hide her disappointment.

It was only then that Lauren realized how little time she had spent with her family lately. Her mother, Diana, had been working overtime on the Chilton apartment project. Lauren wondered if they would miss some of the springtime rituals they had enjoyed in years past: taking walks down Park Avenue and admiring the first tulip blooms, strolling through Central Park and watching the first boats go out on the freshly thawed pond.

A day after her sister arrived home, Lauren took the subway down to Giroux New York. Sebastian was on the sales floor and had just finished conferring with Sabrina about a floor display.

"Can I talk to you?" Lauren asked. Her mouth had gone dry. She and Sebastian had become so familiar in recent months, and now he already felt like a stranger.

"Of course," he said. "Come with me. How's my favorite designer? Are you packing for Paris?"

Lauren took a deep breath. His charm was making this difficult. "Sebastian," she finally said, "I can't go on the trip."

"No—Lauren! You must! You'd be missing such an opportunity."

"I understand that," Lauren said calmly. "I just—"

They entered his office, and she sat down. Sebastian looked at her sternly over his desk that was strewn with papers and sketches.

"The Colette people will be so disappointed. Can I ask why? Did something happen?"

"Sort of," she said. "I just feel like I need to focus on my schoolwork." It was a weak excuse, but she didn't know how to voice her real feelings.

"But, Lauren, my dear, you're already on break," Sebastian said. "What kind of schoolwork would you possibly have?"

"It's not only that. I need to start feeling like a real person again," Lauren said. "People my age don't fly to Paris to launch a jewelry line. I don't need all the stress in my life. I thought that I wanted it, but I don't. I know that I can do it, and I have the rest of my life to try, but I'm never going to get this time back again."

"Lauren, you're losing out on a tremendous chance. Don't you realize what other people would give to be able to do this?"

"Yes," Lauren said, nodding. "I do." That was exactly the point: she knew what she had needed to give up.

"The buyers at Colette were so pleased with your designs. But I can't guarantee that they'll be so happy if they know that you can't attend the unveiling."

"I guess that's a risk I'm going to have to take," Lauren said. "I'll pay for the airline ticket, if it's not refundable. It's the right thing to do." She thought about how Thad wouldn't be able to go, either. But he would understand. As long as she was tied up with Giroux New York and with Sebastian, she would be connected to the Society. As much as she tried to pretend that wasn't the case, she couldn't deny it.

"It's not about money!" Sebastian said. "It's about the experience. What about the rest of the line?"

"That's another thing," Lauren said. "I love doing the line. I really do. But I need to take a break. The work doesn't feel original anymore, not to me. It's inspired by earlier pieces, tweaked with my own touches. That may sell because people like it, but that's not what I want to be doing."

Sebastian was silent for a moment. "Well, this is certainly unexpected. I had no idea. I don't really have a choice except to drop the line."

Lauren nodded. "I understand."

Sebastian buzzed Sabrina on the intercom, asking her to come to his office.

"Lauren, we're going to have to ask you to clear out your office," he said. "We'll have a town car waiting. I'll be in touch with our legal team tomorrow so that we can sever the relationship."

"Thank you, Sebastian," she said.

An hour later, she walked out of the building on 14th

Street, followed by two security guards carrying boxes filled with her sketches, notebooks, and personal effects.

In the fashion world, she may have lost everything, but at that moment, she had never felt more free.

CHAPTER FIFTY-EIGHT

After the conversation with his father at the town house, Nick spent the night at Patch's apartment, as he figured it was the only safe place for him to be. Once Nick and his friends were officially released from the Society, he hoped he would feel secure going back to his parents' place, but until then, he wanted to stay out of their apartment. He had removed his computer and any significant personal belongings from his bedroom, and he was camped out in Patch's living room.

Most of all, it felt important to be close to his brother.

The following morning passed slowly. Genie didn't feel the boys should leave the apartment until they knew what was going to happen. As of noon, word still hadn't come.

"This is just like them," Patch said. "Everything at the last minute."

"At least we're prepared," Nick said. "I've called Lauren and Thad. If the Council doesn't comply, we send out the DVDs and the emails."

"What about Phoebe?" Patch asked.

Nick shrugged. "I don't know where she is. Lauren said she was out of town, but she couldn't say where."

"Girls," Patch said, groaning. "I haven't told Lia anything since you spoke with Parker. I didn't want to scare her." He paced around the living room. "God, why can I not call him my *father*?"

Genie stood at the door to the kitchen. "Because he's not, Patch. Your father is the man who raised you. Parker may be your father in a technical sense, but not in the emotional one."

Patch nodded sadly and looked at Nick. They both wanted so much to have a connection with their father, and yet he had made it impossible. Perhaps all they would ever really have as family was each other and Genie.

The phone rang in the apartment, and Genie answered it crisply. "I believe it's for you," she said to Nick.

Nick answered the phone.

It was Charles, asking them to meet at the town house at two o'clock.

In front of the town house was a security camera aimed at the front door. Patch pointed it out first.

"I didn't notice that yesterday," Nick said, "but maybe I wasn't paying attention."

"I'm surprised," Patch said. "What's the purpose of it? I thought they specifically didn't want a record of people's comings and goings."

Nick shook his head. He was tired of trying to speculate on the Society's methods.

Up the street, Thad and Lauren were walking east toward the building. The four of them had agreed that they would enter together. They had told Genie that if they didn't report back to her in two hours at a specific meeting place, she should call the police as well as drop all the DVDs in a mailbox.

Nick had a sinking feeling as they ascended the steps of the sandstone building. He had hoped that Phoebe would return, that she wasn't really still out of town.

"Hold on," he said to Lauren. "Phoebe. Is she still away?"

Lauren nodded. "I'm sorry, Nick. I'll tell you where she is after this is all over. I promised her I wouldn't, but you deserve to know."

It sounded so grave. Where was she? Had she met someone else? The thought sickened him.

When they reached the top step, the door was opened by Charles Lawrence. The lion's head knocker rattled slightly in the breeze as he held it open for everyone.

Two of the Guardians, members of the Society's private security force, stood in the vestibule of the town house on its kilim runner.

"We're going to need to check each one of you," one of them said. "No recording devices, you understand?"

Nick nodded to the others. "It's going to be fine," he whispered to Lauren and Thad. He didn't really know, though, if it would be.

Patch was looking around frantically, as if trying to figure out what was going on. Nick gave him a friendly squeeze on the arm as they each were patted down by the Guardians.

"Come with me," Charles said. He led them down a hallway, past the main staircase. After pressing a panel in the wall, a door opened, leading to an elevator.

"You want us to get in there?" Lauren said. "You must be crazy."

Charles shrugged. "If you don't want to do this, you don't have to."

Nick stepped forward. "It's fine," he said. "It's an elevator. We've been to the upper floors. We know what's up there, more or less."

The four of them stepped into the elevator along with Charles and one of the Guardians. The elevator car was large, but it was still a tight fit.

Charles pressed a button, and to everyone's surprise, the

creaky old elevator started going down. Nick grasped Lauren's hand, as he sensed she was the most frightened by it all. He didn't know what was giving him the confidence to proceed, but he felt in his gut that they were going to survive this. He was reminded, though, that he had felt a lot of things in his gut in the last six months, and many of them had not gone his way.

The elevator went down what felt like two stories, and then everyone got out. They entered a long oak-paneled room. On its walls were bulletin boards containing newspaper clippings, maps, photographs, printouts of emails, and assorted lists. A bank of file cabinets flanked the wall on the left, and on top of them were multiple flat-screen televisions, one of them monitoring the front entrance, the others turned to muted news channels. A bookshelf nearby appeared to house yearbooks and other directories. On the right were four old-fashioned secretarial desks, lined up neatly in a row. On them were computers, printers, a fax machine, and multiline telephones. Across from the desks was a large oval oak conference table, a Harkness table similar to the ones they had in the Chadwick classrooms. Nick noticed that running along the walls and in front of the desks were brass curtain rods that were attached to the ceiling. Velvet curtains in a deep shade of burgundy were pulled aside at all four corners.

It was a conference room in which the meeting participants could either be privy to the mechanics around them, or be completely partitioned off from it.

"You are probably wondering why we have left the curtains open for you." It was Nick's father, standing at the other end of the room, in front of a doorway. "We call this the War Room. Some of the Elders wanted to hide our operations, to keep it all under wraps today. But I thought you should see what goes on here before you leave us. I wanted you to see how much work goes into this organization. This room is rarely empty. It is where everything happens, where all your text messages are sent from, via the latest technology. Where we decide when and how we'll meet. How we have connected you with opportunities. Most of your classmates will never see this."

The room was a contrast of old and new. The computers were the latest models, but the Edison bulbs and fixtures lighting the room could have been a hundred years old. The burgundy curtains looked like they were from an old Broadway theater house.

Nick looked at Patch, and his brother could merely shake his head.

"What do you think?" Nick whispered.

"I don't really know," Patch said.

Nick decided to speak up. "Why are you showing us this?"

"Good question." Parker looked at the group of four. "I am showing you this because I never want you to take for granted the chance that you were given. The Society is a machine that could have worked for you. But sadly, you have all chosen to throw that away."

He motioned for them to follow him.

Through the doorway was yet another room, but this one was filled with people.

CHAPTER FIFTY-NINE

Lauren was last in line as the four of them were led into the next room. It was octagonal, with black-and-white-striped walls, a glossy white floor, and a dimmed chandelier in the middle. She braced herself for what was to come.

On one side, standing in a row, were their mentors: Charles, Emily, Anastasia, and Hunter, who had been Thad's mentor.

On the other side was Parker Bell, standing with Katherine Stapleton, the Administrator.

"I think we all know why you four are here," Parker Bell said. "You have been a disappointment, and so we have decided to grant your wish to be released from the Society."

"Wait," Nick said. "What about Phoebe? You promised that Phoebe would be released as well."

"Miss Dowling will be released by proxy. Her mentor is

here. You will all be witness to her de-initiation."

Anastasia looked as if she was wiping away a tear.

"My five Infidels," Mr. Bell continued. "I'm sure you know by now that we have called you that. An infidel is a person who doesn't believe in a religion. You also know the word *infidelity*. Being untrue. Not being faithful. All of you lack faith. You lack faith, and you lack trust."

To his left, the four mentors looked dour, as if they, too, had failed.

"Hector, open the doors."

One of the Guardians opened two of the panels. It revealed an unfinished basement, at the center of which was a giant furnace with an iron door.

"Mentors!" The four mentors stepped forward. They each held forward a plastic mask, the ones from the Night of Rebirth that had each Initiate's face printed on them. Emily handed Lauren's to her, and Anastasia handed Phoebe's to Lauren as well. Hunter handed Thad's to him. Charles had both Nick's and Patch's masks, even though Patch had never been part of that night. He handed one to each of them.

Hector opened the iron door leading to the furnace room. "As you burn the masks," Parker said, "you will destroy your identity as a member of the Society."

"Should we do this?" Lauren asked Nick quietly. The heat from the furnace was flowing into the room, raising its temperature.

"I think so," he said.

Each of the four of them went forward, one by one, and threw his or her mask into the opening of the furnace. The toxic smell of burning plastic was released into the air.

"Now, the scrolls," Parker said.

The Administrator handed out five scrolls, each representing one of the members, to them. Again, Lauren took Phoebe's for her. They were the same scrolls they had been shown at the Night of Rebirth.

At Parker's direction, they each threw the scrolls into the furnace. With an ominous clang, Hector closed the door, which fanned the flames even more.

"The burning represents your forgetting—your forgetting all that went on in the Society. You've experienced consequences inside the Society, and now, outside the Society, if you reveal your exploits, you will experience consequences as well. You may wonder why we aren't asking you to sign nondisclosure agreements." He paused. "I think you understand that all of this is above the law."

"What about our tattoos?" Patch said. "How do we get rid of them?"

"We can't remove your tattoos. You are welcome to try. But as I understand it, faint traces will always remain with you."

He turned to Nick. "I won't ask for a copy of that ridiculous film that you all made. I know there are multiple copies out there, and confiscating one copy won't change that. But I can assure you, if the Society ever sees that film in the public domain, there will be grave consequences for all five of you. If I were you, I would destroy all the copies. That's the only way you can ensure that your heirs don't do something silly with them someday.

"Charles, I believe we're done here. Please escort these four back up to the street."

In a few minutes they were back on the street. The entire thing had happened quickly, but Lauren still found herself hyperventilating. Her face was warm from the heat in the room, and the cold air outside was bracing. She held on to Thad, as she felt faint.

"That was quite a production," Patch said.

"I don't even know what to think about it," Thad said. "I guess they couldn't just cut up our membership cards or something, right?"

Nick smiled grimly at Thad's attempt at a joke. Of course, they all knew that they had no membership cards. They had nothing to prove they had ever been members at all, Lauren realized, except for the tattoos on their necks, markings that could have been obtained at any tattoo parlor.

"Can we start walking?" Lauren said. "I swear, I never want to go down this street again."

The four of them started up the block.

"Lauren, can you do something for me?" Nick asked.

"Of course."

"Please tell me where Phoebe is."

"I'm so sorry I couldn't tell you, Nick," Lauren said, turning to him. "She's in LA. She went to stay with her dad for a little bit. Her mom called me this morning, actually. She was really upset that Phoebe left without calling her, and she was trying to figure out why. I told her it was because of Daniel. I know that wasn't the only reason, but I think Phoebe would have wanted her mom to know that she doesn't trust him."

"Will you call her for me? Will you tell her what happened? I want her to come home." He paused, looking behind them at the town house. "I want her to know that I tried to make things right."

"I will," Lauren said as she gave Nick's arm a squeeze. "I promise."

CHAPTER SIXTY

Patch and Nick were walking north on Fifth Avenue, headed in the direction of the Met. They had parted ways with Lauren and Thad, who were going to hang out at Lauren's apartment. She was still pretty shaken up by the entire ordeal, but Thad promised to keep her company. Now Patch and Nick were going to meet Genie at the agreed-upon place. Even in the crisp March air, what they had just been through didn't feel real to Patch. Everything with the Society had an air of unreality to it—the rituals, the meetings, the parties—and the past hour had seemed the strangest of all. Patch was hopeful that they were free of the group, at least for now. There was still, of course, so much they would have to contend with. Patch didn't know if he would ever have any sort of relationship with Parker Bell. He even wondered if

Nick could ever be around his parents again. Perhaps Nick could move in with Genie and him—that is, if their father didn't try to get them kicked out of the building or threaten them in some other way.

Patch sighed. It was all too complicated, this mess they had gotten themselves into, starting last fall. Or perhaps, because they had been born into it, they had never really had a choice. He wished they could run away from it all, from the Society, from their lives, from New York City. Maybe someday they would be able to.

For now, he decided that he had to be thankful for the important things. For the possibility that the Society would leave them alone. For Lia. For Genie. For Nick.

They entered the Met, cheekily paying a dollar—the usual twenty-dollar fee was merely "suggested"—and winking at the cashier as they were let through. The two of them had agreed to meet Genie in the Chinese Garden in the Astor Court, on the second floor, directly above the Egyptian wing. Patch didn't exactly know why they had chosen this particular room at the Met; maybe it was because Parker Bell hated Chinese art, or so Nick claimed.

Genie stood in the middle of the little faux courtyard that had been re-created inside the museum, a replica of an actual seventeenth-century courtyard in China.

"Oh, thank God!" Genie said as she rushed forward to greet the boys. "I have been standing here biting my nails for the past half hour. I was ready to call the police."

"Let's go sit down," Patch said as he took his grandmother's arm.

"The Petrie Court?" Nick asked, referring to the café in the museum that looked out onto the park. Patch and Nick had spent a good portion of their childhood enjoying free hot chocolate from the friendly waiters there who were amused by the two little boys who were barely as tall as the tables.

When they arrived at the café, Patch looked up. "Nick, um . . ."

In front of them, outside the glass windows of the café, was Cleopatra's Needle, the monument where Jared Willson had been killed. It was in the distance, but it was visible nonetheless.

"It's okay," Nick said, pulling out a chair. "It's a monument. That's all it is. Nothing more. What happened to Jared doesn't change that."

Patch got Nick's point. They had to stop being afraid of everything. It was part of the argument Patch had overheard Nick and Phoebe having in the house in Southampton, and it seemed as if Nick had given it some thought.

Genie ordered hot chocolate for the three of them, and an assortment of miniature desserts, the fancy kind that were served on a tower of three plates. After the waiter left, Nick looked nervous.

"Patch, I need to tell you something," Nick said, first

348

looking at Patch, then at Genie. "Actually, I need to tell both of you something. I owe you both an apology."

Patch frowned. "I don't understand—what for?"

Nick took a deep breath. "I knew about you and me and the whole brotherhood thing before you did. My father told me about your mother and him and what happened the day after you were initiated on Isis Island. I wanted to tell you, but I didn't know how to deal with the information. It was too much to handle, and I had to make sure our friendship was solid again. And then everything with Palmer's challenge—there was just never a good time."

Patch looked at Nick angrily. "Nick, you could have told me anytime! Can I ever trust you? This is just like last year when you didn't tell me what was going on with the Society—"

"Boys—" Genie interrupted. "You two have to trust each other. Frankly, you don't have a choice. And for God's sake, Patch, I kept that secret from you for nearly seventeen years. You think I didn't know all that time? You think I didn't want to tell you, that I didn't agonize over every moment whether I was doing the right thing? Ever since your mother left, it was in my hands. I kept it from you as well. Nick didn't tell you for a few months. You need to let it go."

The platters of small desserts arrived, and the boys picked a few each, choosing miniature raspberry tarts and currant scones with lemon curd.

Maybe Genie was right. Maybe Patch needed to give Nick a break. Nick had tried to do what was right, and he was obviously under a great deal of pressure.

"What I want to understand is, what really happened between my mother and our father?" Patch asked. "Why would she do this? Why would she not have told my father—that is, Patch, Jr.—about it?"

"Your mother was ashamed," Genie said. "But she wanted to have a child so badly. She and your father were not able to have children, or at least, they hadn't been successful yet. When she became pregnant, we were all so happy. I had no idea at first. She only told me halfway through the pregnancy. It was a strange piece of news, but in the end, what mattered most was that she and Patch had a son."

Patch nodded. "But why . . . why Parker? I mean, no offense, Nick, but he's such a monster." A monster, Patch thought, who was his real father.

Nick looked dismayed, though not surprised. He turned to Genie. "I can't answer that," he said.

"He was delightful back then," Genie said. "So handsome and charming. All the ladies flirted with him. And in retrospect, he and Esmé seemed to have a curious connection. They hit it off. I think it was only later that your father became—I don't know the right word—I guess he became nasty, hardened. Maybe Palmer did it to him."

"And my father knew about it?" Patch asked.

"I believe he found out," Genie said. "There was a fight between the two of them. It was a terrible time when that happened—it was like two halves of a family breaking apart. And then your father drowned. That weekend was supposed to be a reconciliation. And it never happened."

"I need to show you something," Nick said. "Both of you. Genie, you may have seen it, but Patch, I'm not sure if you have. It's a memorial marker for your father, for Patch, Jr., on the beach."

"I've seen it," Genie said. "But I think Patch should see it as well."

"I don't ever want to go back to that house again," Patch said. "I'm sorry, Nick. I just feel weird about it, after everything your father has done."

"I understand," Nick said. "I'm feeling pretty ambivalent myself."

"Genie, I want to know more about my mother," Patch said. "Before she went crazy."

Genie sighed. "Patch, I feel like it's not for me to tell you these stories. You never heard back from Esmé, did you?" Patch had left her a message but received no response.

"That's right," Patch said.

"I think we need to visit her," Genie said. "I know you don't want to, but it's something we need to do. She was always so fearful that you would find out. I think having her know that you have learned about Parker, and that you understand—or at least, that you understand as best you can—I think it might help her."

"Do you think she'll ever be able to come home?" Patch asked.

Genie looked uncertain. "I don't know," she said. "I guess we'll see. But the first step is for us to go see her. I think we should do that more often, together. I've tried to protect you from it all these years, but you're getting older, and it's time that we try to make this work. You need to have some kind of relationship with your mother, fractured as it might be."

"When should we go?" Patch asked. "Today?"

"I think we've had enough excitement for today," Genie said, frowning. "Let's take a break. How about tomorrow? Let's do it tomorrow."

Patch nodded. As he sat there with his grandmother and his half brother in the warmth of the Petrie Court, he started to feel that maybe, just maybe, the disparate threads of his life were coming together.

CHAPTER SIXTY-ONE

Nick, Patch, and Genie stepped out of the museum. It was nearing closing time, and tourists were gathered on the sidewalk in front of the Met. The strange, sweet smell of pretzels, kabobs, and roasted chestnuts was in the air.

"You both go ahead," Nick said. "I want to stay here for a minute." He sat down on the steps as he watched Patch lead Genie across the street to the building where they all lived.

Nick wondered if he could go back home or if he would have to live at Patch's for now. He had almost forgotten, but he was scheduled to leave town in a few days. Months ago, before any of this had happened, Nick's mother had booked him on a college tour, twelve schools in seven days. He should have been excited for this fresh start, but at this moment he wanted to start putting back together the pieces of his life before he embarked on something new. More than anything, Nick longed to buy a ticket to the West Coast, to go and seek out Phoebe. After thinking about everything they had been through, he understood now how much pain she had been in, and how she had spoken honestly, even in the kitchen in Southampton, even when she had said those hurtful things. She had been right: he had put his family ahead of everyone else, ahead of her, and he never wanted to do that again. As much as he wanted to run after her, he understood that he needed to give her the time she deserved to figure things out. He trusted that Lauren would call her, and eventually, she would come back home.

He glanced across the street at his apartment building. The landmarked building had always been an emblem of all that he thought the Bell family represented: strength, tradition, security. Ever since he had learned about the Society, however, and all that it stood for, it had seemed false. Would anything ever seem real again, or would it all seem as flimsy as those Society rituals, cheap theatrical tricks designed to scare people?

His grandfather's legacy, too, felt false. Palmer had built up a dubious empire, respected by so many, and yet, what was it? Was it anything more than lying, conspiracy, thievery?

Nick walked across the street, carefully taking the cross-walk. As he approached the building, his brother Benjamin stepped out of a black town car. Nick hadn't realized that he was in town.

"Ben!" he called. "I thought you were in Florida." He was supposed to be on spring break with some of his college friends.

"I had some business I needed to attend to," Ben said. This was unlike his brother. His main business in life seemed to be partying with his friends.

"Did you hear about what happened?" Nick figured he could talk about it to his brother. What could they possibly do to him?

"I did, Nick." He seemed downcast, but not in the odd, selfishly disappointed way that the mentors had. This look was different, a genuine sadness.

"What's wrong?"

Ben looked at him. "There's something Palmer always used to say, and now Dad says it as well. It's a Latin phrase: *Alea jacta est*. 'The die is cast.'"

"What do you mean by that?"

Ben glanced anxiously at the building's doors, as if to make sure that no one could overhear.

"Nick, you may think you're out of the Society, but you never really will be."

His brother opened the back door of the town car and got in, shutting it behind him. Nick stood on the sidewalk, speechless, as the car pulled away from the building and merged into the river of traffic going down Fifth Avenue.

ACKNOWLEDGMENTS

I am extremely grateful to my friends, colleagues, and mentors for their support during this novel's creation.

To my agent, Kate Lee, and her assistant, Larissa Silva, at ICM.

To my editor, Sarah Shumway, and my publisher, Katherine Tegen.

To the entire HarperTeen publicity, marketing, design, and sales team.

To my assistant, Susanne Filkins.

To my friend and fellow novelist, Melissa de la Cruz.

And of course, to my husband, Drew Frist, who was there for the entire ride.

I also had the privilege, during the research for this novel, of experiencing two tours that would impress even the most jaded Egyptologist. The first was with Dr. Catharine Roehrig, curator in the Department of Egyptian Art at the Metropolitan Museum in New York, who answered all my questions about the museum's collection. The second was with Dr. Renée Dreyfus, curator of Ancient Art at the de Young Museum in San Francisco, who guided me through its *Tutankhamun and the Golden Age of the Pharoahs* exhibit. Both were invaluable in helping me learn more about Egyptian culture, which provided a rich background for the mythology of the Society. Any flights of fancy or inaccuracies relating to Egyptian art in this novel are entirely my own.

Finally, I am grateful for the following works of non-fiction, which helped inform this story: *The Metropolitan Museum of Art Bulletin: The Temple of Dendur*, by Cyril Aldred; *Rogues' Gallery: The Secret History of the Moguls and the Money That Made the Metropolitan Museum*, by Michael Gross; *The Gardner Heist: The True Story of the World's Largest Unsolved Art Theft*, by Ulrich Boser; *Confessions of a Master Jewel Thief*, by Bill Mason with Lee Gruenfeld; and *Egyptian Revival Jewelry & Design*, by Dale Reeves Nicholls with Shelly Foote and Robin Allison.